MYRE HAMLET &

Copyright © 2018 Dan Tunnelly

The Moral right of the author has been asserted.

All rights reserved.

Apart from any fair dealing for the purposes of research or private study, or criticism or review, as permitted under the Copyright, Designs and Patents Act 1988, this publication may only be reproduced, stored or transmitted, in any form or by any means, with the prior permission in writing of the author, or in the case of reprographic reproduction in accordance with the terms of licences issued by the Copyright Licensing Agency

****

The characters herein are the product of the author's imagination and any resemblance to real persons, living or dead, is purely coincidental. Events are the product of the author's imagination.

MYRE HAMLET & THE ICE WOLF

Chapter:	Title:	Page:
One:	The Blue Pig	1
Two:	The Homecoming	16
Three:	Harvest Home	39
Four:	The Home Leaving	52
Five:	The Sea and the Breeze	66
Six:	Scar Bringer	90
Seven:	Pulse	109
Eight:	Sentinel	126
Nine:	Respite	144
Ten:	Dunbeck	153
Eleven:	Blizzard	166
Twelve:	Icemere	187
Thirteen:	Sharfell	203
Fourteen:	Boy	220
Fifteen:	Bright Messengers	236
Sixteen:	Passing Moon	249

CHAPTER ONE

The Blue Pig

The moon was past the full, but still in all her pale glory. Her face peered down, when the fleeting October clouds would allow, on the creaking sign that marked the door of an inn... the Blue Pig in Myre Hamlet. A lone shadow crossed the windy street in a swirl of leaves. Passing over the threshold, the figure disappeared inside, shutting in the warm flood of firelight that had escaped from the door.

"Evening Felix," the robust figure called jovially as he took off his coat. Making his way over to the blazing log fire, he rubbed his hands in the welcome warmth.

"Evening Barny," replied the ostler from behind the old oak counter.

Felix Cavey had been the innkeeper at the Blue Pig for as long as Barny could remember. He too was robust and even more jovial beneath his curling grey whiskers which had been grey for almost as long as they'd been curly. He had cheeks like ripe apples, and a nose to match. His generous middle was held in place by the worn leather apron which protected a well lived-in shirt and breeches. The sleeves of the shirt were rolled to the elbows of strong arms, arms that had lifted many a cask in their time. Short though his legs were, the breeches barely reached his boots.

"The usual is it?" Felix said, grinning as he handed Barny a mug taken from the low beamed ceiling and already filled to the brim, too late for choice. "You're late tonight."

"I *am*," came the reply from behind the tilted mug, now half-empty. "Fourteen nags today and six of them were plough horses. The entire Hamlet must be ploughing fields or else making for the Corn Market at Westhorn." He added this in explanation after tipping the mug completely and wiping his

1

Myre Hamlet & the Ice Wolf

lips along his sleeve, forgetting for a moment that it was his best white shirt.

Barny Hensman was the farrier in Myre Hamlet, and a skilful smith by any standards. In fact he was the only *real* smith in the area. With his young apprentice, Tom Bridger, he'd only shoe perhaps a half-dozen horses on a normal day, for there was much other ironwork to be done. Being the smith, busy as he was, he'd rarely be out of his working aprons and his old boots, except of course while sleeping. So for the few spare hours he had between working and sleeping he'd change into something more formal and catch up on the gossip and on the news that came to the inn. This he'd do in the company of a few good friends and a mug of ale. He lived alone in the cottage adjoining the forge. Making each of his frequent visits to the inn an occasion, he'd wash away the dirt and the aches of the day and put on his 'party clothes' as he always called them. Tonight he was wearing green breeks and a white shirt with matching stock. The stock was fastened with a gold pin set in the shape of a horseshoe. His waistcoat was brown as were his riding boots, though the boots were rarely used for their intended purpose.

"Still, the extra trade will help to keep these mugs filled of a cold October night," said Felix, smiling as he replenished the mug. "Seth and Will are in the smaller room discussing news brought with the coach from Fenny away up north."

The Pig, as it was often called, was a homely inn and was used by many of those who lived in the village and the Hamlet's farmers found time when they could to sample the hospitality of Master Cavey. The inn was built on the main street which followed the line of the old coaching road running from the larger towns and ports of Sudneck, through Midvale and on to the more remote and smaller harbours of Nording. The road was used little by the villagers, for very few of them made a

The Blue Pig

habit of travelling great distances. The Hamlet being a farming community, the only real reason for travelling far was for seasonal dealings at the corn and cattle markets at Westhorn, within a day's journey each way. This journey would usually be made on horseback or by horse and cart. Some perhaps would visit friends or relatives who'd moved out to more distant and independent farms, but generally the people of Myre Hamlet, who for the most part were generous and warm-hearted, kept themselves to themselves and to their daily routine. They knew little of the lands beyond the Hamlet unless from news brought with supplies from the south or by occasional travellers on the coach road. The coach itself stopped regularly, but the coachmen rarely found the time for gossip.

The Pig had been built many years before to provide rest and shelter for travellers, more frequent then, on their journeys through the village and as a staging post and hostelry for the coaches, made use of by many of them. Set on the eastern side of the road, it had a long frontage. At one end, the roadside had been ramped to enable people to alight or board the coaches with ease. The inn, built mainly in the local stone and with a grey slate roof, was surmounted by five stone chimneys. The windows were squat and small, to keep the heat in on cold winters' nights and the doorframes were low enough to have caused a few sore heads. Several brick built outbuildings had been added in later years to cater for increased stabling needs. The inn had always boasted at least one bedroom available at short notice for any unfortunate who might arrive after dusk. Nowadays, the rooms where all too often empty. The stables formed a courtyard to the rear of the inn which had been paved with cobblestones, laid in varying shades, depicting an enormous purple-blue pig. Three mature oak trees to the northern end afforded shelter. These, the only trees to the east of the road, formed the south-eastern tip of a small copse which at its far end joined with the Westwood.

Myre Hamlet & the Ice Wolf

The trees of the copse and the nearby areas of the wood were mainly oaks and elms. The wood however, which was in reality a large and very dense forest, stretched for many miles to the north, and few in the Hamlet ventured more than a mile or so under its eaves, and so it kept its inner secrets from the farmers.

The main street served the needs of any small commerce in the community and housed Barny's forge. Also to be found here were the Village Hall and several small workshops and stores. There was the saddlery and the wainwright's yard, there was the apothecary's shop and there were the cobbler's workrooms. And there were others too, all of which served some essential need of the people of Myre Hamlet. Most of these places were, like the inn, of stone and slate. The whole village was set around the main street with no more than two score of neatly thatched houses, placed in small plots of no particular order. These were linked with the street by rambling paths between hedges of quickthorn and elder bushes. An abundance of wild plants and herbs spread at the foot of the hedges, natives of the nearby wood. These houses were in the main those of people concerned with the shops and trading places.

The remainder of the inhabitants, who must have totalled some two or three hundreds, lived further out in hamlet farmhouses among the outlying hills and on the skirts of the nearby Westwood.

The farms of Myre Hamlet had been built much earlier than the village itself. Farmers came many generations before from the south attracted by the area's rich and fertile soil that spread for miles in the valley of the river Bucklebank. There'd been early problems though for the first settlers, who'd found this fertile land often waterlogged and boggy. Much ditching and other drainage work eventually remedied this though even now after heavy rains, the fields held some of their old character. The farms sprang up mostly on the western side of

The Blue Pig

the river, afforded some shelter by the Westwood, but as sheep and cattle were gradually introduced, more farms were started on the gentle folds to the south of the wood, which were the northern limits of the Sudmoors.

The village itself had developed some hundred years or more after the early farms as the need for dependence on each other grew.

The road from the south, which had existed in more primitive form even then, skirted the Sudmoors and crossed the Puddle Stream which issued from the Westwood to run into the river Bucklebank. The road then ran north from the stone bridge, following the eastern side of the wood and eventually, after crossing the river again at Weatherford, reached Fenny and Pebblebank on the shores of Nording.

The smell of wood smoke greeted Barny as he entered the smaller room. Felix squeezed through the doorway behind him with a tray of bread and cheeses and two more foaming mugs.

"Hello there, Barny," called Will Sparrow from a chair set at an old oak table that almost filled the room. "Had another easy day?" he added with a hint of friendly sarcasm.

"Oh, yes," winked Barny in good spirit. "Evening both," he sighed as he spread himself in the deep cushions of a chair in the corner, reserved for him by his two friends.

"Evening, Barny," said Seth Linden absently, as he eased his feet down from the edge of the table and shuffled an old map to one side to make room for the welcome tray. He tapped out the contents of his pipe on the beam over the fireplace into the crackling fire and joined the others in sampling the bread and cheese as Felix closed the door on his way out. The chatter from the outer room retreated with the click of the latch.

Seth and Will were two of Barny's dearest friends. Seth lived about three miles to the west, on the edge of the wood. He and his wife, Sarah, farmed cattle and pigs for meat, hides and milk at Puddlefork. Both the beef and the dairy herds were small, but of good quality by local standards. The summer just past had been a favourable one which had produced a good harvest of lush grass for the winter hay. Stocks were abundant this year and all in the Hamlet looked forward to a comfortable winter.

Seth Linden was tall and slim, akin in stature to his slender pipe. His lengthy chin was further lengthened by a feathery brown beard and his face looked all the more chiselled thanks to his long brown hair. He dressed plainly in a pair of aged breeches and a comfortable drab-coloured coat with leathern elbows. His boots were just as comfortable. His wide brimmed hat hung on a peg on the door. He was good hearted even by Myre Hamlet standards but tended to be more inward than the other two. At thirty-five he was ten years or so younger than both Barny and Will.

Will was a builder and an experienced mason, used to working the local stone, though most of his work was in repairing the existing buildings of the Hamlet and in repairing and building paddock and field walls. He was muscled and of fair complexion. His hair hung in tight curls about his weathered face. He too dressed comfortably.

"Felix tells me we've had some news from the north," said Barny, inquisitively, expecting small talk of Fenny or nearby Ambleton.

"That's right, Barny," said Will Sparrow between mouthfuls of bread and cheese. "Samuel the coachman reckons that our expedition is back to the mainland, and should be back here before the winter sets in too deep. Before the end of November with any luck."

"And with the finest beasts we'll have set eyes on, I'll be bound," added Seth, enthusiastically.

"The expedition eh!" cried Barny. "Then their troubles are over. Felix had better save a mug or two of this ale then, for Amos and Ely," he joked. "They'll have found nothing like it to

The Blue Pig

the north."

The expedition that Birdie, as he was often called, spoke of was one that had left the Hamlet in early spring for the northern land of Greylar, across the sea. The local people had been excited last winter at news brought by travellers from Southmould, a more restless people than the Myre folk, some of whom had travelled in Greylar on occasions. On their way back from such a visit, they'd related a tale that had provoked the curiosity of the farmers in the Pig. They'd told of fine and abundant herds of wild cattle roaming free on the southern plains of Greylar. They'd come across the herds quite by chance on their travels near to the abandoned Greymills on the northern coast of that land and to other parts of Greylar. Although the southerners had expressed some small interest, they were not farmers themselves and relied on other means of earning a living.

Intense interest had buzzed around the Hamlet farming community at the prospect of introducing some of these cattle to their own herds to improve the stock. Being contented as they were however, some had taken a deal of persuading that such an adventurous plan might really be beneficial, or even practical, since it would involve a long trek to a place that no one had more than dreamed of. None of them had ever seen a seagoing boat and certainly would never manage the sailing of one. However, after having discussed the difficulties of such a journey with the travellers before they'd left and having learned that boats might be hired with willing crews from Pebblebank or Fenny, they'd decided that a serious attempt, if successful, would indeed benefit the community as a whole.

After further consideration among themselves, they'd set off on what was expected to be a journey of some five or six months at most. They'd set out on horseback, rather than by coach, so as to avoid others learning too much of their quest's intentions.

All had been assumed to be going well until news had reached the Hamlet in June from Fenny that hired boats had dropped the expedition in Greylar in mid-April and had waited as asked. But with no return of the travellers after three weeks, all the boats had left for home save one, which went back to Fenny after a fruitless further two weeks. By all accounts they were to return again with fresh supplies, and news of this had convinced those in Myre Hamlet that all would be well, although a regret for considering the idea in the first place was growing in and around the Hamlet. By September, there'd been no further news. Then towards the end of that month they learned that two of the trekkers had returned to Fenny from Greylar to move the boatmen into setting out again for Greylar. In truth the sailors were reluctant to travel far from their home port... particularly for strangers and particularly to the east. The travellers from Southmould had in fact crossed to Greylar by means of improvised rafts and had never actually enlisted the aid of hired boats.

So it was that, before this latest news, many had despaired of success and felt that they may never see the travellers again. But now it was known that they were back on the mainland, despite the difficulties, and with cattle at that. Indeed they'd sent word for some of the villagers to meet them at Ambleton.

"First or second week in November," explained Birdie. The excitement rekindled, all three laughed and joked and talked of the practicalities of sharing out the cattle between the various farmsteads. Seth retrieved the map, which showed the farms, and they studied it at length.

In burst a short, sharp figure of a man in black cloak and hat, with bushy black eyebrows and expression to match. He stood at much the same height as Barny, but was almost as thin as Seth was. His sallow complexion emphasised his eyebrows and his black hair hung straight and fringed about his face. A thin moustache added further to the vexed impression. White knuckles gripped a thumb stick, which he carried for company rather than out of necessity.

"Damn the weather!" he stormed. "Raining all week, until yesterday. Ploughing's almost impossible."

"A man of your height should be careful ploughing fields in that kind of weather. You might disappear in the mud," chuckled Barny, his smile pushing up his cheeks to meet his laughing grey eyes.

"Leave off, Barny Hensman," snapped Kaleb Moody. "It's alright for you, working indoors most of the time, and by that blazing forge fire of yours too."

Kaleb Moody was another farmer who lived further south, on the first folds of the moors at Brackenridge. Like most of the farmers around, he was competent and hardworking and, if truth be known, quite pleasant under his hard exterior. Barny and the others knew that his bark was worse than his bite and knew that their taunting didn't really bite deep, but that this was the only way to bring him out of his mood.

"We won't share our new cattle with you if you don't brighten up a bit," said Seth, straight faced.

The sudden realisation of what Seth meant brought a forced smile to Kaleb's face and soon all four were laughing as they continued to talk of the prospects for the herds.

It was around midnight, a not unusual time, when Seth left the Blue Pig to a cheerful good night from Felix. He stepped out into the stony road and shivered, greeted by what was turning out to be a sharp frost. The wind had fitfully carried away the clouds to the east and had died with the lights in the nearby cottages, leaving the pale disc of the moon descending into a clear sky in the south-west. She had a halo of iridescent mist to keep her company on her journey, which would take her down over the green folds of the moors and disappearing out of sight to the south of Puddlefork, where the moors met the woods.

Seth turned his gaze from the beauty of the moon and cast his eye across the sky towards the north. Above his glance were the Plough and the Pole Star, and below it was the road which Ely, Amos and their companions had taken. His thoughts went out to them and to the north itself. He wondered what adventures they'd had on their quest for the northern herds and his heart felt the pull of adventure to distant lands, to travel under moon and stars across lands he'd never seen, never known and never even dreamed of.

'Perhaps one day,' he thought, 'I might venture forth on such a journey.'

He shook his head and smiled. "Must be the cold air, and the warm ale," he whispered quietly to the silent street.

Turning his collar to cover his ears and his thoughts back to the west, to home and a warm bed, he stepped across the road into the Westhorn Lane opposite and leaving the now silent sign behind him, he headed for home.

The moon lit his way to the welcome farm gate, but he'd completed his homeward journey without a conscious thought for the way, turning the right turns, crossing the right paths, skirting the woods with its familiar trees. Tawny owls hooted and an unusually late nightjar purred. These, the occasional crack of dead branches underfoot and the chatter of the Puddle Stream were the only sounds he heard until he entered the gate to the farm. Here the barking of his dog, Ruffles, greeted him but the dog was at once quiet when he recognised the farmer's even footfall.

Seth gave a last thought to the North Star, shot the bolt, and turned to climb the creaking stair. He was weary from the day's work and the walking from the inn, and the ale hadn't helped to keep him wakeful. After heaving off his boots and throwing his hat at the peg, and after making the effort to pick up the hat from the floor to place it in its intended place, he stretched out

The Blue Pig

onto the soft bed beside Sarah. She was sleeping serenely beneath warm blankets, awaiting his return. But *he* couldn't sleep, despite his weariness, for his thoughts wandered again to the expected return of Ely and Amos and to the prospects and problems ahead for Myre Hamlet. At length, he set aside his thoughts and, greeted by Sarah's warm and slumbering embrace, he slept. His thoughts turned then to dreams. He dreamed of summer's swaying meadows, of the chatter of the willow finches and of the winding brook they haunted. Overhead, billowing white clouds rolled across azure skies on a ragged breeze.

Morning dawned fair and fresh, accompanied by eager barking and much wagging of the tail by Ruffles. The dog had left his night shelter and was watching the door at the rear of the house, head cocked expectantly on one side. The farm's crested cockerel rose to call... in his true tradition, *after* the dog had alerted *him*. The door opened with a reluctant creak of its hinges, as if yawning and stretching to meet the new day and there stood Sarah, silent for a moment as she took in the scene that greeted her.

Sarah Linden was two years younger than her husband was, but at thirty-three, she was still as attractive as she'd been when Seth first met her some eighteen years before. She'd lived on another of the outlying farms. Standing only a little less in height than Seth did, she was slim and quite delicate in appearance. Her features were neat and her complexion was fresh and fair, yet her hair was dark and fell to her waist. A bow held her hair tied back, as it did each morning, out of the way of her chores. Her eyes were wide and grey. She wore a plain dress of coarse linen, suited to a day's work and her feet were clad in laced leather boots. For all her delicate appearance, she was stronger than most women were and was a great help to Seth in working the farm. She was of a gentle nature, but on occasions, when Seth annoyed her, could display a temper which was fiery though nearly always justified.

Before her, lay a small cobbled yard, slippery with white stars of morning frost. To her left was a well, surmounted by a circular stone wall and a sloping roof of slates. At the far end of the yard a small wall of the same stone, that was typical of the area, held back the rolling greensward which yielded some forty paces beyond to the thick, almost overpowering eaves of the forest... the Westwood. A stone step from the yard leapt onto a winding path which lazily twisted to the wood's edge. The hen run was fenced off to the right of the lawn, and housed three coops of solid timber, built sturdy to thwart the foxes which would often leave the wood to hunt.

Sarah stepped down from the door and after drawing water for breakfast she returned to the yard, crossed the cobbles, and strode out onto the frosty turf, joined by a scampering Ruffles. Together they entered the hen run. The hens had sprung to life with the first call of the cock. Sarah unlatched the doors, one by one, and the hens swaggered clucking from their coops and meandered around the run, scratching for worms, whetting their appetites for the corn that would soon be scattered.

The sun had risen already in the east and hung hesitantly above the lane by which Seth had returned the night before. Its burning disc threatened to scorch the outstretched fingers of a dead tree on the north side of the path.

At the foot of the tree, the Puddle Stream issued forth, bringing news from the depths of the wood. It chattered cheerfully into the open air as if, after keeping the secret for many a mile, it had come across ears willing to listen to its small talk. After discovering the bridge under the path, it wended its way around to the east and out of sight. After finding its way to the south side of the village, it would eventually tumble reluctantly into the silent rolling waters of the Bucklebank. There its chatter would cease as abruptly as it

The Blue Pig

had begun.

As Sarah turned to fetch the feed for the hens, the sun was already paling from its fiery hue to a watery yellow, as it rode higher into the morning sky. She re-crossed the yard, but turned to the far end of the house, passing the adjoining stables which housed Seth's two plough horses, Tag, his bay gelding who at sixteen-and-a-half hands nearly matched the plough horses, and Meg, the roan pony which he used to pull his small cart and which Sarah often rode.

The stables and other outbuildings, food stores, workshops and barns, were all built around a further, larger yard at the western end of the farm and the farm's land stretched in the main, beyond these buildings, to the south and west.

Before stepping out from the house, Sarah had prepared to start breakfast on the stove and after feeding the hens and leading out the horses and pony to the nearer paddock, she returned with fresh eggs and soon the kitchen smelled of bacon sizzling in the large open pan on the stove. She'd also prepared mushrooms and bread and soon the table was made ready and the plates were warmed. Seth stepped down from the stair which opened into the living room and without the need to think, ducked through the low doorway to the kitchen. Scratching his waking head, he approached Sarah and embracing her gently he kissed her. She answered his good morning with a loving smile. "Hungry?" she asked, placing a mug of milk on the table.

"Of course," he replied, strolling to the open door and taking a draught of the crisp air. "I'll need that meal inside me this morning," he added cheerfully, "I thought I might take Ruffles with me down to the clearing and chop the last of the logs for the winter fires. I can take the cart down there after noon to bring the rest of them back. It'll be a job well done."

They sat down to eat, joined by the dog who enjoyed scraps from the day before and who gnawed on a favourite bone for good measure.

"How are Barny and Will?" remarked Sarah, as she carved two portions of the crusty bread.

"Fine," answered Seth, pouring milk for them both. "Barny's very busy, though that's to be expected this time of year and Will is his normal self. Mind you, they were both a might merrier last night than usual. So was I, come to that. He spread the bread with fresh butter from an earthenware pot, and continued. "The coach brought news yesterday evening from the north. Ely, Amos and the others are safely on their way back."

"The expedition!" Sarah exclaimed. "That's wonderful news... after all our fears. Their families will be so relieved to learn for sure that they're all right."

"Yes. And what's more, they've met with success. They're bringing back cattle. That'll make everyone in Myre Hamlet happy. There may only be a couple of the beasts for each farm, but we'll soon have herds finer than ever they were. The finest in all Midvale at a guess."

"And when are they expected back?"

Sarah was now as excited as those who'd discussed the news the previous night.

"Before the end of November, Sarah, according to Samuel the coachman. There'll be celebrations then. They've sent word asking some of us to meet them at Ambleton in about three weeks' time. They warned of perils on the road at Weatherford, but that can be no challenge compared with *their* arduous journey."

"Celebrations! But of course. We must delay the Dance to be sure they don't miss it, Seth.

They talked of the celebrations in prospect as they finished breakfasting. Sarah pushed back her chair and carried dishes to the wash tub by the stove, pouring water which had been heating. Seth reached for his pipe and tobacco and leaned back

The Blue Pig

in his chair savouring the smoke and contentedly working up a new appetite, for log cutting. Soon he was ready to start on his way to the clearing with Ruffles. He left the kitchen and shouldering his wood-axe, set off by the outbuildings, along the southern edge of the woods towards the east.

"Don't be late back," called Sarah as she prepared the pails for the milking. "There'll be a meal waiting for you both around noon."

CHAPTER TWO

The Homecoming

It was still well before noon on the twenty-fifth of November. Dogs yapped and barked excitedly, cattle lowed and men and children alike danced and cheered as they rushed out to accompany ten weary men and forty or so weary head of cattle down the old stone road into Myre Hamlet. The southbound coach had brought news over a week before that the herd had left Ambleton and had been seen making steady progress southwards. The party had each refused transport with the coach, all saying that they wanted to see the achievement through to the last step. They'd taken all of fifteen days to travel from Ambleton, accompanied by the four others who'd set out to meet them there some weeks before. Although weary and badly in need of long rest the men had preferred to move on from the town in the north as soon as was possible, so as to enjoy their rest in the company of their fellow villagers. They knew too that even the last miles were not without possible perils, for their journey out of the Hamlet had had its dangers even close to home.

Weariness was cast aside for the time being and they joined in with singing and the general chatter concerning their travels. As they reached the heart of Myre Hamlet, more people thronged to meet them, until quite a crowd stood round them as they came to a halt outside the Blue Pig. The cattle were herded hurriedly into the inn yard, for later consideration. Benches had been fetched from the inn and Felix had been summoned to the aid of the great thirsts that had arrived outside, at a time when he'd normally have continued to sleep contented before opening his doors, towards noon.

Barny Hensman, on hearing the commotion approaching his forge, had rushed into the street leaving young Tom holding

The Homecoming

the awkward end of a somewhat enormous chestnut mare. On seeing the cattle led by Amos Spivey and Ely Blackmore, he'd dashed into the inn and, shaking Felix from his slumbers, had almost carried him to the large tuns of ale, shouting with elation.

"Quick Felix! Here come Amos and Ely for those mugs I told you to save. Must have them poured. They're almost here!"

As Felix had come to his senses, he'd found himself reeling across the road with a tray of full mugs followed closely by a beaming Barny, who carried a similar load.

Birdie Sparrow had now joined the crowd, along with Kaleb Moody who'd come into the village from his farm to see Will about repairs to the crumbling stone of his farmhouse. Seth Linden was not to be seen. He was at Puddlefork urgently mending a broken gate, fearful of losing stock.

"Amos! Ely!" cried Barny in jubilation. "Thanks be that you're back safely. We'd given up hope almost at one time."

Will, Kaleb and many others joined Barny in shaking the hands and slapping the backs of Amos and Ely and of all the others who'd returned. Meanwhile, Felix handed round the mugs from both the trays, achieving the almost impossible, by not spilling a drop of ale amidst all the hustle and bustle. He was about to congratulate himself when someone handed back one of the trays... it had been trampled underfoot in all the excitement and now resembled a half spent moon.

"Ah well!" he sighed, a frown replacing his earlier smiles. "At least it went to a good cause."

He picked up the other tray and went off chuckling to himself, having decided that the best thing to do was to open the doors early, to save losing any more trays to good causes.

Barny now looked deep in thought as he talked quietly to Ely Blackmore to one side of the gathering. When shaking hands with the returned travellers, he'd noticed that of the twelve men who'd set out, only nine had returned and an additional, rather wild looking character had returned with them. Barny had never set eyes on the likes of him before. He certainly wasn't from Myre Hamlet.

"Where are the other three?" he asked Ely with some consternation.

Ely sighed with resignation, "I thought you might know. We *did* send word ahead. I'm afraid we lost them on the journey," he explained. "We were lucky more were not lost with all the damned troubles we ran into."

He looked drawn and weary to the point of exhaustion, unable to offer more in the way of explanation for the moment.

"I know it's important, but perhaps Amos and I could tell you more in the Pig tonight after we've rested awhile. Perhaps you would let their families know if they didn't get the sad news. I don't think we're up to it just yet ourselves."

Barny couldn't take in all he'd heard and absently assured Ely that he'd let them know as soon as may be if they'd not already learned the dreadful news. But what he would tell them, and how, he didn't really know. Yet he was still puzzled over the addition to their numbers.

"But what of this stranger who's with you, Ely? Where's he from?"

"Perhaps that too will wait until tonight," sighed Ely with great effort. "Suffice it to say for now that he's both hindered and helped us on our way back here, and that he's harmless enough. We met him in Greylar. He'd travelled there from his homeland, a land unknown to us, a place which he calls Icelar. Oh! and his name... his name is Kelman.

Kelman, despite Ely's assurances, struck Barny as rather an unfriendly character. He stood about the same height as Barny, but the crouching stance he adopted made him look a little shorter. His dark brown hair and beard were wild and matted and his brown eyes were deep set below a frowning brow. His jaw was square and his build was solid and muscular... squat

The Homecoming

but powerful. He wore improvised clothing of leather and sheepskin, little more than a loincloth in nature. He was shod in tough hide, laced to form boots. Perhaps his unfriendly look was a reflection of fear and uncertainty among so many strangers. No doubt he too was weary, but these thoughts didn't allay Barny's uneasiness at this strange interloper.

Ely was wainwright by trade and lived with his wife and three children in one of the cottages in the village. The cottage was already overcrowded, but he'd decided that Kelman should lodge in his workshops on the main street for a while.

"I'll keep him with *us* for the time being," he said. "Until we can perhaps find him a more suitable home."

"Very well," said Barny. "Perhaps you should all get off home and sleep to ease your weariness. *We'll* see to it that the cattle are moved to nearby pasture for now. We've discussed how we might share them out among the farms and if you all agree with the plans we'll start moving them tomorrow. You know, it really is an amazing achievement. Everyone is in your debt. And by the way we've put off the Dance to make it a celebration for your return. I understand it's to be on December the sixth. I hope your blisters have all healed by then. We all know you're the finest dancer in all the Hamlet."

"Away with you," said Ely, forcing a smile. "But I'll be there, to prove you wrong. First though, *I* need a good sleep."

"Then maybe we *won't* see you tonight in the Pig, then?" Barny offered thoughtfully.

"Don't you worry about that, young farrier. I know I need a good rest, but I'll feel a lot happier if I get the last few months off my chest as soon as may be. I'll be in the Pig tonight, even if I need propping up in the chair."

With this Ely made to cross the street.

"But watch those cattle… *they're* tired too at the moment," he said, "but given a rest and half a chance they'd stampede and you'd be all night catching them."

Most of the closer relatives of the travellers had arrived on the scene by now. Mothers, fathers, wives and children. First had come those who lived in the village itself and then those who'd been called in from the nearer of the outlying farms. Those who found no one to meet were consoled in their desperate shock and grief by friends who led them compassionately from the scene, joining them in their sobbing. Barny, though he tried, could do little to help. Among the assembly of villagers was Helen Blackmore with two of her young children. Having rushed from their cottage, they couldn't at first reach Ely, but now Helen greeted him warmly, sobbing with relief on realising that her husband was safe home again. Ely embraced her and then in turn picked up each of the girls and hugged them.

"Where's your brother?" he asked them.

"He's watching the stove," Helen replied on their behalf. "I thought you might be hungry," she smiled.

"Yes," he answered, hugging her again. "And then to sleep awhile is all I ask. I'm sure I'll never want to use my legs again."

No other words were spoken, for the joy they all felt was enough. They turned towards home, Helen on Ely's arm and the children on either side of them.

"Ely?" a questioning voice called from behind them. Kelman had been gazing all around him at his new surroundings, lost and lonely in the crowd. No one had paid him more attention than a cautious glance and although he could sense warmth around him, he felt that it did not, and could not, belong to *him*.

"Kelman!" called Ely as he turned. "Forgive me! I'm forgetting you in my weariness and my newfound joy. Please, come and join us. My wife and my children must meet you, since you're to lodge with us for a while. Helen, this is Kelman, from the north."

He explained that Kelman had joined them on their travels

The Homecoming

and would need accommodation for the time being. Helen's first thoughts were of the overcrowding this would cause, but after Ely explained that Kelman would sleep in the workshops, she smiled afresh. There was no caution or concern in her voice. "Welcome to our home Kelman," she said warmly. "I'm sure you must be as weary and as hungry as Ely."

At this Kelman's heart lifted and the questioning look in his eyes melted.

"Thank you," he offered, somewhat haltingly.

He joined them and together they walked along the neatly hedged pathways between homely gardens to Ely's cottage.

Slowly, the gathering dispersed in all directions, the most favoured of these being into the Pig, leaving Barny Hensman, Will Sparrow and Kaleb Moody sitting on one of the benches that Felix had left behind.

"Well," said Barny, "was it really worth it... the lives of three men for forty head of cattle? I suppose..."

"Of course not," interrupted Will, showing great concern. "But none of us realised that such a journey would take so long or be so perilous. Now that the journey has been made, we can't change what's happened, however painful and sorrowful it seems. Let's at least make good use of what we now have, so that lives won't have been spent entirely for naught."

"I guess that you're right, but it just seems such a waste," replied Barny.

Kaleb, for once, remained silent.

"Anyway," continued Barny, "I must get back to young Tom. In all the excitement I left him holding a mare back at the forge. It'll have probably dragged him half way to Westhorn by now. By the way, Ely reckons on being in the Pig tonight to tell us more of Greylar and about this fellow Kelman from up north. No doubt Amos and a few of the others will be in too if they can be woken."

"And what of Seth?" asked Will. "I'm sure he'll want to hear the tales to be told."

"Yes, he's sure to be in tonight, but I'll go over to Puddlefork before then to tell him and Sarah the news. I don't think they even know the men are back yet."

"That's alright Barny," Kaleb said, with his usual frown. "I'll drop in on my way back to the farm now, to let them know."

"Fine, I'll see you both tonight then."

Barny's mood lightened at the prospect of a long chat over a mug of ale. He turned and paid a brief visit to the Blue Pig. Forcing his way through the merriment he found a stool to stand on and with some difficulty persuaded several in the crowd to leave their mugs and see to it that the cattle in the yard were moved to pasture close by, as he'd promised Ely.

Barny's eyes bulged in amazement when he returned to the forge. Young Tom *hadn't* been dragged half way to Westhorn but *had* in fact finished shoeing the mare single-handed and was just leading her into one of the stables.

"Well, I'll be blowed," chuckled the farrier after inspecting the horse's shoes. 'That's as good a job as I'd have made and no mistake. *I'll* be the assistant soon and that's a fact."

"Steady fella," Seth's gentle voice urged, as he encouraged his gelding along the path to the village. A sudden encounter with the fluttering and hooting of a startled owl had unnerved the creature for an instant. Seth had chosen to ride to the Pig tonight for, by all accounts, he might be leaving much later than usual on his return home. It was a dark evening. The moon, which had waned to a crescent, hadn't yet risen and Seth carried aloft a flickering lantern, tied to a strong wooden staff. The lantern burned with a reassuring light but the twisted shadows of gnarled, finger-like branches darted and fled from its approach and were not so reassuring. Boughs groaned and creaked before a sharp wind, which was growing from the north. Seth, wrapped inside a thick cloak, leaned forward and

The Homecoming

deftly taking staff and reins in one hand he patted the horse's neck, gently urging him forward at a walking pace.

"Now then, Tag, think of that hay waiting for you at the Pig. I'm sure there'll be company there for *you* tonight as well as for me."

The horse snuffled at the wind, whinnied as if in anticipation of the promised feed and responded to Seth's encouragement, now stepping with enthusiasm towards welcome lights.

When the farmer had stabled his mount alongside the many other horses, he plunged forth into the warmth of the inn to find the outer rooms comfortably filled, indeed more than comfortably packed, with chattering folk. The air was thick and pipe smoke floated like a mist above their heads, curling in delicate wisps around the beams before being lost in the general haze. Many were listening to some of the returned travellers who were recounting details of their quest. Others laughed and joked, paying little attention to this topical business. Seth jostled his way to the smaller, quieter room to find Barny and Kaleb already chattering with Will Sparrow, speculating on tales to be told. They greeted the new arrival and before long Ely and Amos arrived as expected too. The din sprang forth then receded as the two entered and closed the door behind them.

Amos, another farmer, had joined his friend Ely at his cottage and they'd come from there together. Each had returned from the north with a growth of beard, but both had shaved now to reveal their old selves. Ely's craggy face was even without the untamed drooping moustache that he normally wore. His hair, now washed and free of grime, was black and long, tied back with a small bow. His thin well-defined nose was raw, as were his cheeks, from the winds and weathers of the north and his lips were cracked and dry, though not so severely as to keep him from the ale mugs that were before him on the table. The others noticed that his steady brown eyes stared as if from some distant world, only dreaming of what they now saw. He had, it seemed, been deeply affected by the rigours of travelling and by the tortures of delays and uncertainties.

Amos however, who was a man of great moral stature and would make decisions and stick by them, usually to the benefit of all, looked as confident as he always had. He was one of the more vehement approvers of the quest. His watery-grey eyes and his wisps of greying blond hair belied his nature. Both his nose and chin were unobtrusive and his cheekbones couldn't be detected in his unusually smooth and rounded face. Yet *his* face too had been weathered by the elements, though not with rawness as Ely's had for he'd worked all his days in the face of the weather. Unlike Ely, he was of slight build. Amos had often spurred his companions on through despair in adversity on the road.

Both men, who were thirty years or more of age, wore clothes of the sort popular with the people of the Hamlet at this time of year. Each wore a white stock and a waistcoat, breeches and brown leather boots suitable for riding. Each had discarded large-brimmed hats and high-collared coats of heavy cloth on entering the room.

Amos viewed the gathering of friends with confident approval and placing his mug on the table and his foot on the chair before him, he smiled and laughed heartily.

"Well," he said, slapping Seth square between the shoulders, "It's good to be back in the Pig after so long, and to see you all together looking so hale."

Seth, recovering from the unexpected blow, nodded in agreement as he coughed and spluttered over a mug of ale. If truth be known, apart from still feeling weary for want of more rest, Amos was now more fit than anyone else in the room.

"What about these cattle then?" remarked Ely somewhat absently from the corner where he'd settled.

And so the cattle were discussed. Proposals had been well

The Homecoming

mooted before they'd ever set out and since all that had changed were the numbers available, little more needed to be said.

"We'd thought on similar lines ourselves on the last few days between Ambleton and the Hamlet," Amos pointed out. "I'm sure our travelling companions will be more than happy with what's been suggested."

"But what of your travels?" burst out Barny who, not being a farmer himself, could withhold his enthusiasm no longer for a tale of less essential but more attractive content than this.

He always liked a good tale and tonight had promised to be a night abounding with such absorbing talk. He'd heard Seth and Amos discuss the cattle relentlessly on so many prior occasions until he'd even dreamed of shoeing line upon line of them, each beast to be taken from his forge and either ridden home under saddle or harnessed to some cart or other. He'd even seen the coach from the north come wildly galloping through Myre Hamlet under a ghostly full moon... pulled by no fewer than six white cows.

Amos sat down in his chair, took a draught from his mug and looked across the table at Barny.

"Hmm," he mused. "It's a long tale to tell if you want to hear it all. So, I'll do my best in the time we have tonight, and perhaps Ely will help me if I go astray... and we did enough of that as you'll soon find out," he added flippantly.

Seth chuckled and with feet upon the table, a favourite pose of his, he lifted his pipe and rekindled it in anticipation of a long account from Amos.

"You'll remember we set out on horseback from Myre Hamlet in mid-March. Well, I'm sure we'd have reached Fenny in just over a week, but we were waylaid at Weatherford. All of our horses and many of our supplies were taken. The wild men who attacked us seemed hungry and wild enough to have eaten the horses as well as our food. About fifteen of them, mostly on foot, came upon us from a small copse on the western side of the road after we'd crossed the ford. They fled like the wind towards the mountains in the east. This is why we warned of perils there, when we sent word for you to meet us on our return, though thankfully they were not seen again. Our first thoughts had been to follow them, but it would have been folly to leave the road, we being on foot and all. We'd two other choices... to head back for the Hamlet and set out afresh later, or to try to make it to Fenny on foot where we could find new mounts for our travels in Greylar, as well as fresh food and gear which we'd intended to obtain there anyway. We decided on the latter since any further delays could mean winter might catch us.

"We made it to Fenny on foot but we were unfit and with little food we were slowed considerably even though we followed the road when we could, still avoiding the coaches for secrecy's sake. The weather was kind, mind you, and we reached the coast and Fenny a fortnight after leaving you here. For two days there we rested, and after restoring our food stocks and finding new mounts we were ready for the sea. With some difficulty and more silver, we persuaded the masters of three large sailing boats to take us along the northern coast to the east and along to Greylar. Sorry days followed, for the sailors were ever reluctant."

"So much for willing crews." agreed Ely.

"Yes," went on Amos. "Being the superstitious folk they are, they'd not normally be away from port overnight and in any event wouldn't leave sight of the coast for fear of never again finding it. Some sailors indeed. But we promised we'd find a mooring along the coast each night or we'd never have found a boat in the whole place."

Birdie, shuffling his chair nearer to the fire. "There *was* vague news of your ambush in April," he said, "so we had some warning of perils on the road already. But we were happy to

The Homecoming

hear then that you'd all set out for Greylar soon after your arrival in Fenny."

"Everything considered, things were going quite smoothly until we found the wild herds," said Ely, who still gazed vacantly and said very little.

"That's no lie," continued Amos with a nod to the wainwright acknowledging his comment. "We had some delays whilst sailing though, but nothing more than delays thankfully. They'd never sailed far east before, these sailors. Most of their trade, it seems, is done in Fenny Bay or west to main ports of the continent. They doggedly followed the coast around another large bay. We were held up with strong tides and unfavourable winds for more than a few days and the additional burden of anchoring every night at dusk meant it took us all of eighteen days to reach Greylar and our landing place at the Greymills. Even so, it was now only mid-April and we were in high spirits for we were nearing the plains. The boat crews agreed to wait three weeks for our return to the Greymills should it prove necessary and if we still hadn't returned, for at least one boat to wait for a further two weeks in the hope we might still return.

"We travelled on horseback great distances over the plains of Greylar in search of the cattle, camping for brief rests at night. We were all much fitter now and missed the comforts of home much less. We sheltered when we needed, but the weather was more than kind. All the same, we soon became anxious, for time was short and we'd not found the cattle. Then, on the fair dawn of the sixteenth day we saw them... far off, on the edge of sight. An incredible sight it was too, like the shadow of some dark, brooding storm cloud drifting across the wide plain. We had little difficulty, once we came upon them, in splitting a hundred or so from the herd, though the sound of the thundering hooves of so many left us in awe. The worst task was the keeping of a careful eye on our few for a day or two, for they'd have returned to the herd if given half a chance."

"That's when our troubles *really* began," Ely interrupted, his eyes staring blankly into the blazing fire.

Amos continued, "Sure enough, that's when our troubles *did* begin."

He too was now staring at the fire. The flickering flames cast fickle shadows and he fancied that in them he saw the herd, moving first this way and then that, but always together, always guided by some unseen leader.

"Several days later, the cattle took fright at the wind in unfamiliar trees," went on Amos, dragging his eyes from the fiery vision, "and they stampeded, not for the last time, into the darkness of a cloudy and moonless night. It took days of tracing and retracing them and still we didn't find them *all*. Then the wind turned and with it the weather for with the new wind came continual rain, for days, for weeks. Torrential, soaking rain.

"The cattle, when they weren't stampeding, were happy enough to graze on the abundant grass, but we were beginning to go round in circles chasing them and achieving little progress in our intended direction. Even makeshift fences were no help.

"Being concerned that we'd miss the last of the boats, John Farley and Jud Fielding set forth on our strongest mounts to ride with all speed for the Greymills. By now we'd almost spent our food and our spoils from hunting were proving sparse, so reluctantly we resorted to the slaughter of some of the beasts. We could ill afford to waste them to this purpose, and with no decent way of preserving meat, much was wasted.

"The weather dried as we left the pasturelands and we crossed a desolate moorland, sparse of vegetation. We neared the coast now, but were confronted with another, greater peril... we could find no water, for ourselves or for the cattle. Both we and they took sicknesses and, as if our ills were not

The Homecoming

enough to make us lay down and give up completely, we came upon a horrifying sight."

Ely endorsed this with a shiver and uttered a cry of revulsion, but couldn't, or wouldn't find words.

Amos gripped the arm of the chair, "A horrifying sight. Half-eaten corpses lay before us... John and Jud."

Tears welled from the depths of his eyes, but he stifled them and went on.

"Both they and their horses had been attacked by wild dogs, not more than five miles from the Greymills. Five bodies of the viciously fanged creatures lay about them, either killed by brave John and Jud before they'd fallen, or felled by their own filthy cannibalistic pack who'd fed on these five and the horses too."

The others in the room were taken aback by this unexpected revelation. Barny, who'd been enjoying the conversation, turned as if to vomit in the hearth, but held it back, managing to overcome his horror, gasping for air.

"We wept long and sorrowfully for them," said Ely, who seemed hardened to the tragic loss, yet still he gazed into the flames. "We buried them as best we could, feeling now that all was lost. It was possible that they'd reached the boatmen before the tragic end, yet it was unlikely, and if they'd all left without us, there would be no hope now for the cattle and little help for us. And yet Amos seemed strengthened by this evil fortune. He insisted that we'd make it back, even *with* the cattle. He resolved that he'd take two others willing and head south if indeed it proved that all the boats had left. He'd find the place where the southerners had crossed and so travel by land to Fenny and bring back boats. 'We'll not give up! Not until we're all dead!' he'd shrieked, as anger overcame resolve."

"But we thought that they intended to return to you," interrupted Seth, surprised. "At least, that's the news *we'd* had from Fenny. Why didn't you consider waiting for them,

Amos?"

"Consider waiting, Seth?" protested Amos. "We were desperate, and if they'd any intention of returning, *we* didn't know of it. At the time of our parting from them we'd not even seriously considered the possible need for the one boat to stay alone. The boats had indeed all departed by the time we reached the Mills, so Jamie Hunter and Sam Rushey set out with *me*. Poor Sam. He too lost his life out in the accursed north, though at least he was spared the dogs as you'll learn.

"The cattle were led back to the edge of the grasslands, where food and water were sufficient and there the return of the three of us would be awaited."

"But before we'd found that the boats had left, and before Amos set out on this desperate mission," said Ely, "we had yet another encounter, though this turned out to be less harrowing."

"Kelman!" announced Seth, leaning forward.

He'd wondered where Kelman might come into the story and he settled back into his chair as Amos confirmed that he'd guessed aright.

"Yes, Kelman. A being who, at first, seemed as much a threat to our safety as any wild dogs might be."

"I almost brought Kelman here tonight," Ely said, "to give his story to you himself, but he's wary of our village and of our ways, and he's not well versed in our tongue. Their language is a broken, simple form of ours."

"*Theirs?*" questioned Birdie. "Who are *they*?"

"Give me time. Give me time!" Amos insisted, taking up the conversation again. "I was coming to that shortly... Kelman at length explained to us that he'd ventured into Greylar from the place that they call Icelar."

Birdie, still impatient to know who *'they'* were, was now perched on the edge of his chair and listened intently as Amos went on.

The Homecoming

"As we'd approached the Greymills by boat, many weeks before, we'd seen what we took to be a small island to the north. Gulls were flocking around the sheer cliff faces that were its limits. We paid it little attention yet this, according to Kelman, was Icelar, a much larger land than we'd imagined. The cliffs that we'd seen were merely the south-eastern tip he assured us, and stretching across this land into the north-west is a great range of mountains. In a sheltered valley on the eastern side of this backbone is Ironmound, the homestead from which Kelman had come."

Birdie now relaxed a little, having been partly answered. Amos took a swig of ale before answering him further.

"His people are hunters, it seems, living in a harsh land. Food, especially after a hard winter, is difficult to come by for they're not skilled in curing their hard-earned meat. Kelman explained that by early spring this year things had become so desperate for his own family that he'd attempted to steal food from someone else, for the autumn sharing had been done and he knew that no more would be given. His attempt was discovered, and great anger fell upon him. He was taken to a hill cave, and knew that an ugly death awaited him. And so he plotted his escape and that very night broke free, unnoticed by his guard, and headed south with all the speed he could. After eluding his eventual pursuers he slowed his pace and took some time in reaching the southern shores. He'd been south before, for he's a restless man and he'd stood on the cliffs that we'd seen from the sea in the past. He knew of Greylar and even before his need for escape, he'd half thought of leaving cruel Icelar to seek a better land. Yet in his way he loved his family, for it shows itself in what little he's said of them. He would never have left them had he not been forced to.

"Reaching the cliffs, he'd found his way down to the shore of a small cove on the northern coast of this outcrop of land and to his amazement had discovered old boats in nearby caves. They were rotting, but by now he was desperate. He'd heard legends of his people that spoke of their ancestors coming to Icelar over the waters many years before. Some had said that many had settled as fishermen on the coast while many had moved inland and at last had settled where Ironmound had grown. *'Could these then have been the boats of recent fishermen?'* he'd thought. He'd then picked the best of the boats and, with some improvised repairs, had attempted the crossing. From what he's said, he was washed ashore on what was by then no more than a half-sinking collection of planks. He was desperately hungry but, with spring's full arrival and with his skill as a hunter, he soon had enough fresh raw meat to feed on... hare, rabbit and even wild pig."

"A blue one I shouldn't wonder," chipped in Barny with a smile, having regained some of the colour in his cheeks.

"When we met up with him in mid-June," went on Amos, "he'd been wandering around for more than a month. I reckon *he* was in a sorrier state than *we* were, if only for want of company. Seeing a chance of ending his lone trek, he jumped into sight with such enthusiasm that we at once thought we were under attack. His untamed locks did nothing to help, and he and I nearly killed each other before we sorted out our little misunderstanding. But shortly he explained what you now know."

Ely took the story on as Amos quenched his thirst again.

"Kelman seemed a pathetic creature, in need of nothing more than company. He insisted on staying with us, in spite of our own great plight. So when we'd travelled the short distance to the Greymills and had seen no sign of the sailors, Amos, Sam and Jamie set out for Nording and for Fenny, while Kelman came back with the rest of us to the plains. He showed us water he'd found and reminded us of many hunting skills, to spare the cattle. There we waited.

"Each day brought more hopelessness, knowing that if Amos

The Homecoming

wasn't back before winter started creeping on, we'd have to abandon the cattle and do what we could to return without them. We'd have left them sooner, but after all we'd been through we hung on as long as we dare. We knew Amos and the others had a long and dangerous journey to undertake and that even if all went well, it would take well over a month to return to us."

"In fact," informed Amos, taking up the tale again, "it took us much longer. We were delayed and bedogged with trouble almost from the outset. We reached the coast easily enough, but having rested and having made what we hoped was a reasonable raft, we had to wait for more than a week for favourable conditions suited to such a flimsy and ill-controllable craft. We knew it would be folly to go otherwise, for a rash crossing might destroy our purpose completely.

"Once on the mainland we were weakened by shortage of food. Our shelter was poor and we shivered with sickness for it rained relentlessly along that north coast. We were in no condition to hunt, but abundant streams and springs saw to it that we didn't fall short of water.

"Woodlands to the south made the rough terrain more difficult at times for often they stretched out to the coast and caused us to track and re-track in deep valleys matted with brambles. It was on such a misadventure that poor Sam Rushey had a disastrous fall. He slithered and fell to the bottom of a deep rill in a densely wooded area. Until he'd called out in surprise as he lost his footing, we'd not detected the peril. He'd broken his right leg and badly twisted and bruised the ankle. He tried bravely to continue, but the pain was so bad that we had to stay put and tend him as best we could. We tried to reset the bone, but it seemed badly shattered. He was in dreadful agony and sobbed with pain through many nights. We just couldn't leave him, even though the others were depending on our return. We felt that they'd be safe enough in numbers.

Finally we resolved that Jamie or I must go alone but to our despair Sam died, his leg all poisoned and swollen, saving us only from our small dilemma of who would go and who would stay with him.

"We'd no hope of burying him properly, so we made a mound of stones under grey skies and thought on it less than our hearts demanded.

"We finally reached Fenny and after recovering, we persuaded our 'friends,' with great difficulty, to return again. They said then that they'd intended to return but in the end they'd felt that the dangers were too great. The superstitious fools! *'If only they knew,'* I thought. We now resorted to desperate threats and although they could easily have ignored the two of us, for our threats in truth were impotent, this approach seemed to stir them into some understanding of our plight. We set out for Greylar once more with boats."

The door sprang open and in came a smiling Felix with a young lad at his side. They both carried trays… ale to replenish drained mugs and the usual feast of bread and cheese. It was hungry work, both talking and listening, and all in the room had appetites to prove it, except perhaps for Barny who still dwelt heavily on the evil news that the story had brought them. Nonetheless, they continued their discussions between mouthfuls of the welcome food.

"So," remarked Kaleb, venturing unexpectedly from his silence, thumping the table with clenched fist. "The news we had in June played us false indeed. We were led to believe then that the last boat had returned, but to turn again after a brief rest and restocking in Fenny. It wasn't until late September that we learned of your further plight, and it seems that plight was overcome by then. If we'd known in time, we too would have sailed the northern sea. So much for Fenny."

Amos nodded in agreement, but he'd thought on this much of late and knew that the sailors, though reluctant to return,

The Homecoming

had perhaps done as much as should've been expected of them.

"They had at least been patient enough to wait for five weeks," he replied. "Or so it seems. And eventually we *did* win more of their respect and confidence. They said that they'd changed their minds about returning *after* news that they *would* go had reached you here in Myre Hamlet and were afraid to admit to anyone that they were not to set out again."

"But they could have ruined you all," insisted Kaleb. "If they *had* set out again, maybe poor Sam at least would still be with us."

"And why didn't the coach bring news that they'd not set out again?" added Will.

"They could quite possibly have sailed out of port for some other destination," explained Amos, "and little would have been reported to the coachmen. The folk of Fenny will help when they have to, or when they're paid to, but not so for other reasons. They're not as close a people as *we* are, for the closer your neighbour sometimes the further you are from him."

"Miserable wretches," Kaleb went on, now mumbling under a brooding cloud of anger. "I hope their boats go down on top of them."

"They almost did," remarked Ely, with an ironic smile, "though to be correct it was *beneath* them. When they'd arrived back at the Greymills with Amos, we were soon herding the cattle to the shores of Greylar once again. There we loaded without too much difficulty and though we were precariously low in the water, the weather was fair and the sea was quite calm.

"We made good progress considering the burden we carried and the stops they still insisted on, until one day we found that water was leaking badly into one of the boats. The other boats looked like going the same way too, although we were now nearly half way to Fenny. We kept close to shore, but we knew now that we'd never make it all the way as we were. Then, the weakest boat shuddered to a halt and listed violently. We'd run aground in shallow sandy-bottomed waters, some two furlongs from the shore. Then we could see that the tide was ebbing rapidly leaving vast expanses of sand all around us. Previous journeys must have taken the boats past this point at high tide.

"Perhaps the worst of this peril might have been avoided had the boatmen not been preoccupied with the first grounded boat, but soon all three were high and dry. The cattle unloaded themselves and we desperately herded them in wet sand on foot, for we'd left the horses in Greylar to avoid further overloading... we'd been sure they'd find the pastures of the grasslands and would thrive there happily.

"Now a decision was needed, and a quick one at that. Should we leave some of the cattle and travel on by boat when the tide came in or should we travel on by foot, having at least reached our own mainland? Or perhaps split the herd and travel some by boat and some by land? To some extent our decision was made for us, by the boatmen. They now protested more strongly than ever at the increasing danger to their craft and felt it nothing short of madness to go on with all but a few of the cattle. The skies portended evil weather too. And to be fair to the men of Fenny, we'd caused them much inconvenience already.

"None of us wanted to part company, but, although the land route would no doubt take longer, we all felt confident with our feet on land. We didn't relish the thought of driving the cattle back onto the boats again, what with the wet sands. So it was that we drove our charges over the grassy sand dunes that marked the permanent shoreline. The boatmen occupied themselves with temporary repairs, taking some advantage of their running aground, so that when the tide returned they might float on it and not be washed away *under* it.

"Having made camp on the dunes, and leaving the others to tend the cattle, we helped with the repairs as we could. They

The Homecoming

agreed to pass on news of our route when they returned.

"That evening we sat and watched the boats carried away as the tide rushed to meet them. Out of necessity they'd become confident enough to sail by night this once."

"Then this must have been in early October," Seth calculated. "We received news on the eighteenth that you were safe on the mainland and hoped to reach Myre Hamlet by the end of November. From what we heard, you hoped to reach Ambleton by the first or second week of the month."

"Yes. We thought it would take less time than it did," said Amos, "for we hoped for no more ill fortune. We looked to surprise you all by reaching the Hamlet before you set out to meet us."

"Then what kept you?" asked Barny. "Surely not more trouble?"

"Not exactly trouble, but difficulties. Our main concern when we'd decided to leg it was that we may never control the little herd we'd established, but I think they'd learned to know better for they were little trouble to us now. Perhaps they were grateful for being free of the sea, though Ely reckons some evil must have taken them before, when they were so much trouble in Greylar. It certainly seemed that way. But now, the horses were not missed except for want of saving our own sore feet and of course our time. The weather too was kind but we took a deceptive path that led us deep *into* the mountains rather than through them. It proved to be a dead end after we had some promise of a way through. We retraced our path and soon we came across a more obvious way through the foothills, with no real mountains before us.

"So with all our trials behind us, we arrived in Ambleton after our welcoming party had made it there. Two days after in fact, on the tenth of November. Such was our joy at seeing people we knew, that we were tempted to rest and celebrate there and then. But we felt at heart that we should press on, for once you rest near to the end of a task it's hard to set to it again. At last we'd broken free of Ely's 'evil forces' and that in itself deserved the respect of an immediate return. We met with no further real delays, though we lost one or two more of our cattle through sickness of their arduous travels. Perhaps forty-five head is not as much as we hoped for?"

Amos finished his story with a sigh and a shake of his head, but the others soon reassured him that he was wrong to feel dejected.

"Forty-five's more than enough for what we need," Seth insisted. "And if you'd loaded a hundred, I reckon the boats would have sunk without trace."

"Oh, yes. I'd like to see you keep an eye on *that* many, Amos," laughed Barny, knowing full well that he and the others had done little short of it for many months.

Amos and Ely smiled feeling at last that their ordeal was over, now that their story was shared with friends.

"You can both rest from now until the celebration Dance," said Will. "Then we'll expect to see you dancing as lightly as the rest of us."

He stood up and demonstrated with a brief jig, made even more brief by his tripping on the rug and spilling a full mug of ale over Barny's upturned face. Raucous laughter gripped them all and they settled once more to chat further of what had been said and to talk of other things besides that concerned the Hamlet.

CHAPTER THREE

Harvest Home

"Kelman!" shouted Josiah Cavey. "Take these boots over to Barny Hensman will you? He'll be at the forge *now*. He'll want them for the Dance tonight you know. Don't you dawdle now.

"Yes Josiah... I go now," stammered Kelman, a little unsure as he tore himself from the window where he'd been watching the rain.

Josiah Cavey was the cobbler. He was Felix Cavey's brother though less good-natured at times. In one of his more generous moods he'd offered to take Kelman into his care. He'd more room at home than Ely and he and his wife were happy enough to provide food and lodgings for Kelman, on the understanding that he'd run errands for the overworked Mr. Cavey. He, like Barny, always had more work at this time of the year than at any other. Kelman had spent two nights in Ely's workshop but since then had slept in a comfortable bed in the Caveys' cottage nearby. He'd cleaned up, and had been given clothes more acceptable in his new surroundings. He'd shaved at the insistence of Mrs. Cavey, but had retained the wild growth of hair on his head. He was still rather wary of people, and the day-to-day goings on in the village were still very strange to him. He still seemed to be fighting with his inner feelings to achieve any noticeable self-confidence. Unfortunately Josiah already took Kelman's help a little for granted, which made things even harder for him.

The morning had dawned chased by clouds rolling in from the east swallowing up the promised brightness of morning and, as the day passed to noon, they'd become a grey, oppressive blanket that had threatened to pour forth its contents like an overburdened sponge. Now, a soaking drizzle fell, drenching the road, the buildings and the hedgerows and gardens.

Kelman wrapped a cloak around him and, picking up the parcel from the bench where Josiah busily attended more boots, he splashed out into the rain and made for the forge.

Everyone in the village was disappointed with the weather that had forced itself upon them today. The Dance wasn't just an occasion for dancing indoors in the evening, but festive attractions took place during the day too, some indoors and some out. Though late in the autumn, it was usually dry, but the few weeks of delay this year has landed them in the lap of an impatient winter.

The Dance day was never generally admitted to be a holiday, but for the most part, people concerned themselves with attending to essential work only and always seemed to manage to combine it with visits to the various attractions.

Tents and small marquees had sprung up along the street and in the gardens, offering wines made by farmers' wives, and breads and cakes from the same source. There were also cheeses and pies, smoked meats and pickles and all drawn from abundant stores that had been prepared against the winter. There was ale too, of course, which helped the more reluctant to join the antics of the small troupe of dancers who reeled and cavorted giddily up and down the road, along the paths and through the gardens, accompanied by a pipe and tabor. After a brave effort to ignore the rain, they were forced under cover to continue capering in a less noble but no less vigorous effort. Nonetheless, there was still an atmosphere of happy celebration, helped perhaps by its extra purpose this year.

Kelman passed the boisterous, noisy tents on his way to Barny's forge, but didn't venture in, for his lack of confidence still outweighed his curiosity. He now knew and trusted a few of the villagers but he'd had little contact with the majority of them.

Harvest Home

"Hello, Kelman. Got my new boots, I see," Barny greeted him with a smile as he wiped his hands on a grimy cloth having just attended a pony that had slipped a shoe. Putting aside the cloth, he attacked the parcel with enthusiasm.

"Hi, Kelman," nodded Tom as he led the pony out.

"Hello Barny. Hello Tom," Kelman replied, with some measure of confidence. Barny seemed much more easily trusted than some of the others and with the forge being close to Josiah's workshop, he'd spent as much of his time here as he may. He'd watch Barny at work, spellbound by his craft and would talk with him, learning a little more of the ways and traditions of the villagers. Barny and Tom also learned something of the ways of the folk of Ironmound, though Kelman spoke of his native land with reticence. Certainly they didn't shoe horses there, though they did *use* horses, or their close relatives as beasts of burden.

The boots that Barny now held before him were indeed a work of art when compared with the collections of hide that Kelman was used to.

"Beautiful," declared Barny. "In these tonight, I'll dance everyone off their feet... or blisters will dance me off mine. *You'll* be there won't you Kelman?"

"I... No! I think I not go tonight. I not know how you dance," he managed, unsure of himself again.

"Come on now," replied Barny, slapping him on the back. "No need for that. We'll soon show you how. To tell the truth we all fall over ourselves enough times, when we're full of ale, so I'm sure no one will worry if you fall over with us."

He smiled and demonstrated with a little jig which sent him careering through a doorway and crashing into a pile of old horseshoes. He reappeared, still smiling, and rubbing his rump.

"Ouch! ...even when we're *not* full of ale," he added painfully, having demonstrated more the falling over than the dancing.

At this Kelman laughed aloud, and could find no way of refusing to attend the Dance. He returned to the cobbler's workshop in the drizzle, still chuckling to himself.

"Welcome to our annual Dance!" shouted Seth Linden.
He hammered loudly on the table before him and repeated his greeting as the din responded to his request for silence.
"Welcome to the Dance! I've been asked to say a few words before the dancing starts. As you all know, we've a special reason for celebrating this year. We celebrate the fact that we now have cattle that will improve our herds and will also make our celebrations special in the years to come."
A unanimous cheer of approval went up from the already jovial gathering. Seth continued.
"We celebrate the return of the men who brought this bounty to us."
Another, louder cheer.
"But alongside our rejoicing we must remember that three of the men who set out *didn't* return."
This was answered with thoughtful murmurings.
"While this is indeed a sad loss to us all, and more so to their families, and though we mourn, we must at least rejoice in their great courage in helping to make the journey a success and in aiding, while they could, the safe return of their companions."
Subdued murmuring continued, but having already thought on their loss for some days, they saw the need to forget sorrow.
"So, please join with me in saluting their bravery," bellowed Seth, rousingly.
Another cheer rose from the gathering.
"And let's celebrate, as always, our good fortune in that we're well stocked with food for this winter."
Yet another cheer.
"Finally, I'd ask you all to welcome one new member into our community, indeed to our land itself... Kelman of the

Harvest Home

north, for he too helped in bringing back those who returned. Perhaps we can now help *him* by accepting him into our village, and into our hearts, so that he may find no need to steal food to survive, as he was forced to do by the tragedy of Ironmound."

A further cheer almost lifted the roof, perhaps more because Seth had finished speaking than in acknowledgment of his words. And the cheers turned to laughter and applause as Seth concluded by asking the small band of musicians in the corner to strike up their music, and by asking the gathering to enjoy their dancing.

The band comprised players with fiddle, flute and several lute like instruments along with the pipe and tabor borrowed from the travelling party of the hedgerows and tents. They played their tunes so merrily as to make them soon irresistible to all but the most reserved of the Hamlet folk. And their simplicity encouraged even the most incompetent and drunken of merrymakers that the evening could produce to try their skills.

The Dance had taken place ever year in living memory and always occupied all but a handful of the inhabitants of the entire Hamlet. It was always held in the village hall, which was itself always well decorated on Dance day with colourful streamers and with dried flowers. The flowers were set in windows and in baskets. Lanterns flickered warmly overhead. The merrymakers always made a point of admiring these when first entering the hall since later most were oblivious to the existence of the hall itself, let alone the decorations.

Soon, the floor was teeming with joyous dance, much of which was improvisation to suit each person's skill in dancing, or indeed each person's lack of it. The general idea was for the men to partner ladies, but often the erratic progression from partner to partner would produce a pairing of two women, or even two men accompanied by roars of laughter from the entire gathering.

Barny was there of course, sporting his new boots. And young Tom too, proudly attached to a new beard... his first, grown but recently. Felix served ale, little change for him, between dancing. Kaleb and Will talked in a corner, each rising to dance less often than most, but as vigorously when they did join in. Ely Blackmore and his wife, Helen, chatted to Seth and Sarah.

Kelman too had come, as he'd promised, talking and laughing with Barny, when Barny wasn't bounding across the floor inside his boots. Kelman took some persuading to join those out on the floor, but once there, he was no longer reluctant and took part in the falling over as well as the dancing. He even won the prize of a small leather purse for the most original improvisation of the village's favourite jig, which was renamed Kelman's jig on the spot by Barny. Amidst the warmth of the festivities, Kelman felt at last that he belonged here.

It was early morning. The winter sun was too weak to melt the frost that the stars had left behind them. Kelman cleared the thin smear of ice from a windowpane and sat, head in hands, gazing across the waking street from the workshop. The cottages beyond the road caught the slanting shafts of the eastern sun, which gave gold to the sleepy windows where shutters had been neglected. His breath hung in steaming clouds as it drifted from his yawning mouth. He was reminded much of the winters in the north.

Two months had passed since the dancing. Things were back to normal now. Josiah, and hence Kelman, had been busy since the Dance and today, it seemed, would be no exception.

"Come on Kelman. Look lively! Take these hides to the storeroom now, and bring me that last from over there in the corner."

Kelman remained motionless despite Josiah's calling, lost in some deep anxiety or other.

"Are you deaf man?" Josiah bristled, shuffling over to Kelman. With a prod, he repeated his request. "Store these hides and fetch that last. There's work to be done."

Kelman swung reluctantly away to comply with the request and Josiah caught a glimpse of Kelman's mood.

"What's wrong Kelman," he enquired, taking hold of the northerner by the arm and spinning him round acknowledging that his helper may have some reason for sulking.

The cobbler's mouth fell open, letting out a gasp of amazement. There upon Kelman's neck he spied a sight that at first sickened him and then frightened him. A horrible scabby presence, dry and crusted in parts, festered there. A revolting purple sore, the like of which he'd never seen. Josiah stared in disbelief and Kelman darted a look of hurt at him, turning away weeping to himself.

"What is it?" choked Josiah at last.

Silence.

"What in Midvale *is* it Kelman?" he repeated, overcoming his initial revulsion and placing a reluctant hand on Kelman's shoulder.

Kelman made no reply but continued to sob.

"This must be shown to the apothecary. He may know what this pox is… perhaps he may treat and cure it."

Kelman, who'd at last felt wanted back in December, was turning out since to be more and more inward and now in February he'd become lost in some immense internal conflict. This festering had at first shown itself on his body and was well hidden but gradually, as it spread, it became harder for him to conceal from those who might see and be horrified. And so it also had become harder for he himself to think it might leave him free of its awful manifestation.

Josiah had put on his coat and was dragging Kelman out of the workshop and along the street before the poor man knew it.

In his dilemma, Kelman now followed almost willingly and found himself standing before John Arden, the apothecary, who peered at him through spidery spectacles from behind a dusty counter littered with phials and crucibles.

"Yes Josiah, can I help you?" he asked, placing a small pestle delicately beside its mortar and affording Kelman a cautious glance.

"Perhaps," replied the cobbler, encouraging Kelman to the counter. "Our friend here has something you must see. He seems to have caught some infection or other. I insisted that he came to you, hoping you may know its cure or at least its cause."

The aging chemist moved to the side of the counter and, pulling back a heavy curtain which cloaked a doorway to the rear, he beckoned them both in to a dismal and musty room, lit only by a small lamp. He motioned to Kelman to sit on a couch by the lamp and turning up the wick examined the infection closely, opening the front of his patient's shirt to see its full extent. An air of recognition came over him.

"Is this the outcome of what I've seen on others in the village?" he asked gravely. "Is this what *their* small marks will become?"

"On others?" repeated Josiah. "On what others?"

Even Kelman had startled with surprise at John Arden's remarks, for here was sudden realisation that he wasn't the only affected one in the village.

"Why, Martin Wileman and Jack Marsh each first came to see me more than a month ago with such marks on their bodies, yet theirs were very much less severe and certainly haven't spread in such a way as this. How long have you had these marks, Kelman?"

"I not say!" cried Kelman, for his head was by now spinning with confusion.

Once more the fear of rejection and of being cast out

overwhelmed him... unsafe, insecure again in the company of these two astonished men.

"I not say, except to Barny."

Barny, being the first and only really trusted friend of Kelman's, was remembered now above all the confusion in his mind.

"Well," said Barny, who'd arrived at the mercy of Josiah's grip, as had Kelman, "what's all this about? It surely can't be as bad as it all sounds," he said reassuringly. "How long have you had these marks that Josiah tells me of? When did you first notice them, my poor friend?"

Kelman, with reluctance in his voice, began slowly to explain.

"I first notice marks after I meet Ely and Amos in the north... in Greylar. I know it soon get worse, like others... in Ironmound. I... I even know I might die, like others."

At this the other three gasped.

"Die?" said Barny, in grim disbelief, and not at all reassuringly. "You mean this thing can *kill*? Why on earth didn't you tell us before? Why did you let them bring you back here at all?"

There was now a note of anger in the farrier's voice which Kelman had never known in it before.

"I was lonely... and lost. I not want to be left alone forever. I though disease might only be in Icelar and not be here where it warmer. I not know 'till now others have disease here in Hamlet."

And with this Kelman wept bitterly.

"But these, and others, might die," said John Arden. "Unless we can find something that will cure them."

"And what of Kelman, apothecary?" snapped Barny changing his mood with Kelman's words. "Will you not cure him too? He may have brought this dreadful thing hence but it seems he didn't do so with purpose. Does he not deserve some thought as well? And besides, those two other men that have this thing were on the expedition with Amos. Maybe they'd have caught it without the help of Kelman here. And could it still not be that catching it depends on being in the north?

"I guess so," acknowledged John Arden. "We mustn't panic about it. We must see what can be found in the way of a cure... keep Kelman and the other two isolated as far as possible and hope that no more of us become infected."

Kelman was so remorseful to find that he'd seemingly brought the disease to his new friends that he insisted he leave the village and not return, but Barny wouldn't hear of it, since there might be a cure for him along with the others. And so Kelman, Martin and Jack were found alternative lodgings in an unoccupied building in the village and the people of the Hamlet waited and wondered and their fear grew with time.

Seth Linden talked further with Kelman, before he was rehoused and learned that the man from the north hadn't been accused of stealing food after all. It seems that Kelman's family, his woman and their four children, had all died of the disease, yet Kelman had shown no sign of infection. The others in Ironmound, which was fully in the grip of the illness, had blamed Kelman for the outbreak, since he'd seemed immune. He'd fled a savage attack by a screaming mob of folk who were once his friends. He also told Seth that in Ironmound legend had it that this disease had struck before. This, Kelman had learned from the older men of Ironmound who recalled legends from the distant past. *They* at least would not lay the blame on Kelman. Indeed they spoke of a cure that may be found somewhere in the distant north of Icelar. Yet no one now would listen to the elders... no one but Kelman... and for him it was too late, for his loved ones had gone and he'd no need of such a cure, or so he'd thought. The younger generations would hold no store by those legends of the 'Ice Wolf' that roamed the frozen north, and their apathy did naught but breed, until Kelman was set upon in frustrated rage, and so it was that he'd fled south.

Before long, they knew the worst here in the Hamlet. Others who'd travelled north were falling foul of the pox and, despite *them* too having been kept apart from others for much of the time, more of them soon showed signs of the infection. It was April now and it seemed that people were contracting it well before it showed its dreadful face. Amos Spivey now was taken with it and Martin, Jack and poor Kelman were worse. Kelman's face was a hideous sight and he swathed it with scarves, hiding what he could.

The tenth of the month came and a meeting was called in the Hall. Seth took the chair.

"This meeting..." he called, thumping the table hoping to be given some attention.

The noisy chatter that filled the Hall died to a murmur and he started again.

"This meeting has been called so that we may best decide what's to be done about our dilemma... the dilemma we've all come to know these last few weeks. We're in the grip of disease which, as we now know is taking a tight hold of our community, for some among our number who *didn't* go to Greylar are now stricken. We know that the village itself is worse affected than the outlying farms and we know from Kelman that the disease will kill."

The mention of Kelman's name brought murmurs back to the lips of the crowd and a new air of anger could be felt. Several shouts of resentment echoed above the general noise. Seth knew that in the face of this adversity, the people of Myre Hamlet could be cruel and heartless, against their usual character, and he thought of Kelman's flight from his own home.

"We also know," he continued, and in his voice there was no compromise, "that Kelman could be the first to die."

The hard tone in Seth's voice eased the tense atmosphere and he went on, with a more attentive audience.

"John Arden has laboured long to find a cure, yet it seems at last he despairs of finding what he seeks. The only ray of hope appears now to lie in the legends of Ironmound... in Icelar, with the Ice Wolf in the north of that land. Though we've learned of the dangers and unforeseen delays that such journeys bring, I feel we must consider setting out once more in the hope of bringing back this cure... for we must hope it's more than legend. Kelman has told us something of the geography of his homeland and he wishes to come with us should we decide to go, for he's regretful of the ill fortune that's followed him here and would make amends for what we now face. Indeed, he carries a double burden now. I say we should decide to go, for I at least have resolved to travel and, along with us, Barny Hensman and Will Sparrow would also come. You may say that we are too hasty, for no one has yet died, but the signs don't bode well and I for one don't wish to spend a single life before we're moved to action. If we departed even now, I'm sure we'd not return to see all those we left behind."

"But surely to take Kelman wouldn't be wise," protested John Arden. "For he'd lessen your chances of success and increase your chance of becoming afflicted."

"I think not, John," said Seth, acknowledging the apothecary's genuine concern. "For though we now know more than we did of the terrain in the north of our own land and of Greylar, and indeed of the seas off our northern shores, Kelman's knowledge of Icelar would be valuable indeed. And I count Kelman among those who I'd not expect to see on returning, for he's quite ill now and to take him *to* a cure would be faster than to bring it back to him."

In truth, Seth was also concerned now for Kelman's safety

were he to be left among the Hamlet folk without Barny or himself. He went on.

"We'd travel lighter than those who went before and with another summer on its way should be back well before winter sets in. So you see, this is more in the way of an announcement than a seeking of decisions. But we who've decided we must go are looking for your endorsement of our intentions, though we also look for several more to join us. Ely Blackmore and Amos Spivey wish also to come, and we'd have them, for their knowledge of the north will be important enough."

Though those present had shown animosity at first, they were at least some way from total apathy still and saw the need for action. So, many volunteered their support and those chosen to go were no keener than those who were not chosen. Kaleb Moody would go. So too would Abe Arden, John's brother, for although a farmer he knew something of the apothecary's craft. Later, when told of the decision, Samuel Dale a carpenter and Jake Foxton another farmer who'd both been on the previous voyage insisted on going again. These two had been to see John Arden but recently, so that five of the ten who would travel had been in the north already and four were afflicted. In truth, the disease took a good while to develop and the knowledge of those four would surely outweigh the danger of their condition for the others.

It was decided to set out on horseback, again for Fenny, on the fifteenth of April allowing them little less than a week for preparation.

CHAPTER FOUR

The Home Leaving

A drenching rain greeted Barny as he stepped into the road from the forge. He cast a glance at the grey rolling blanket of cloud above and pulled the hood of his heavy cloak over his balding head. Avoiding most of the deepening puddles in the road, he made his way hurriedly to the Hall. Outside the Hall, ten restless horses stood soaked in the pouring rain. Each was saddled and all but one were mounted. The nine men who were to set out with Barny sat waiting as he slung a small pack across his back and mounted to the empty saddle. There were in addition four ponies, laden with necessary food and essential equipment for their journey. It was intended that they stock up more fully after reaching Fenny.

The few days since the meeting had been spent well in preparing and the companions were now as ready as they'd ever be. Each had put on a heavy cloak which covered coat and breeches well. Each had spare clothes packed. The mood of many in the Hamlet was one of misery and despair at being held in the grip of the disease. Some were now deep in apathy seeing little hope in the mission to the north and in some the sharpest emotion was anger towards Kelman. He himself looked as drenched and as reluctant as the grey horse he sat astride. A cold wind was now rising from the north-east and the rain bit into his face despite the hood draped over his brow and the scarf across his mouth.

They'd said their goodbyes to loved ones who now stood close by on the wide steps of the Hall. Ely had said a long farewell to Helen and to his children. Seth, reluctant to leave Sarah but anxious to guide the company on their desperate quest had said his parting words. Sarah held back her tears as best she could so that he might find strength in her parting smile.

Barny turned to young Tom who'd followed him from the forge in shirtsleeves and apron.

"Farewell Tom," he offered light-heartedly. "Remember what I've taught you and you'll manage well enough while I'm away. You may well be busy, but I'm sure *I* shall be too, with these to look after on the way," he joked, pointing a thumb at their reluctant mounts. "Still, we'll all be back in time for those log fires in the Pig come autumn."

They were ready. Seth spurred on his horse and at last they were on their way north. They started at a brisk walk, Seth at their head with Tag, his gelding, now striding out as if to escape the relentless downpour. The others followed now quite spiritedly. Ely and Amos rode close behind Seth. Will Sparrow and Kaleb were next, followed by Barny who was chatting quite merrily to Kelman, speculating on a change in the weather and looking forward to an enjoyable journey through a pleasant summer. Kelman had said no real goodbyes, other than to Tom, for his only other two real friends, Barny and Seth, were with him on the road. Barny's conversation helped to cheer Kelman but his heart remained chilled to know that he least of all could hope to return.

Abe, Samuel and Jake, who'd turned to wave a last farewell as the travellers reached the eaves of the wood, made up the rear.

Noon was approaching and the heavens, it seemed, had no intention of ceasing their persistent drizzle. The ten men now spurred their horses into a comfortable trot and continued with some urgency, sometimes trotting, sometimes at a brisk walk hoping to make reasonable headway that day before nightfall.

After a while, most of them found themselves mesmerised by the rhythmic stride of the horses and by the occasional swish of a tail. Seth however, leading them, gazed at the dank hedgerows as they glided past, step after step, mile after mile.

The hedges, which followed the road on both sides for some miles north of the Hamlet, became more and more wild and overgrown as they travelled on. Presently, they became no more than bramble and briar thickets, losing orderly shape as the farmland fields gave way to wilderness. The sodden grass showed here and there the yellows of primroses and of celandine. A myriad of tiny silver droplets clung to the slender branches and lethal spines of blackthorn bushes enticing the buds to break into blossom, and all seemed sharp and clear in the rain.

Soon the light dimmed and night fell quickly, aided by the shade of the outreaching eaves of the wood. With the coming of night, the rain melted away. The travellers decided to ride on into the darkness for some miles, lighting lanterns to aid their path. All the same, they were soaked and cold so before too long they halted and, wending their way some distance into the trees, they made camp for the night in a suitable clearing. The horses were unsaddled and the ponies freed of their packs. They lit a fire with the aid of a tinderbox. At first the flames were reluctant for, though abundant, the dead wood about them was damp. However, once persuaded, the fire danced and flickered merrily and the twigs crackled in the heat. Fresh clothes were taken out and wet ones were hung up to dry. With, blankets wrapped about them, smiles soon returned to glum faces as the smell of cooking meat floated before their noses. With the meat they ate fresh bread and shared out ale mulled in the fire. Though there was little grass, the horses and ponies browsed contentedly and all seemed more bearable than it had just a few hours before.

Seth leaned back onto the bole of a convenient tree and filled his pipe from a pouch of tobacco hidden beneath the folds of his blanket. He turned to Will who sat nearby with hands outstretched to the fire.

"Well, Birdie, with a fairer spell of weather we should reach

The Home Leaving

Fenny by the twenty-sixth and when we find a boat we'll be under sail before the end of the month, as we planned."

"All being well, Seth," agreed Will. "This part of our journey should at least prove trouble free, for we're on the road, we know what lies ahead and we know we can restock at Ambleton or Fenny. No, it's the sea crossing and the traveling in Icelar that worry me."

Seth lit the pipe, "I fear you're right, Will. And what shall we find in Icelar, I wonder? The Ice Wolf indeed? The legend tells us little enough and we'll be in a land strange to us. Trap this wolf we may, but what then? How should we use it for our need? A potion no doubt but made from what?"

He drew smoke and contemplated what he'd said.

"Still," replied Will, "all we can do is get there first and then worry about tracking it down when we need to."

The two of them turned at a sudden burst of laughter from the others. Barny was recounting some of his favourite stories. He'd often do so at the Pig much to the delight of everyone whose ears they fell upon and although most had been heard before, they always went down well. Seth and Will perceived that Barny was recalling the night the chimney at the Pig had been blocked by a fallen piece of masonry. Will remembered it well. He'd been called in to put it right afterwards.

"...Old Felix spotted the smoke backing out of the fireplace," continued Barny, "and when he tried to look up the chimney to see what was blocking it, he was met with a face full of soot for his trouble. It was a bit hot mind and he got more than a black face... he got a blistered nose as well."

Raucous laughter filled the clearing. Soon they all settled beneath their blankets and before long were lost to the world.

A fair dawn blessed them next morning, the sun smiled all that day and for the next few days the weather was as kind as they'd hoped. After dawn on the third day, they'd left the woods behind altogether and after making camp in the open for the next two nights the faint chatter of running water came to their ears. They'd reached Weatherford where the road passed through the waters of the Bucklebank. They crossed the ford and dismounted to replenish their water from the fast-flowing shallows, filling the leather bottles with care. The horses and ponies drank at will from the flowing waters.

At the fording of the river grew a cluster of trees on the gently sloping banks, which was a welcome change in the bare country through which they now journeyed. The road ahead would offer little shelter in the next few days. Seth cast a wary eye on the thickening clouds above as great shadows crept across the landscape before them. This seemed an ideal place to rest and eat, but Ely and Amos had already reminded the others of the ambushers who'd waylaid them here the year before. They were all anxious to fill the bottles and move on as soon as may be.

'Crack!' The resounding snap of a dead twig echoed through the trees. Birds startled and fluttered noisily from the branches and then there was silence again. Seth's horse reared, others whinnied and the party crouched low, peering all around them, wide eyed in anticipation of attack. But there was no further sound. Seth calmed his horse and Barny smiled in realisation, pointing to one of the pack ponies which had roamed under the trees to sample the lush grass which was strewn with dead branches dislodged in forgotten storms.

"Come on, Little 'Un," called Barny as he walked towards the wayward beast. "No more frights like that, if you please."

They mounted, now somewhat ill at ease with the strange silence which hid thinly disguised by the gentle hiss of the swaying trees and the ever-rolling waters. Seth and Ely turned their horses and urged them on into a swift canter northwards along the road. The others followed in a ragged hurry, leaving the trees to murmur to themselves.

The Home Leaving

They now rode into a country that became flatter with every mile, especially in the east where a great plain opened up stretching almost to the edge of sight.

"*There* are the great mountains," shouted Amos to his fellow travellers, checking his steed. "They stretch far into the north, where we took our misleading path last year."

Onward he spurred his mount and soon after nightfall they perceived great, grey shapes to the right of the road.

"There's shelter for the night," called Amos to the leaders of the party. "We camped among these great boulders on our journey out before."

So here they made camp, unloading the packs and pegging their mounts, giving special attention to Little 'Un as Barny had now taken to calling him. Soon after, a fire was lit and they ate a frugal meal, for their food was now more than half spent and they were still some way from Ambleton. A watch was set and Samuel Dale took the first stint for he had some knowledge of the place. He woke Kaleb after two hours and in his turn Jake Foxton relieved Kaleb. Seth was to be woken by Jake to take the next watch, but instead he was woken by a sudden shout of alarm and by a confusion of horses galloping off into the night.

"Hoi!" cried Kelman, again. "Stop!"

For it was Kelman who'd been roused from his light sleep by the unsettled horses as raiders mounted them and fled. Soon all the party was assembled, staring blankly after the echo of hooves in the distance to the east. A hurried survey discovered that seven of the ten horses were gone and worse than that, Jake was gone too. They'd overwhelmed him, or else caught him sleeping. The packs had been left undisturbed in the main, as indeed had the ponies.

"We must give chase, quickly, before we lose them."

Amos was saddling up as he called to Seth and Kelman to do likewise. He knew that Seth and his gelding were as swift a team as any, and he also knew that Kelman was a hunter.

Within moments they were gone, chasing the rumour of the attackers and calling for the others to wait for their return.

The moon, in her last quarter had risen some hours before and, peering down here and there between the clouds, she gave a little light for the three desperate men to follow. Still, pursuit was hard and demanded many halts, for even Kelman had much difficulty reading the signs of flight.

'They're surely heading for the mountains,' thought Amos as they galloped on once more across the never-ending plain.

It now seemed to them these raiders must live in the shelter of the hills, if indeed they were those who'd attacked the earlier company. But why the raids? They must be a desperate, wild people and now they had poor Jake.

Soon the pursuers were despairing of ever finding their companion for the trail became harder still as the ground became drier and more barren.

New hope came with the daylight though, for Kelman was aided in his search for clues and after several false trails and many anxious hours they drew near to the foothills and still they had the scent.

The wild men, oblivious to pursuit were not cautious in their flight and even now a column of white smoke high in the hills gave their camp away.

"Here," Kelman called to the other two, pointing to the ground before them.

Seth and Amos dismounted to study what Kelman had seen. Here were the signs of a scuffle.

"Look, the bushes over here are crushed and trampled, Amos," Seth remarked and here also they found shreds of clothing… Jake's clothing, blood stained.

"Maybe he got no further than this!" exclaimed Amos. "Let's hope this blood isn't his."

"Animals!" cried Seth, angrily. "Why Jake? Why not just the horses, or even the food?"

The Home Leaving

"Perhaps," said Amos, "they thought despite their haste to take him as a hostage should we follow them or, more likely, they hoped to escape from our camp undetected, taking Jake to avoid our discovering their evil deeds before they were away. It's thanks only to Kelman's keen ears that we were able to give chase at all."

"But what can we do now we're here, Amos?" Seth was despairing again. "There must be at least a dozen from what Kelman saw of them and no doubt they've returned to a whole nest here in the hills. We could never hope to take him from them by force."

"True enough. We must hide here in the lower hills until nightfall," Amos answered with reassurance. "Then we must find out what we can of their camp."

They decided that Amos and Kelman should go on foot and Seth should stay behind with the horses, for the one advantage they had was their undetected pursuit.

Dark night fell. The moon hadn't yet risen and if she had, the clouds would have left her hidden. Amos and Kelman set out, stumbling up the steep, rock strew paths with little light to guide them. They picked out landmarks on their route as best they could so as to mark their return path to Seth and the horses... an unusual boulder here, a twisted tree there, but all the while making for the column of smoke above them which glowed red now at its source.

"How can they ride horses up here, Amos?" whispered Kelman.

"They live in the hills, Kelman," he replied. "They must know ever rock, every twist, every turn, by day or by night."

They could now faintly hear many voices clamouring and chattering in some strange tongue. Now and then, it would break into a sinister chant that floated now louder, then soft again on wisps of a breeze that blew gently over the hills.

As they drew nearer, the two men wrapped their dark cloaks

around them tighter, hats pulled down to hide their faces from the growing light of the fire, lest a guard perhaps might catch sight of them. They said little more to each other, knowing that they must stay close together. Signs would have to suffice now. They soon reached a point where the path levelled out and then descended. It seemed that the fire was below them now. Moving to one side of the path, peering cautiously from behind a huge outcrop of rock, they could see the fire itself.

They were right. Their flight had led them to a veritable nest of wild men. Below them the hills gave way to a large shallow bowl. The fire was to the nearer end. At the far end were the eaves of a wooded area whose trees marched into the shadow of night. Between the fire and the wood lay a flat area of short, dry grass. On either side of this were rows of primitive huts. These dreadful creatures looked as if they'd seen no civilisation for many generations, yet there was a hint that they might once have done so, for some had shaved their faces. All had shaved their heads and though some wore skins, as Kelman had, many wore clothes fashioned of woven cloth.

'Perhaps the coats and breeches belonged once to the likes of Jake,' thought Amos, turning to the reason for the chase. "Where *is* Jake now, I wonder?"

Many of the wild men crouched close to the fire. Others moved to and fro between the huts. Women carried drink to those around the fire who ate with ferocity continuing their grisly chants between hungry mouthfuls, while tearing meat from bone. Wild children joined the frenzied throng. The scene was aglow in the intense firelight and the heat overflowed into the faces of the two secret watchers. Amos watched horrified. It was a nightmare beyond his comprehension. Kelman grimaced but said nothing.

The fire crackled and hissed, fanned by the breeze and the two men detected the smell of scorching flesh. Amos stifled a cry which rose in his throat at the thoughts which came to his

The Home Leaving

mind, but the thoughts were whisked away when Kelman pointed at the far side of the camp. There in the shadow of a hut, Jake was propped against a lone tree that stood out from the eaves of the wood. He was tied by the ankles and by the wrists, his arms held above his head by a rope which was slung over a low branch. He looked badly treated though at this distance they couldn't be sure of his condition.

'There are too many of them for us to consider a rescue here and now,' thought Amos. *'Too many crawling about their sickly nest. And if Jake is no better than he appears, he would be a heavy burden indeed. We could never run should we need to.'*

It now seemed clear that the purpose of the raid had been to obtain food, for a carcass or two could be made out, near the fire though why the mountains didn't offer enough hunting, Amos couldn't understand. Apparently they'd not yet decided what was to become of their captive.

'Perhaps a rescue wouldn't be pursued too far,' thought Amos. *'But there are far too many of them to take such a risk. No, we must bide our time.'*

Convinced, he beckoned Kelman and they turned quietly and made their way back to Seth.

"What do you propose then?" said Seth, after Amos had told of all they'd seen.

"I wish I knew," replied Amos. "Perhaps we'll see more clearly tomorrow what's best done. We'll be rested then, and more able to follow through any plan we may have."

"But tomorrow may be too late," protested Seth.

"I know," agreed Amos. "I intend to go back now to our hide. I'll watch as I may, though I think nothing will happen this night."

"No, *I* shall go this time," Seth insisted.

"Better that *I* go Seth. If things go wrong you'll be needed by the others more than I will. You've a good head on your shoulders."

"Then take Kelman back with you Amos," said Seth, reluctantly.

"Yes," said Kelman. "We go together, Amos. Back to see the baldies."

"Very well," said Amos, smiling at Kelman's remark.

"Over two days they've been gone now," snatched Barny, bringing his clenched fist down on the saddle which lay beside him. "We should follow, to see what's befallen them," he went on, as he got to his feet and paced to and fro.

"No, we can't do that," argued Will. "None of us here could follow their trail very far and if they *are* on their way back to us we could miss them. We must wait here as they insisted."

"But they may be in need of help by now," replied Barny, slapping his sides in desperation and sitting down again. "Surely two or three of us could at least attempt to find them, while those who don't go could head back for Myre Hamlet."

"But we only have the ponies, Barny, and it would be a cumbersome trek even if we were to pick the right direction. I say we wait. And besides, we'll not turn back to the Hamlet for we've only just begun our journey. All's not yet lost, and we'll be in for harder decisions than this on the way, if I'm not mistaken."

In the absence of Seth and Amos, Will had assumed charge of those remaining and felt it his duty to keep some calm prevailing.

"Then let *me* go alone," went on Barny. "And if they return before me, I'll head back for Myre Hamlet if I return and find you gone. All I'll need is one of the ponies, and very little of the food. We can't wait here forever, and there's no way I could leave without at least a try."

Ely, looking thoughtful, joined the discussion.

"Perhaps he *should* attempt it, Will. At least we might find out what has become of them. Then the quest could continue,

The Home Leaving

without them if needs be. We need them with us, but if they're lost or slain then we must go on with all speed, and make the best of it ourselves."

"But what could Barny do that the others couldn't achieve themselves?" Will demanded.

"He could answer our questions, one way or the other," said Ely, still thoughtful of what may have befallen their friends.

Will reluctantly conceded that Barny ought perhaps to go after all, but as Barny grasped a nearby pack, Kaleb, who was standing atop one of the boulders nearby, uttered a cry, pointing to the eastern horizon.

"There! Dust rising from the plain."

Sure enough the dust throw up by galloping horses could be seen below the haze of the distant mountains. Soon, the dust clouds enlarged and the horses could be made out clearly, racing towards them at great speed.

"It must be Seth and the others," called Kaleb. "There are three horses."

But where was Jake? Had they not found him? Had they found worse?

As the riders neared, Seth and Kelman led the way. Amos followed close on their heels and to their delight Jake clung wearily to his companion, sharing the willing mount.

"Well, I'll be," cried Barny, cheering as he dropped the pack. "They've done me out of a trip across the plain and all."

Seth dismounted as his horse came to a halt, and urged them all to the cover of a standing stone, peering back over his shoulder as if expecting followers.

"We found Jake tied and half-conscious in a camp of wild men in the mountain foothills. It was night on the day we took chase," catching his breath, he went on. "We daren't make a move until early this morning for our flight had wearied us. Then Kelman moved in quietly and with a reassuring word he cut Jake's bonds and whisked him away clear of the light of a dying fire and past the slumbering guards. One poor fellow woke, but the sight of Kelman's angry face sent him screaming into the night. The others stirred and gave chase, but I don't think they'll trouble to come this far again. We lost sight of them many hours ago. Still, just in case, we'd better move on north a way before dark. We *should* find shelter somewhere, and we can think about Ambleton tomorrow."

"How's Jake?" called Kaleb to Amos as he came down from the rock to greet the last of the horses to reach them.

"Not so bad, now that I'm back with you all," sighed Jake. "A bit tired and bruised, but nothing that won't mend."

Soon they were all ready, and off they moved at a brisk pace, though forced to move no faster than those on foot, anxious to leave the boulders behind. Before dark, they found the shelter of an abandoned, ivy-tangled house by a clump of trees not far off the road. The house had been unused for ages and was now but a shell, with little even of the roof left, so they were at the mercy of the skies.

They set a large watch and daren't light a fire. Abe Arden did what he could to ease Jake's bruises. They ate a meagre meal and slept uneasily, hoping to make an early start, at dawn. The night sky was kind to them.

They arrive near Ambleton some six days later, having seen no more sign of the wild men. Barny had needed to see to a slipped shoe on the third day, but this was the worst of their ills. On the journey between the boulders and Ambleton, coaches had passed twice... the southbound shortly after they left the derelict house and the northbound only the day before they reached Ambleton. On both occasions, they'd avoided being seen, retreating to nearby trees and bushes, for they'd agreed from the start that their journey should remain unnoticed for as long as possible. Besides, they all agreed that news carried back home of their evil encounter so early would only serve to dishearten those left in the Hamlet. As for the

The Home Leaving

prospect of news of their coming reaching Fenny before them, that would only put them at a disadvantage, they thought, in bargaining for a boat. Now that Ambleton was before them, Seth thought, as he had many times before, what a disaster it would be if Ambleton or Fenny were taken by the Scar. It had been with great difficulty that the secret of their plight had been contained within the Hamlet anyway, but at least no mention had come with the coach of any such illness in the north. Seth knew though that, come what had and come what may, the less fuss made here, the better.

Ambleton wasn't dissimilar to Myre Hamlet village, in that it was a small settlement set around the road and was built of similar stone. But it had more dwellings close by and no outlying farms. It relied instead on the ports such as Fenny for many of its needs. The people, some hundred or more were, in the main, from Fenny or Pebblebank originally, the village having been established to quarry stone found in the area. Now it was traded in the ports, only two days ride to the north.

The folk here were friendly, but not as warm as those of Midvale were. They'd turn a cold shoulder to strangers, as would the people on the coast.

As the travellers approached, they aroused a cautious interest and Seth felt that the sooner they passed through, the better. Seth, Barny and Kaleb stopped briefly to buy a few essentials for the next couple of days while the rest walked through. The storekeeper looked at them suspiciously as they discussed the weather.

'The disease?' thought Seth. *'Does he know of the Scar, I wonder?'* His thoughts rambled off, back to Puddlefork and to Sarah and to his kinsmen so far away.

"Thank you kindly," the fellow grunted. "Will that be all?"

"Er, yes... Thank you," stammered Seth aided by a nudge from Kaleb.

Barny gathered up what they'd bought and the three

remounted, cantering on to catch the others.

CHAPTER FIVE

The Sea and the Breeze

Two more days passed and sea air greeted them on a stiff breeze blowing from the north-west. The road had swept in a long curve to the west and in the distance ahead it fell to the lowlands south of Fenny, meandering as it did so until it brought the company to the skirts of the fishing and trading port. The sea, now in view from the high point on the road was something that Seth had never seen, though some of his companions had already seen more than enough. They'd told him of its magnificent power... something to be marvelled at and to be respected, but it was only now that he took in the stark and overwhelming beauty of the wide waters.

The sun was setting somewhere hidden and the sheet of cloud that hung over them cast a grey melancholy shroud on the seascape before them.

Fenny in fact was set in a deep, sheltered bay which stretched for fifteen or twenty leagues before yielding to the open seas, so that before them and below them, the town lay between two projecting arms of the coast running to the north and to the north-west. To the north ran low cliffs of stark rock... the timeless sea of waves had pestered them leaving debris from its ceaseless ebbing and flowing, wave upon rolling wave leaving boulder upon crumbling boulder. To the north-west the coast stretched away with *no* cliffs. A beach of shingle hissed on the retreat of the waves only to be smothered on their return. Behind the beach stood a flank of sand dunes, bushed with gorse and with wild grasses, which sloped steeply but evenly down from the inner lands to the coast. In the angle between the two coastlines was set a small harbour, with stone breakwaters... outstretched arms sheltering the town from the might of the tides and enclosing calmer waters. The road took a path to the east of the town down to the harbour and passed between the quayside and the town itself before emerging to the north-west on its way to Pebblebank.

A sea mist was rolling in now as the light dimmed and the coastline's end drew near to them as they looked across the township below them. Flickering lights sprang into windows... golden, homely lights. All were glad that they'd come to a place of shelter, where warmth and a decent bed were in prospect.

"There! On the north coast," said Amos, pointing into the thickening mist. "There lie a few fishermen's cottages and those of others concerned with the harbour trade. But the main town lies south of the road behind the dunes. It's there that we must seek shelter. Perhaps the place to ask is at the Ferryboat Inn. There you see it, at the end of that street. Look, the green lantern marks it well."

They'd now descended to a point where the road forked, with the row of cottages about a furlong away. They dismounted and followed the main fork to the east which took the road, now cobbled for the sake of the houses, to Pebblebank near the far corner of the bay some eight leagues distant. There, the wetland delta waters of the Bucklebank crept into the sea, a bleak place compared to Fenny, flat and marshy with little shelter. Fenny, though a fishing port, traded with towns in the north-west of the continent in other foodstuffs and in ores and finished metals. Less of their trade came south.

Soon the travellers turned aside along the narrow cobbled street, their footfalls echoing in the darkening gloom. The green lantern peered at them through swirling vapours like the eye of some watching serpent. The streets were quite deserted. The day's trading had come to a close and most were indoors. They sheltered in the warmth of new-lit fires, for the wind from the north had brought a cold damp upon them, unexpected and unwelcome in early May.

The Myre Hamlet folk had passed little heeded, it seemed,

through the streets despite their numbers, though their clatter had brought a few curtained glances from un-shuttered windows.

At the corner of the street they halted and Seth beckoned them to gather close to him.

"We'll enquire after shelter at the Inn as Amos has suggested," he whispered. "But we must keep our quest to ourselves, for if they perceive our plight, they'll surely offer us little aid or sympathy and may even drive us out. Kelman will be a problem. He must stay hidden."

"I go find shelter in dunes," Kelman replied. "I used to sleeping in hills, beneath stars. I have warm clothes. Meet you in the morning somewhere out of sight."

Kelman was quite at ease with the company by now, but had already been hiding his face for fear someone in the town might peer out and see him. Seth had been dwelling thoughtfully on how Kelman might be hidden since first they'd entered the streets, but until now had delayed its mention. They were well aware that it would be better for all concerned had they been able to pass the town by altogether but they could do nothing without a decent seagoing boat. They craved rest and food too. They needed to make provision for the weeks ahead before travelling on and though they hoped to be on their way the next day or at the latest the following morning, Fenny couldn't be avoided.

"Thank you Kelman," acknowledged Seth. "It's unfair to expect this of you, but I'm sure it's the only way. Tomorrow in the light of day we must *also* keep you hidden."

At this Ely spoke, "But Seth, I think there's another way, with a bed for the night for Kelman into the bargain. Do you remember, Amos? The room we stayed in for one night before... the big one on the ground floor. There was a window facing the alley to the rear. With any luck, if the room be ours, we could let Kelman in through that window and with so many of us, one extra wouldn't be noticed. He could stay there hidden with us tomorrow."

So it was that Kelman hid in the alley and waited.

"There's stabling in the yard opposite," said Amos, as they approached the inn on foot.

Seth, accompanied by Barny and by Amos, entered to enquire after the room. As they walked into the common room they felt no warmer than in the outside air. The room was brightly lit with oil lamps, which hung on hooks from the lofty, bare ceiling. The walls were stark and the furniture basic.

'Not a lot like the Pig,' thought Barny.

They trod the bare, creaking boards to the bar counter and felt the gaze of penetrating, unfriendly eyes. The dozen or so characters who'd been drinking and talking at tables around the further end of the room fell silent and now stared at the intruders. It seemed that the occupants of the room were as cold as the room itself.

"Hello there!" exclaimed the bespectacled landlord. "What can I do for three weary travellers?"

The chatter gradually returned and the stares and glances were retracted after meeting with those returned by Seth and Amos.

"Good evening. We're hoping for a bed," offered Seth, omitting to mention the others for the moment.

"Indeed? Well, as long as you can pay the price, there's a room upstairs for you," came the reply.

"Good," Seth responded, not liking the sound of 'upstairs', "though there are more of us. Nine in all to be precise. The others are with our horses outside."

There was some hesitation from the face behind the bar. Barny, who'd stood to the rear, stepped closer.

"Amos here reckons the last time *he* came here there was a big room they stayed in downstairs. That would do fine."

"If it were empty of course," added Seth, cautiously making

The Sea and the Breeze

amends for Barny's lack of tact.

"Of course, agreed Barny, grinning broadly.

"I'm afraid there's a couple of fellows in there," came the prompt reply. "Still," he continued, wiping his hands on his grubby apron, "I *could* move them upstairs. And the room downstairs *is* bigger. Not too comfortable mind, but the only one. Still, I could get nine of you into that room, at a squeeze. Anyway, you look as if you could sleep on a log tonight, if you were forced to."

"Even on a hat peg," smiled Barny.

"So, where are you from?" asked the landlord, eying Amos with suspicion, trying to put recognition on the face.

"Myre Hamlet," said Amos, thinking after Barny's little slip, that honesty in this much at least would benefit them more than it would hinder them. "Just you remember, Jack Roper. I came with others from the Hamlet just over a year ago. We travelled to Greylar."

"Of course. That's right," nodded Jack, acknowledging him with a smile and much rubbing of hands. "I remember now. Amos Spivey isn't it? You were here in the town again just before leaf fall too. Of course, you didn't come to the Ferryboat then, but the news all comes here in the end anyway."

"That's right," said Amos who, although he was on friendly terms with Roper, had met him only once, on that first visit to Fenny.

Jack Roper had seemed more friendly than most in the town, yet Amos was cautious even now.

"We got back eventually, Jack, my friend. But not without the sad loss of lives, as you probably heard."

"We *did*. It was a great pity that your journey turned to such perilous ends. Still, you must stay here tonight. The stable lad will see to your horses and see your companions in."

At this he snapped his fingers at a young, be-freckled lad who'd been sharing talk at a table, but had heard everything said at the counter.

"You must join us for ale and food, while you tell us why you're travelling again. Not more cattle, surely?" added Jack.

"I think we're more tired than we look, so if you'll excuse us, we'd all feel better if we could rest quietly while we eat," explained Seth, for the moment avoiding the landlord's question.

'Of course, of course!' Jack insisted

And calling to two men at a nearby bench, he ushered them out to a dark hallway and into the downstairs room, apologising as they went. Soon the two men came out and made their way up the stairs that led from the hallway, followed closely by the efficient Jack who made a smart detour to the kitchen to shout for food for the Hamlet folk.

The others now entered, led by the young lad, their packs slung on tired shoulders and again the conversation died, but soon returned as Jack welcomed them in.

"Ale and bread will join you in there," Jack confirmed, as they went through into the hall followed by Barny who'd had quite enough of the common room.

"Now then," said Jack, scratching his head and turning to Seth. "As I was saying, what brings you here again?"

Seth deliberated, drawing a pipe from his pocket... a somewhat shorter pipe than he normally smoked, more convenient for travelling. He drew out a pouch and took a fill of tobacco, offering the pouch first to Amos who accepted taking out his own pipe and then to the innkeeper who declined explaining that he'd avoided 'the smoke' since giving up the habit at the age of ten.

Lighting the filled pipe, Seth took several draughts to ensure it was burning and offered a pensive explanation.

"Having been successful in bringing back cattle for our herds last year, some of us were set to thinking that such fine cattle could be herded and maintained in their own homeland, in

The Sea and the Breeze

Greylar. We felt that a visit this summer might prove useful in planning a start there for ourselves and others from our homestead, perhaps next year."

Nothing was further from the truth of course, but Seth had discussed this deception with the others before they'd entered Fenny for he felt, and the others agreed, that the truth must be hidden at all costs. Their fears that news of the Scar might have reached here before them had been allayed when the room was offered to them.

"Good luck to you, *I* say," offered Jack, as he filled mugs and a stoop of ale. "There's enough to do at home I reckon, without running all over the place."

And with that, he took the mug-laden tray and passed it to the serving boy who rushed away with it.

"Tell them not to let Barny get his hands on that jug until *we're* in there," laughed Amos with a wry smile.

"Of course, we'll need a boat," Seth went on, turning the conversation necessarily back to business, "and provisions too."

"Well!" declared the innkeeper. "That could prove to be a problem. Alan Wooley keeps the best stocks in Fenny and *he* lives next door. His stores are at the far end of the street, but being this time of year and us having had a long, cold winter the whole place is rather low on food, except maybe for fish. And as for a boat? That may prove even more difficult. Last year's travels to Greylar did little to endear foreign folk to the seafarers. You'll know that they rarely travel east and then only a little distance if they can. And they're yet *more* reluctant now."

"Still, you could do worse than get yourselves down to the harbour at first light, and with the right purse, you'll no doubt find someone daft enough to take you. After all, the calmer season's on the way and the weather is warming. Tide's in at daybreak though and they'll all be out soon after light. You'll need to be abroad early."

"A nightcap and a good sleep will see us well. But first I'll be off outside," said Seth to Amos, "to see that Tag is well bedded down for the night."

"You'll find them all comfortable," assured Jack. "The stable lad will have seen to that. Bran and oats too, no doubt. He loves horses. Speaks to 'em more than he does to his folk, no lie. He reckons they're more reliable than men are. None as peculiar as folk, eh?"

"Still, I'll nip out just to be sure," said Seth.

"I'll come too," said Amos. "I know the yard well enough to find the stables."

Sure enough, Tag and the rest were munching happily on wholesome feeds, anxious to start on fresh hay slung in the corner racks. The beds were thick and clean. The lad was nowhere to be faulted, by man or beast.

"You look happy enough, fella," Seth stroked Tag's neck. "But then at a guess, you miss Sarah and old Ruffles less than I do."

Amos looked over his own mount and the others and thought of home as well.

Soon, both Seth and Amos found themselves indoors again and, after thanking the innkeeper for his hospitality, retired to the large room they'd procured to find it with much the same cold feeling as the outer room. Amos shivered in recognition.

Spare beds had been improvised and now, with one for each of the party save one, the room resembled more a dormitory than a private room. The others had seen to it that Kelman was let in from the darkness outside unnoticed and had huddled him into a corner with the packs.

They were already sharing out the ale and food which had been brought in. The fare was left wanting compared with Felix Cavey's efforts in the Pig, but after two weeks travelling with ever lightening packs, it was welcome enough.

The Sea and the Breeze

Those who'd not already done so heaved off heavy boots and made ready for sleep. Seth lay back on one of the comfortable beds and with hands clasped behind his head he stared at the darkening ceiling as Barny, the last to settle, turned down the wick of the lamp.

"Sleep well, Seth," said Barny.

"You too," replied Seth.

With the dying flickers of light, Seth fancied he saw Sarah, her gentle form no more than a shadow, walking to and fro in the twilit rooms of their farmhouse and he almost cried to think that she was so far away at such a time of peril for them both… for him the peril of a journey and for both of them the peril brought by Kelman. Yet Seth's thoughts were for Kelman too, for he knew that Kelman, who was worse with every day, wouldn't see the Hamlet again. Until recently, his disfigurement was the only outward symptom but now he'd wince with pain at times and he started to sicken. Then Seth's thoughts turned to Amos, dearest of friends, for he'd confided in Seth. The signs of *his* illness too were spreading, slowly but with grim sureness. Seth wondered if they ever would find a cure and was taken with great anguish at such a desperate prospect. And so, Amos worsened. Sam and Jake showed worse signs too and it must be certain that Seth and all the others would soon fall foul of the dread thing. And Sarah?

'What of Sarah?' he thought. *'Surely she'll escape its attentions, for she's isolated at the farm.'*

Again he saw her pacing up and down, ever turning on bare boards, pausing now and then to gaze from a window… a familiar window, the window looking out on the yard at Puddlefork. But her face? He couldn't see her face.

His weariness overcame his restlessness and he drifted into sleep, though it was the uneasy sleep of dreams. He found himself in barren hills, on a rough track which wound through rocks and boulders strewn about. Beyond were mountains, snow-capped, to the north. The path stretched out before him in the dying light of a grey day. He sensed that the others were with him there, but the heavy air left him drowsy headed and suddenly, before him stood a figure. The cloaked form stood motionless, head bowed as if staring at the path between them, but the face couldn't be seen for it was be-hooded. The robe was heavy and of dark brown cloth, tied about the waist. Seth turned at last for reassurance that he wasn't without his friends. They were there and they motioned him to speak with the stranger. Seth turned again to speak, but the figure was gone and with it the dream faded and Seth slept in peace.

Morning dawned fair. The sea mist had heralded fine weather and as Seth, Barny, Amos and Will wended their way through the sunrise streets all was quiet but for the distant barking of dogs, the overhead call of gulls and their own footfalls echoing along the walls of the houses off the harsh cobbles.

The sun was rising red above the cottages to the east. The streets took a steep winding path on their way to the harbour and they were slippery with dew as Barny found out, almost to his detriment when on more than one occasion he slithered and tottered on the brink of falling.

As they neared the harbour, a gentle breeze met their faces and noises grew in their ears. The gulls were nearer now and the chatter of the boatmen vied with the toing and froing of the sea on the pebbled shore. Having decided that their first need was a boat, they'd risen early and breakfasted along with their companions in their dormitory. The four had then made haste to catch the fishermen and traders before the ebbing of the tide, when the boats would all be out and away under sail.

Most of the boats were deep hulled, suitable for net fishing in deep waters. Some were open decked with a central hold and a well to stern which afforded some shelter for the steersman. There was often no cabin, for the fishermen always returned

The Sea and the Breeze

before nightfall. The favoured sail was a simple mainsail supported by a single mast and its boom, the mast rising fore of the hold. A few boats however were larger... those used for trading to other ports to the north-west and these few sported a larger hold and a cabin to berth a crew of four or five. Some few of these were double masted. This latter type had served for the cattle herding the year before.

Seth and his friends had spied a fellow attending to a boat hauled clear of the water on the beachy shore at this eastern end of the harbour. The fellow was busy tarring the hull. A diminutive man, white haired and in late middle years, he'd looked friendly enough and they hoped he might direct them to a likely boat owner, if not able to offer his own services.

"Morning," greeted Seth. "Busy I see."

"I *am*," said the sailor sharply, sizing up the strangers with a suspicious eye, neglecting his task for no more than a second. "No trip out for me today."

"Actually," offered Amos, "we were hoping to find a boat to take us east, to Greylar. We have a fair purse for the right boat."

"Then I shouldn't go asking them as took you before," the fisherman replied, with a recollection more sure than that of Jack Roper at the Ferryboat. "They've a doubled dislike for eastern waters since you helped them ground their boats. And besides, they're mostly carrying cargo out today for the west."

'No, we were hoping for a smaller boat this time. No cattle to bring back. Just a travelling party of men and hopefully some of our horses."

"And a few horseshoes," added Barny, who'd taken an instant dislike to the man and his manner.

"Well, I reckon you'll be lucky. People don't like travelling far, though fish don't like the nets these past few weeks. Maybe some would welcome the change and the purse."

He pointed along the harbour, mentioning names as he picked out several boats whose owners might be worth an enquiry. The foursome acknowledged his help and moved on.

"Pleasure," was the sailor's parting comment, though Barny felt sure it hadn't been.

The first boat they tried brought them little encouragement. The owner made excuses that he'd promised customers the fish he hoped to catch for many weeks to come. The second boat owner refused even to reply to their question, but the third seemed quite interested and, when a generous purse was revealed by Seth, he was asking them what exactly was involved.

When Seth had explained that they'd need the boat and a crew for no more than a month while they paid a brief visit to Greylar, and had told him of their numbers, he remained in favour of the deal.

Henry Harding was the boatman's name, a mere twenty-five years of age, though he stood more than six feet tall. His clothes were drab and stank of fish oil, inherited from many a catch. Greasy hair covered his ears and neck and an old kerchief added to his generally unkempt aspect. He was well muscled with work on the nets, throwing and hauling.

Seth knew that a month may be optimistic, but they were desperate enough for such a deception.

The captain insisted however that he'd take no horses aboard, for fear of overloading.

"And we must anchor close to shore each night," he added.

After some bargaining, Seth persuaded him to take one of the ponies, primarily for the packs, and that he was to make preparations during the day so that they might bring provisions on board later with a view to setting out next morning.

Whilst they'd hoped to take horses with them to Icelar, they'd always expected difficulties and were quite prepared to attempt their quest on foot if needs be. This single opportunity couldn't be squandered, for they'd found little joy so far and this offer of a boat mustn't be lost. Seth agreed in good faith to pay half the purse now and half when they'd returned, but insisted that two of their party slept on board that night to safeguard the provisions they were to bring.

The four now turned to make their way back into the streets of Fenny, hoping to find the food and stocks they needed. People were now out and about seeing to the day's business. The group was now more light-hearted than they'd been since before the ambush at Weatherford for, although possible peril lay ahead, things seemed at last to be going to plan.

"One thing troubles me," said Seth who alone among them was looking pensive. "You know, we ought really to tell this Henry Harding of our real plan to make for Icelar. After all, we'll be putting him in danger enough merely by travelling with him."

"All too true," agreed Will. "But despite the pox, or indeed because of it, we must keep our secret at all costs. At least until we've sailed. Then we may at least persuade him to our cause. If not, then we may do what we must. I know it sounds ill, but remember Myre Hamlet. Our errand must be done at all costs. It's *that* important. However we attempt it, we can't do it without involving others, fairly or otherwise."

"He's right, Seth. It's the only... Hoi!"

Barny was cut short. He'd turned to notice a young scruffily clad youth dart down a narrow jitty.

"The purse!" cried Seth. "He's taken the purse!"

Sure enough, as they'd walked engrossed in conversation, the young thief had crept behind, picked Seth's pocket and had made a dart for it. The four gave chase, half because of the valuable purse and half for fear that the rascal had heard mention of their true intentions. The latter might prove more costly to them than the former. Amos led the chase, followed by Will and Seth. Barny trailed behind, for he wasn't built for running and wasn't used to such exercise at all. Luckily for him the cobbles were dry now.

Through the alleyways they went, the boy clattering across the cobbles some distance ahead, turning corners this way and that, now skating by shops in and out of the peopled streets of Fenny. The townspeople on the streets now grew in number. Most turned to see what brought the commotion but with no endeavour to halt the boy or to interfere in any way with his getaway. Several people were barged out of the way, first by the boy and then, on the verge of recovery, by the faster of the pursuers. By the time Barny reached them, puffing and panting, they were well prepared and sidestepped smartly to avoid his red-faced approach.

'If we lose him, we're done for,' thought Seth, *'and no doubt.'*

The others shared his thoughts.

They'd been heading uphill into the heart of the town and now, after several more alleyways and detours, they were approaching a neglected area to the west of the town. Many of the buildings were deserted. It was a sad-looking place. The cobbles here were ill maintained, as were the buildings. Soon the pavings disappeared altogether as they chased their quarry across waste ground towards open grassland and a small, isolated and derelict house.

'We must have him now,' thought Seth. *'He can't lose us here.'*

It seemed this was where the urchin 'lived' and as such came home with apparently no thought for the fact that there he'd be trapped. He disappeared into the ruin, now followed closely by Amos. As Seth and Will approached, they heard a muffled cry as Amos grabbed at the lad. Then there came a cry from Amos, cut short by what sounded like a heavy blow. The others slowed their pace and, reaching the house, peered cautiously round the doorway. There was Amos lying unconscious on the floor and over him stood two men. They were unkempt like the lad. One stooped and reached out for the purse, now clasped in Amos's right hand. The boy cowered in a corner, muttering and

The Sea and the Breeze

mumbling, too out of breath it seemed to warn of the presence of the onlookers. Seth and Will lunged forward together. Seth hit one of the men with full force and sent him crashing into the far wall. Before he had time to recover, a sharp blow to the face saw the villain reeling senseless onto the dusty floor. At the same time Will had grabbed the other man from behind by the hair and securing his strong right arm around the fellow's neck had shook him and choked him unconscious.

As the dust settled, in panted Barny, wheezing and spluttering, more red-faced than ever. He made for the corner and sat down on a boulder, for the moment speechless. The boy still stood in the far corner cringing.

Seth attended Amos who soon staggered groggily to his feet, still clutching the purse in one hand and fingering his sore head with the other. Grimacing from the pain of the blow inflicted by a gruesome chunk of wood, now lying by the door, he raised the purse.

"Got it!" Amos smiled, shaking it to show that the coins were still within.

"Well caught, Amos, but what about our friend in the corner there," said Will. "We'll have to take him with us, lest he opens his mouth, but that'll cause problems in itself."

With this, Amos now coming more to his senses grabbed the lad by his thick-matted hair and jerking his head back sharply caused him to cry out.

"Come on young 'un. What did you hear back there? Speak up! Now! Or we'll have your tongue out."

As he said this, he unsheathed a dagger that he wore on his belt. The boy blubbered and gurgled out, but offered no intelligent reply.

Amos wrenched his head further back. "Speak!" he insisted.

Again the gurgling, but this time the thief pointed to his mouth, gagging as he did so.

"Easy, Amos," cautioned Seth. "Don't you see? He's dumb!

He can't speak a word. If he heard, he'll not repeat it."

"Dumb?" exclaimed Amos. "The poor little beggar must have run back here to these two good-for-naughts to give them the purse. And precious little *he'd* have seen of it I'll warrant."

"Surely you wouldn't have used the knife would you, Amos?"

"Of course not, Seth, but I thought I'd better find out for sure if there was a danger. Our secret must be kept."

Seth now looked at the youngster standing quaking and pitiful in the shadowy room. A beam of dust-filled sunlight slanted from the broken roof onto his forlorn face. He knew they could do nothing for him. They'd leave him to the mercy of his two acquaintances. His face cried out for salvation from this prisonlike existence, but he knew he could look forward to nothing better.

Seth took the purse and prising out a large silver piece, he pressed it into the lad's hand. He darted a glance at the sleeping partners as he did so. The boy understood. Bending shyly he hid the coin in one of his boots wiping away a tear as he stood upright.

"From the men of the Hamlet," Seth said to him.

Turning to the others, he added, "We'd better get back."

Barny, now almost recovered but still rosy cheeked, stood up to comply with Seth's suggestion. He opened his mouth as if to say something, but being overcome by a fit of coughing and spluttering gave up the idea and followed the other three outside.

By now the morning was passing towards noon. Bright sunshine poured down early summer warmth on them as they marched with purpose down the streets, back into the centre of town. Halting, they gazed below them over the rooftops of Fenny across the harbour. Far out in a calm sea sailed a haphazard collection of boats. They wended their way through the day's business, some tacking against the fresh sea breeze, some sailing upon it. Some were anchored far out in the bay, others glided gracefully to its northern extreme on their way to other ports. Yet, haphazard as they were, they formed a spellbinding scene... a patchwork of many coloured cloths on a blue canvas, speckled white.

Up on the hillside, the airs wafted about the companions.

"There, just beyond the horizon..." Amos stretched an arm vaguely at the scene, "is the open sea, where the coast turns east. Following that coast we'll come to Greylar, but away from the coast, to the north, is Icelar and our fate... *and* that of the Hamlet."

"Do you think we might sail direct to Icelar?" enquired Seth thoughtfully, emphasising the urgency of their quest.

"Best ask Henry Harding that," offered Will.

"After *he's* asked all *his* questions," added Barny, with a grin.

"As I've said before," cut in Amos more seriously. "I couldn't be sure what lies beyond the coastal waters. You know that even Kelman knows little of those waters and what little he *does* know would surely be too little. Much would depend on chance."

"All true," smiled Seth in mild frustration. "And much will depend on our speed. But now we must find our stores."

They'd spoken earlier with Alan Wooley but even with the mention of Jack Roper's recommendation, their visit to his store had borne no fruit. The rather unapproachable fellow had refused to sell them anything other than salted fish despite his seeming to have reasonable quantities of other foodstuffs.

Touring the numerous narrow haunts of the town now, they found similar attitudes. Here in fact, despite the promise of all manner of fare, little seemed to be stocked. Very few vendors had much to offer. This was primarily due to the short stocks, but such commodities were seemingly reserved, perhaps understandably, for the townsfolk. Even fish was hoarded. Harvests were still some way off.

So, their immediate quest became a tiresome affair of having to take what they could get from several hard-earned sources. They'd secured only half of what they'd hoped to obtain. They now had ample fish, some fresh but mostly smoked or salted. They had little in the way of meats, pickled vegetables, oatcake, bread or biscuit. They *had* however managed to come by equipment for the sea crossing... utensils, lamps, blankets, water skins, to add to the packs they already possessed.

The equipment and the food they arranged to be sent to the Northern Lady, the boat they'd hired. And so, somewhat dejected at their disappointing provender, they headed back to the Ferryboat.

"Hello!" greeted Jack Roper as they entered the inn. "How did you find things in the town?"

His manner suggested that he knew they'd not done too well.

"The boat was no problem really," explained Seth, "even though we only needed the *one*. We'll travel with the Northern Lady. Henry Harding seems a fair fellow. The food wasn't such a success."

"No thanks to Alan Wooley either," put in Barny, pointedly.

"But we've enough, if pushed," confided Seth. "We'll be setting sail first thing in the morning anyway."

"That's disappointing news indeed," said Roper. "I suppose folk *do* hang onto their stores at this end of the year. But at least you have a boat... and a good skipper, *I* can tell you. And that's more important than the food... if you must go travelling... you wouldn't float far on one of Alan Wooley's biscuits."

The sympathy in the innkeeper's voice did little to blunt the sharp edge of Barny's thoughts on the matter.

"We won't get far either if we end up eating the boat, shall we now."

"Still, for the time being, I think we need to rest from our day's walking," sighed Seth. "We've plans still unmade and a more tiring time ahead, though I dare say some of us may join you later in brief company."

The foursome ordered food and drink and went to join their fellow travellers. It was agreed that Samuel Dale and Jake Foxton should go down to the Northern Lady to ensure that the supplies had arrived, and to sleep aboard to guard them. This pair had been to the north before with Amos and Ely and knew their way around the boats more than a little from experience. It was also planned that later, in the early hours, Kelman should slip down to the boat to be hidden among the packs and baggage until they set sail in the morning. Seth would go with him to ensure his finding the right boat in the darkness.

All that remained was for Kelman to be hidden on the boat and they were ready for the next day and all it might bring. Those who remained at the inn were anxious to join the townsfolk, to forget their cares for a while. The people of Fenny seemed to them friendly enough after their weary journey from Midvale, but all agreed that danger might be found in light-hearted encounters. So it was that only Amos, Seth and Kaleb ventured forth. Barny, Will, Ely, Abe Arden and of course Kelman stayed behind, and talked quietly of the Hamlet, of their lives there and of their hopes for a swift return. Kelman spoke of his homeland in Icelar, but of the Hamlet he didn't speak, for he sensed that although he now looked upon it as home, he wouldn't return there.

Before long, Amos and Seth were conversing with Jack the innkeeper as if they'd lived in Fenny all their lives, which of course might prove dangerous, for their guard was down and a slip of the tongue could land them in trouble. Kaleb however, was true to his reputation and said very little. He was miserably resigned to the certainty, according to him, that he'd be the first to feel the seasickness warned of by Jack. His face was green with anticipation.

"Barny here reckons Kaleb gets seasick ploughing the

furrows," laughed Seth with a wink.

By now, even some of the cautious locals were smiling and joining in with the conversation.

A group near the counter burst into impromptu song. A man at a nearby table struck up the tune on an accordion. Raucous laughter punctuated each verse of a boisterous sea shanty, obviously well-known as it spread contagiously from table to table. The room became a sea of mirth, the like of which Seth had thought impossible in this place. Kaleb was even roused by Amos and Seth to join in the unfamiliar choruses, when in dashed the young stable lad.

"Quick! Fire!" he shouted. "Fire! Get the buckets, quick!"

"Where? Where?" cried Jack, as the singing died away. The lad gasped for breath, for he'd made a mad dash from the stable yard.

"Next door," he gulped. "Alan's house! The upper rooms are burning. Get the buckets. Quick!"

Jack sent the young assistant scurrying for buckets as the stable lad turned tail.

"Take 'em to the well," he said, and turning to the crowd now clamouring for the door he added, "And you others. Fetch all the pails you can lay your hands on. We'll need a chain from the well to the flames."

Alan Wooley, who'd been sitting in a far corner eying Seth and his companions with a continuing disdain for 'foreigners', had heard his own name.

"My house! My house! It'll be ruined. Help! Help!" he screeched, now in blind panic as he fought his way to the door.

Seth and Kaleb rushed outside to see if they could help in any way. Amos dashed to their room to raise the alarm. "Fire, next door," he explained briskly. "Barny, Will, Ely! come out to the yard. Abe, you stay here with Kelman, but be ready to leave by the window if the fire spreads. And if the need arises, throw out the packs before you."

The Sea and the Breeze

As the four reached the yard, Seth and Kaleb were already running to the fire with the first buckets, before a chain could be formed. As more buckets and more people arrived, the men of the Hamlet found themselves near the front of the line, but the water was being wasted.

Flames now leaped high above them, escaping out of upstairs windows. Roof timbers could be heard twisting and cracking in the intense heat. Grotesque, fire-red phantom figures darted to and fro around the yard, which backed onto the burning house adjoining the inn. Flames could soon be seen piercing the roof, devouring the timbers as they took hold. The heat could be felt even down here in the yard, where the fire sent shadows dancing impotent on the stable walls.

"This is useless," cried Amos. "The water's all being thrown into thin air. We must get to the base of the fire. To the base of the flames."

With this he tried the cottage door, to no avail. It was locked. He charged it, but it held firm, solid oak that it was.

"Where's that fool Alan Wooley," he cried. "He *must* have the key with him."

As if in answer to this cry of desperation, up popped Master Wooley, tearing his hair, still crying for help, dancing and fidgeting here and there. "The roof! The roof!" he shrilled. "It's going up! There'll be nothing left. Help! Help!"

Seth made a grab for him as he danced by... and missed. He stumbled, but recovering chased the shopkeeper in circles round the yard and finally caught him.

"The key!" Seth shouted in his ear. "Where's the key?"

Wooley came to his senses momentarily and fumbled in his pockets. He brought out a large bunch of keys and finding the key to his cottage door, he made two unsuccessful attempts to find the keyhole in the half-light then with panic returning, on the third attempt the key was home. He turned it in the lock. Seth, Amos and Kaleb pushed by and making their way upstairs entered a smoke filled room at the rear. Directing the buckets they carried at the fire, they doused the floorboards. Smoke and steam belched forth, but still the roof was ablaze. Amos gazed aloft and an idea sprang to mind.

"Come with *me*, both of you," he called. "We'll do little here. I think I know how we might do better."

Out he dashed and the others followed.

Finding Roper, Amos took him by the arm and between gasping and coughing,

"Quick," he said, "show me where we can find ladders. Long ones, to reach the roof."

"In the mason's yard... four doors away, down the street," Jack offered, puzzled by the request.

"Then get three or four, as long as may be found, and prop them up across the front of the house. Pitch them at the angle of the roof so we can climb to the ridge. We'll be back as soon as we may."

Straightway, Amos herded his two friends out further into the street, turning out of sight of the commotion. Presently, four ladders were set against the roof, and before long three men came back down the street carrying a heavy load... a furled sailcloth, some twenty-five feet long. Without delay, it was dropped and unfurled before house. Those with water buckets were instructed to soak the cloth. Will Sparrow now joined the three and together they rerolled the sail. They shouldered the now heavier load and moved to the ladders.

The crowd stood back with empty buckets in anticipation. Several moved forward to steady the ladders. The four inched their way up in unison... Seth and Will in the centre, Kaleb to the left and Amos to the right. Will's ladder was shorter than the others were. He'd chosen this one since he was a little taller than his companions were. Being used to ladders, he could venture to the uppermost rungs without fear of falling. Kaleb was rather shaky but managed well. As the four neared the top

The Sea and the Breeze

the sail, dripping wet, became heavier with each rung. Now they could feel the heat. Flames leapt into view beyond the ridge. Sparks and hot ashes floated upwards on the rising smokes, falling here and there about them. Smoke was finding its way through their *own* side of the thatch now and flames threatened to break out.

"Now!" cried Amos to the others. "Lift the sail high. Hold the outer edge firm and roll the sail up and over."

As they pushed the sail aloft they realised they were still a foot or two short of their target.

"Higher," called Amos. Will now balanced precariously on the top rung of his ladder, pushing as high as his long arms would reach. The others moved cautiously up, and with a last effort, the sail was launched. Over it rolled, smothering the flames. But with that last effort Kaleb had lost his balance and as he fell sideways off the ladder, he clung desperately to the sail, footloose sprawled on the thatch. His ladder slid sideways, halting threateningly on Seth's.

"Hang on, Kaleb. *And* you others," called Will as he slithered down, feet astride the ladder poles.

Seth called to Roper for more buckets to be taken inside. Will grabbed Kaleb's ladder and struggled to right it. Kaleb lost half his grip and almost fell, but found a foothold on the returning ladder. Its foot was left to its minder.

"Hang on tighter this time," Will left him with, as he dashed back up his own climber.

By now the flames were dying, and soon all that remained was smouldering and sizzling. Building stones were tied to the sail to secure it and then they descended finally, retching, recovering from fumes and heat.

When the locals who'd gathered, some helping, most watching from the street, realised that the fire had been conquered, they cheered loudly as the four men clambered to the ground.

Alan Wooley ran forward, grabbing Amos by the hand, and then the others in turn, thanking each of them.

"You've saved my house," he said. "Thank you all. Thank you."

"We've saved *some* of it," said Amos, reminding the trader of the damage.

The four re-joined Barny and Ely and now returned to the Inn, along with others, leaving Wooley and many of the locals to clear what they could of the mess in the darkness and to continue damping down.

"What on earth made you think of the sail?" Seth asked Amos.

"I noticed it in the yard when we were returning from our chase earlier. It just came to mind in the heat of the moment."

CHAPTER SIX

Scar Bringer

Back in the relative quiet of their room, the men of Myre Hamlet, anxious as they were to rest well, before their sea voyage, returned to their beds to a background of continued merrymaking, the noise of which drifted to them from the common room. All, that is, except for Seth and Kelman, who waited anxiously for the noise to die down and the street and the yard outside to empty before they made a move for the Northern Lady.

Seth talked with Kelman at length by the light of the fire and he now saw more than he had before of this rough heathen character. He was honest and reliable in an endearing way. Any deception he'd practiced was all the more understandable for this. As Kelman, almost in whispers, relived his days alone in Greylar, Seth knew that he'd have taken the same course of action himself in such a situation.

'The sheer immensity of the task of survival alone, not only physically but in his mind, must have been almost unbearable, even for a hunter such as Kelman,' Seth thought.

Seth also saw that Kelman had held a real love for his family... the family he'd lost to the Scar. This loss, more than anything else, had surely made Kelman desperate enough to come south with strangers in search of a new life.

And Kelman saw that Seth was a friend indeed, for he showed concern for him. Kelman the outsider, Kelman the Scar bringer.

Seth listened intently while Kelman talked of Ironmound, his home and his family, and drew comparisons with his own abode. Seth himself talked of Sarah and Ruffles, of the horses and of the hens. And of the chatter of the Puddle Stream. Kelman fell in love with Puddlefork, though he'd never seen it.

They shivered. The fire had died to embers and with the fading of its glow silence had come unnoticed by the two companions. But now they knew they must move and Kelman must be hidden on board the waiting boat.

Seth, used to moving stealthily when the need arose, slipped through the window into the street as quietly as Kelman and the two made their way like cats across the cobbles, down to the harbour and slipped on board the Lady. Seth knocked quietly but firmly three times on the frame of hold and Samuel, who knew the sign to expect, and who sat his turn awake, gently drew back the cover taking care not to wake the captain who also slept on board to the stern in the covered well. Samuel and Seth exchanged brief words and Kelman was hidden, quite comfortable among the packs. The cover slid back into place and Seth turned, stepped neatly to the quayside and disappeared into the dark streets of Fenny.

"Morning Henry," greeted Amos as the party met the skipper on the quayside next to the Northern Lady.

"Morning," returned Henry Harding, still cautious not to appear too friendly. "You've had visitors already. Alan Wooley and his assistant were down at first light with a few choice additions to your supplies, it seems."

"Yes," smiled Jake, peering out from the now open hold and raising aloft a large pack. "There are two like this. Many of the things we couldn't get are here. He said something about being grateful for your help… a fire in the town?"

"That's right," said Seth. "We helped put out a fire that would have gutted his house, next to the Inn. It's a shame it took all that to open his larders this wide."

"True," said Jake, "but at least this is free of charge and quite willingly given, although friend Wooley did take pains to point out that his stocks would be terribly low until the new season was come of age."

Jack Roper had bid them farewell and assured Seth and his companions that the horses they were leaving behind would be well kept until they could be fetched by others from the Hamlet. Seth's farewell to Tag had been reluctant despite the assurances. So that the horses might be returned home, the innkeeper had promised that news of the safe though horseless departure from Fenny would be sent with the next coach, which was due before the week was out. Seth still trusted that his fellow villagers would keep the secret of the Scar, though that mattered less now that they were leaving the port.

They boarded the boat, leading the pony they'd brought with them precariously, and for *his* part reluctantly, across the boarding plank and then clumsily down a ramp improvised from the same plank, into the hold. The skipper and his two fellow fishermen who were to be his crew as always, helped with the few remaining packs brought from the inn, but the travellers were careful not to let them too near to the bundle where Kelman lay.

At least once, their secret was close to being let out, when the pony, led by Kaleb, faltered at the foot of the ramp, half turned and took Barny unawares, bundling him over onto the pile of packs in the corner.

"Ouch!" called out Barny as he hit something lumpy under a tarpaulin. Seth and Will, who'd been helping to manoeuvre the pony, laughed heartily, more to disguise the echoing "ouch!" uttered from under the canvas sheet than through amusement. The lumpy something was Kelman.

"And I thought *you* could handle horses, Barny Hensman," chipped in Seth with a cautious glance at the packs.

"I *can*," replied Barny as he regained his feet, "but Little 'Un here's a right handful at the best of times. Ponies are always cheekier than horses, and that's no lie."

With the efficiency of experience, and with no help from the dry-landers, the three sailors cast off from the mooring and raised the single sail. As it unfurled smoothly, the fresh morning breeze which had seemed quite insignificant caught the cloth strongly and it billowed out before them. For a while, they'd be heading north until they cleared the point that Amos had spoken of the day before. Then they'd follow the coast eastwards. *'Perhaps then,'* Seth thought, *'we might find it best to reveal our true plans, and indeed to reveal Kelman. At last we outnumber them, should they resist, though of course we couldn't sail the vessel without their guiding so easily.'*

Seth decided that the best occasion might be when they lay at anchor.

As they cleared the immediate confines of the quayside the breeze stiffened. It was blowing from the south-east, a dry wind from the mountains of eastern Nording. This brought welcome fair weather... a bright sky of blue azure and a relatively calm sea, specked with white foam as the breeze caught the incoming waves. The sail was set to take best advantage of the wind and they made fair speed, though the boat wasn't designed with haste in mind. A couple of hours after midday saw them clear the point. Now they steered north-east slowing a little, for this put the wind directly from the starboard.

As darkness descended, they were nearing the open sea and with the insistent advice of the captain they decided to moor on the eastern coast of the outer limits of the bay. Henry Harding was familiar with this much of the coast and knew of a suitable retreat in a small sheltered inlet clear of the stronger currents. Kaleb was glad of this news, for although he'd not yet turned green, he was for the moment struggling to find his sea legs and would be glad to find the shore.

They moored at the sheltered mouth of a stream that issued into the sea here from the south. Where it greeted the sea it was deep enough to take the boat, and though its banks had a rocky foundation, the overlying earth was well endowed with an overgrowth of moss and grasses, giving a safe berth for the craft. The mossy banks gave way quite abruptly to pine trees stretching away solemnly into the twilight in each direction along the coast.

The mooring completed, fires were lit in the shelter of a mound close to the stream overshadowed by the trees. This proved an easy task, for there was an abundance of dry, dead wood.

Little 'Un was led ashore by the system of planks and Barny ensured he was tied securely where he could graze after drinking from the water skins, for the stream was salt soaked here, so close to the tides. Packs were brought from the boat, food was unpacked along with bed rolls and the utensils needed to prepare a meal. The sweet aroma of the pines drifted about the encampment. Amos had gathered an armful of pine cones and fuelled one of the fires with them. When all was well settled, Seth and others took to their pipes. Seth sat with Henry and the crewmen, offering them his tobacco. The two boatmen declined, but Henry drew out his own pipe and took a fill.

"We're sure to run short of this before we get back," sighed Seth, anticipating disappointment.

"No doubt," agreed Henry with a laconic smile. "You'll find with sea travelling, the long days and nights, you'll smoke all the more. A month away from Fenny will need an awful lot of tobacco."

"Actually," said Seth, cautiously, "it could be a little more than a month, by the time we get back."

"In that case," replied Henry light heartedly, apparently getting a taste for adventure, "I'll hang onto my own tobacco for a while until we've finished yours."

The four shared the jest with smiles and Seth felt now was the moment.

"You see," he added, "our true destination is Icelar. Not Greylar."

"What?" startled Henry. "Icelar! No one's even *seen* it. It's only a legend."

The two others looked on, surprised but silent.

"*We've* seen it, or at least part of it," a new voice replied.

Seth turned as Ely, who'd strolled over from the other fire, spoke.

"When we travelled to Greylar, we saw Icelar's south-eastern tip, quite close.

"Alright. So you say you've seen Icelar. Then why didn't you tell us that was your destination? And what's your business there? How do you know for sure that it *is* Icelar?"

Seth noticed with interest that although Henry had expressed surprise and some degree of anger at these intentions, it seemed he might have no greater trepidation in travelling there than to Greylar. If only Seth could convince him for certain that the danger wasn't so great.

"The answers to all three of your questions are linked Henry," he replied. "And I'm sincerely sorry that we had to deceive you. We're desperate, and if the folk of Fenny had discovered our quest, they'd have driven us from the town."

"But why? Why?" insisted Henry.

"Well," said Seth. "We need to go there in search of a cure. A cure for a fearsome ill which has hit Myre Hamlet."

He then explained how Kelman had joined with the first travellers in Greylar and had unwittingly brought back the Scar. How he'd told them of Icelar and of the legends of the cure.

Henry, with a patient interest that surprised Seth and Ely, listened intently, drawing thoughtfully on his pipe.

"Sounds like a long trip, all told," he said, after a tense silence. And no doubt there'll be problems galore. Not that I can speak for these other two, but *I'm* willing to help you all I can. I can see you're indeed in dire straits and I know that you would've revealed the truth earlier, could you have dared. I'm sure I'll regret it later, but I've nothing else to do for a while. Actually, when you told me yesterday that you needed us to wait for you at our landing place in Greylar I wondered what we might do for the days you were away. Now, you know, I might even join you. I'd like to see this Icelar myself. But wait," he continued after a brief hesitation. "Then you here have been in contact with the disease? Worse still, *you* may have the disease."

Suddenly, he seemed to lose his enthusiasm to this realisation.

"I'm afraid so," admitted Seth, with genuine misgiving. "Kelman, the man from Icelar himself, is with us. We brought him for his knowledge of his homeland there... he's already told us much of its terrain and of the inhabitants near Ironmound where he lived, but I fear he grows worse. His face is dreadfully poxed now and I wonder if he will ever reach Icelar, even with your help, Henry. I know we've tried your trust, along with that of Simon and Peter here, but I hope you can find it in you to forgive us. At least the disease is slow to act, and may not trouble you at all. More than a few of us in the Hamlet seem immune to it. We could only offer you a normal price for the boat until now, for it would've raised suspicions in your mind. But now the truth is spilled out, if you'll help us willingly, you'll have ten times the purse. And if we're successful, we'll be in your debt always."

This belated realisation of the danger caused Henry to hesitate. He looked questioningly at his two crewmen, who still said nothing and then with final resolve, shrugged his shoulders.

"Well, handsome is as handsome does," he sighed, "and I guess it's a little late now to say no. In meeting you, we've met the deepest danger. If I'm to fall foul of this dreaded thing, the nearer the cure the better. As for my silent friends here, I can't say."

Still the pair said little but, like good sailors, declared their duty to be with the captain and their decisions to be with his.

"Then bring friend Kelman from his hiding place," called Henry, clapping his hands together. "Simon, Peter, stoke up the fire. He'll want something to eat with the rest of us."

Ely joined them in the task while Seth, after heartily thanking Henry, rushed to find Kelman.

Henry refused to take a purse different from that he'd already agreed and Seth was convinced now that had they not deceived the boat master, he'd still have taken them.

Fresh meat and wholesome bread were prepared, intended for the first few days of their journey, before they'd need to resort to less wholesome but more preservable foods. Ale they had also, though no doubt this would soon be spent. But the farmers among them were not entirely unable to hunt fresh meat and, with Kelman's help, they'd not starve. And of course the sailors knew the ways of fish and fishing.

Soon they were feasting, with no thought of running short, though Amos and Jake had been busy. They'd set traps further inland, where the woods were thicker and where the undergrowth may yield more food come morning.

The boatmen were somewhat startled by Kelman's appearance, which couldn't now help but show its ugliness, as he ate, despite the continuing presence of scarves to hide behind. He said little, but ate with ferocious appetite, for he'd eaten little.

The meal over, spirits were high and Seth settled down to his prepared bedroll close to one of the fires, to the sound of others joking and singing. He was well pleased, for it seemed that good fortune had led them to the right boat, and the right boatman.

'Soon the Hamlet will rejoice again' he thought as he slipped into sleep.

The singing soon died and was replaced by the song of the

pines swaying in the warm night breeze.

Seth woke to a sharp blow in the stomach then almost instantly he was attacked by a wild thing that seemed to claw for his throat... a wild furry thing that choked and suffocated him. As he reeled to his feet, flinging the thing from him and standing dazed but crouching ready for the next attack, he was greeted only by hearty laughter from Amos and Jake. Bewildered, Seth turned his gaze to where the creature had fallen. There he saw rabbits. Dead rabbits. The traps had done their job.

"That should at least add to the fresh meat for today," Amos grinned. "Though I'm sure we'll need something larger before long."

Seth returned the grin. Now that he was full awake he knew his life wasn't under threat.

"You're right, Amos. But if you can catch a deer, or a wild boar, don't go throwing it in my direction until it's cooked."

In a short while all were awake and after an unambitious breakfast of oatcake and cheese and a ration of water they broke camp and loaded the boat. Little 'Un was getting quite used to planks by now and, helped by not having Kelman to stumble on, Barny brought the pony on board with no trouble. Barny and Will had taken Samuel and Peter to replenish emptied water skins further upstream where the water was free of salt. With the help of another fair day, and some south-easterly wind, they cast off and headed for the open coast away from the shelter of the inlet.

At first, they made decent headway still, turning the sail to catch the wind, but as they rounded a point of the coast and turned due east, the wind blew against them.

"This is what I've feared since we set out this morning," Henry cursed. "I was hoping the wind might shift. It'll be slow progress now, while this one blows. We'll have to tack and make the best of it."

Most of the company were in the open hold. The awning was stashed with the packs. Kaleb still seemed to be troubled by the swell of the waves... even the pony was travelling better than the farmer was. Seth and Barny were in the well to the rear and Seth had been trying his hand at the tiller. But now Henry took it. Peter and Simon unhitched the ropes which had held the sail steady. Now Henry turned the tiller, first one way, then the other so that the boat zigzagged forward. With each turn, the sail came about and Peter and Simon slackened or took up the ropes alternately.

Seth and the others were amazed that, with such manoeuvring, they could actually travel *into* the wind. But progress was slow and it seemed hardly worth the effort with the upsets it now caused... the pony staggered to and fro with each change of direction, and Kaleb felt worse than ever.

By evening, they'd covered less than ten leagues and seven of those were won before they'd turned due east. With daylight fading, they looked urgently for a sheltered mooring along the sandy coast. They anchored as close as they dare to the land and carefully came ashore through a foot or more of water, carrying what packs they need above their heads to the shelter of the rocks higher on the beach. The pony at first was reluctant to take a dip but, with persistent pushing and pulling, he splashed his way ashore, followed by a bedraggled Barny, who'd pushed when he should've pulled.

Spirits had dropped now for progress has slackened so and they all thought how much easier it would be to turn and drift with the wind, back to Fenny. But the spell of settled weather continued and with it the dry south-easterly persisted.

For three more days they battled on, sometimes with more progress and sometimes with much less. More than once, Kaleb and Barny each received a clout from the boom as the sail jibbed. But Seth insisted that every inch they gained was important, for thoughts of the Hamlet and its plight kept flooding back to him. Henry and his two fellows seemed quite happy to sail back and forth forever and stuck to the task with continued dedication.

On the first day of the three, they'd encountered the second bay, almost the size of Fenny Bay. Those who'd travelled it before recalled how the captain of their boat had followed the coastline, for they'd had no sure knowledge of where the further shore might be. Now, with the assurances of Amos, Henry kept a straight course across it. They almost lost the light before they reached the far side, but were happy that at least they'd crossed it and avoided at least an extra day's sailing. Kaleb had been sick on two occasions, cursing as he wretched. The pony now anticipated most of the twists and turns and kept his feet quite well. Considering he'd to wait for dry land each evening before eating much, he seemed in high spirits. The sky remained clear and blue and for early May, the warm sun and the cooling breezes were the best things they had. But even these became tiresome in the face of constant changes in direction. Of the Myre Hamlet men only Seth, through his deep realisation of their needs, and Barny through his nature, remained optimistic during this trying time.

On the evening of the seventh, they found a cove, sheltered and almost as welcoming as that haven on the first night out from Fenny.

Seth realised that his companions were weary of this slow and tiresome progress to the point of despair and, with no prospect of a change in the wind, he spoke with Amos of something they'd not mentioned since they'd looked out across the bay from Fenny... a direct crossing to Icelar. Seth in fact had discussed this possibility at length with Amos and Kelman back in Myre Hamlet. Amos knew only the eastern route and Kelman, although he *had* looked out to sea from Icelar, could recall nothing but cliffs along its south coast.

"Surely," argued Seth, "that coast must offer some landing?"

"Perhaps," said Kelman, "I not seen one. But then, I only see a few miles of the coast."

"Then we must ask Henry's advice," concluded Seth, feeling a pang of conscience that he might once again have neglected Henry's confidence.

"You're certainly full of surprises, aren't you," was Henry's first reaction when the plan was made known to him.

Then almost predictably now, he fell to silence and calmly considered the suggestion. And after some thought he made his reply.

"If I were ruled by common sense, I'd say no. It's hard for me to leave sight of land, for it conflicts with my instincts. We'd not know what to expect along the coast, and where there are cliffs there will likely be rocks. More haste, less speed, I say. But on the other hand, this damned head wind is driving me crazy deep down. I'm used to a day of it now and then. But day after day, then I'm not so keen. Now, heading north would at least allow us to take the wind into the sails again. If it's still against us tomorrow, we'll change course. Maybe with a good day's sailing we'll reach Icelar. But one thing, and one thing only, persuades me against common sense, and that's because..."

He paused, scratching his chin pensively, as if still weighing the decision in his mind.

"And what's that?" asked Seth at length, unable to wait for him to continue.

"...and that," he concluded, with resignation, "is because, if I refuse, you'll no doubt tie the three of us, or worse, and attempt to sail the Lady without us. And that's something I couldn't stand for.

Seth perceived a hint of a smile in Henry's eyes as he said this and knew that Henry had made up his mind more certainly than he hoped to let on.

Seth took Henry by the hand. "Thank you once again, he

offered. To get to Icelar early will surely be a boon to our kinsfolk."

"Maybe," said Henry. "Maybe."

And so it was they left their course. Seth glance over his shoulder and squinted at the noon sun now high above them. They'd left Nording's coast beyond the horizon and, looking back, all that followed was a wake of silver... tiny sparkling waves in the green-blue sea. They'd bared their backs to the warmth of the sun. A few clouds drifted by overhead and every now and then, when one blotted out the sun's face, the breeze felt cold across their backs as it aired the sweat, only to yield to welcome warmth again as the clouds moved on, losing their silvered edges as they went.

Little 'Un stood patiently in a corner. He now took to lying down when he fancied, for the nights were taken with grazing, but mostly he stood, resting his head on the packs. Occasionally he swished his tail, twitching nose and eyes too, for he was troubled by flies that had joined the travellers on their journey over the sea.

By now, they'd come some six leagues, more than they'd covered the whole of the day before. Though they'd hoped for a change in the wind, all their hearts has lifted with the sail, as it had fluttered and billowed out before them in the early morning breeze. 'A new course for good fortune,' was a proverb they all knew. They'd eaten a sparse breakfast, washed down with the last of the ale which went down well though the lack of it now wouldn't.

Some of them now passed the time with a pack of cards that Simon had produced. Peter attended the various ropes and shackles that held the sail, while Seth, Ely and Kelman stood with Henry who was at the tiller. These four surveyed the forward horizon intently, hoping for a first sight of land ahead.

The clouds drifting overhead from the south-west now

seemed to pass more thickly, yet ever more slowly. Before long they could see that the clouds were collecting ahead of them and by mid-afternoon a vast bank of ominous grey spread itself before them. Below it, on the far horizon, the sky was still clear.

"There!" cried Kelman excitedly, "Icelar, look, ahead."

With this, even those few who'd been sleeping clambered up to see for themselves. Sure enough, on the edge of sight, they perceived land... a thick, dark band on the horizon, hazy in the darkening day. Cheers went up from the hold. Seth and Ely grinned. They'd found Icelar.

Henry Harding looked less pleased. The wind was dying, yet the sea was becoming restless. The water now rolled and churned and the waves became choppy. Foaming spray splashed high as the waves hammered the hull and all aboard now looked around them worriedly. The darkness increased as the sun was lost to the clouds now fingering their way across the sky above. The boat was dragged on fitfully, more by surging currents than by the wind. They seemed to be pulled to starboard... northwards, but always more strongly to the east. The wind had become blustery, fitfully changing direction. The mast creaked and groaned under the increasing strain.

"Lower the sail!" bellowed Henry, "Before we lose it. Stow it as quickly as you can. Cover the hold."

Peter and Simon obliged. The men of the Hamlet got under cover of the hold. Barny steadied and comforted the pony as best he could as the vessel buffeted in the ever more unfriendly waters. Seth and Kelman alone stayed with the three seamen in the well. Peter now joined Henry at the tiller. Simon and the others watched forward as the boat swayed and lurched at the mercy of the current. The air was heavy now. They all sweated in the clammy heat. Forked lightning flashed wildly accompanied by a deafening clap of thunder bursting overhead, the storm ripping through the dark heavens with awesome fury. With it came rain. Torrents poured down on them. The wind tore in all directions and the Northern Lady was tossed about as if she were a leaf in a swirling stream.

Barny needed the assistance of Kaleb and Ely in calming the pony after the thunderclap, for he was already restless in the tottering darkness.

The sea was now enormous. The wind set north-west and a stinging gale blew rain and salt spray into the faces of the steersmen. Henry was battling desperately to keep a course into the main barrage of waves, but was forced always to the east, turning at the mercy of the storm. The boat mounted a huge swell and there below them to port in the enormous trough that followed, Seth and the others spied with horror, jagged razor teeth of rocks... a line of them east to west.

Henry no longer resisted the pull of the current to the east, shouting to Peter as they turned the tiller. For a terrifying moment, the boat hung, teetering on the brink of the trough and then was swept back with the wave she was riding as another ridge of water swallowed the rocks.

As they swung away eastwards, they saw that the rocks were not to be flirted with, for there before them rising in the fleeing troughs of the waves ran a long line... a great reef barring the way to Icelar.

Henry and Peter did all they could to steer away, but were now at the mercy of the currents which, having swept them first towards the rocks then eastwards almost astride them, now flung them south and east away from the craggy danger. They were lying side on to the swell and huge waters pounded as the waves surged back at them from the rocks. The lightning blinded them and thunder crashed again and again in their ears. Then, a crack above their heads, almost as loud as the thunder.

"Look out!" cried Kelman, as he saw the broken mast falling.

As Seth looked up in heed of the warning, he instinctively lifted an arm in a futile gesture of defence as the mast crashed down on them. In an instant, he was struck a glancing blow by the huge timber. It hit the deck, and tearing free from its stump, slithered into the seething waters, tethered only by the trailing rigging which had held the sail.

Kelman recovered from the violent lurching of the boat and looked around him. There were Henry and Peter, still hanging grimly on to the tiller. Simon was floundering in the well, which was awash with the sea. But nowhere could he see Seth.

"Here," cried Seth, "over h…"

He managed no more, a huge wave overwhelming him. As the wave moved on, Kelman spied him in the cold, green water, clinging desperately to the splintered mast which now washed back and forth at the side of the boat with every new wave.

"Hold on," cried Kelman.

And with sharp presence of mind, he grabbed a rope. With eyes half blinded by the salt spray he attempted to tie the rope to the rail of the well. Twice he was foiled as waves broke over him. But at last, it was tied.

"Catch hold if you can," he screamed, tossing the loose end in Seth's direction to follow after his words.

Seth, gasping for air, thrashed at the rope as it passed him, but missed it by an arm's length. Kelman drew in the rope for a fresh attempt, leaning as far as he dare to get nearer his struggling companion. Again waves pounded the boat and Kelman too was overboard, thrust in Seth's direction. He clung desperately to the rope as he somersaulted into the air. The mast surged up to meet him and with a sickening thud took him full in the chest. Slumped over the forsaken spar, half-conscious, he fought for control of limbs and senses, still clinging to the rope. With lungs half full with water, half with searing pain, he recovered enough to see that Seth was close. The two now clung to the rope. Peter left the tiller and Simon, recovering from his flounderings, reached the secured end of the rope and together, hauling with strained muscles and tense grip, they hauled for what seemed like a life or more until Seth, and then Kelman, were each in their grasp. With a last effort from all four the pair were in the well like landed fish. Seth spluttered and coughed. Kelman grimaced in numbing pain, winded by his encounter with the mast.

"Quick, Peter! The tiller!" bawled Henry, "I'm losing her. Cut the mast ropes, Simon, or we'll be dragged to ruin."

Peter made it back to the tiller. Simon fumbled around for a small, sharp gutting knife and when at last he found it clambered to the decks. With precarious agility he cut first one and then another of the ropes. Then another and finally the mast floated free, buffeting the sides once more as if in defiance of its freedom before parting company with the boat.

Carried by the current, and with the tiller's aid, they'd thankfully drifted clear of the jaws of the rocks and what they could still see of the deadly reef was some four or five lengths of the boat away, waves yawning around the awesome teeth. They were helpless on the waves. South-east they went.

Seth lay recovering, retching sea water. Kelman sat stiff and sore. All felt some relief as the storm died. They drifted on ever calmer waters, oblivious to their course. It was as if the rocks had known their purpose and, with the storm as an ally, had fought them off. Now that their attempt was thwarted, the storm fled almost as urgently as it had reared its head.

The men who'd sheltered in the hold had suffered little injury, just a few cuts and bruises. Even the pony had no more than a cut on his flank, inflicted by a rope bracket. The cover had saved them from drowning, but the floor was awash, two feet or more in water. Unlike the stern well, the hold had no drain... a sump for baling was all. Though they'd taken little more than a soaking, most of the packs, and so the provisions, were sodden. When baling had been done, their fears were realised. Much of the food was ruined. They were shattered. As if the rocks were not trial enough, their food was spoiled, and with no mast, they were at the sea's mercy.

Time soon left them bewildered. They became reticent, reluctant to fight for survival, for there seemed to be no controlling their fate.

The wind had changed with the storm, conjuring a drear blanket of cloud. Unable to use the north-west wind, still they drifted steadily south-eastwards. Night had come, followed by day and night again. And on they moved. The time seemed endless, for the sea had become calm now, almost flat. And sea mists followed them from the north, eerie mists that sometimes hung far off in clouds steaming on the water and sometimes engulfed them, echoing every splash and every creaking board in the dank, hollow air.

The next day brought drizzle, and with it the mists had dissolved. Only the three seamen showed any interest in their course or indeed their wellbeing.

"By my reckoning," Henry had said, "we should come back to Norway before long at this rate."

"Yes," Ely had replied, "and then what? We're ruined. No mast. Little food. Some hope of reaching Icelar now. We'll be lucky to get home ever again, *without* an answer to the Scar, let alone *with* one."

Seth too felt that all seemed helpless now. *'The prospect of a long trek back to Myre Hamlet, defeated, is the best we can look forward to,'* he thought. He'd recovered from his ordeal but Kelman, who'd helped him, who'd saved his life, wasn't so fortunate. His affliction had taken an overpowering grip on him now and this, coupled with his painful injuries, found him lying delirious with fever, often close to death. So desperate, yet he clung to life with all his faded strength, for deep in his heart, he longed to tread the earth of Icelar once again.

"Surely," Henry encouraged, "with what tools and

provisions we have, if we reach the mainland soon, we can repair the damage. We can even replace the mast, given trees. At least we still have the sail, and ample ropes and shackles. She could soon be good as new. *Your* skill as hunters and indeed *ours* as fishermen will see us through. We can reach Icelar, even by the eastern route. Why give up now when it's still possible."

This encouragement helped the others mend their thoughts. Amos, realising that Henry took his habitual hopeful stance took up the challenge and carried the others with him.

"All cheers to Henry," he bellowed, and the others echoed his approvals.

Before long, the clouds fled on persistent air, taking with them the drizzle that had bedogged them all day, though they'd been grateful for this salt free water. It was with raised hearts that they sighted land ahead come nightfall. By the light of a moon, now almost full, that rose early before them, the Northern Lady limped to a shallow resting place on open sands, not ten miles from the north-eastern tip of Nording.

"Madman's moon, tomorrow night," whispered Barny to Little 'Un. "Madman's moon tomorrow night," he repeated, louder for the benefit of his companions. Endeavouring to cheer them, he added jokingly, "there's certainly plenty of madmen here to greet it!"

CHAPTER SEVEN

Pulse

Morning greeted them early. A fiery sun rose above the sea, close to the clear reaches of the coastline which stretched away to the east. After hovering reluctantly, the sun escaped the hold of the calm waters and climbed steadily into the pale skies. Soon the hint of frost that clung to the grassy dunes in which they slept was warmed to sparkling dew. Birds chattered in nearby woods to the south and gulls soared above, calling to the sea.

It was a glorious morning, but as the travellers awoke, one by one, there was little greeting wasted on it. The boat keeled on the ebb tide, lying where she'd been left moored the night before. She looked a sorry sight... ropes and canvas strewn about, broken boards and rails and the ripped and splintered stump of the mast. The calm sea flowed around her, sighing sadly on the sands. This sight was enough to convince them that the weather was worth no smiling. They'd unloaded as little as they needed for the night, for although they'd laboured little since the storm, their bodies were as weary as their minds and spirit of heart was hard to find, despite Henry's reassurances.

Little 'Un had been tethered safely under the eaves of the nearby woods, though he found little grass to comfort him and it was well that he was patient, for many of his kind would have argued with the rope and been off to find better grazing.

Kelman, still in a feverish dream, had been made as comfortable as possible by Seth and Abe Arden. Abe administered what medicine he had with him, hoping the fever would be overcome. A hasty fire had been lit and pans boiled for Kelman's sake as much as anything else and, after a welcome but rushed and inadequate meal, they slept almost where they sat. Birdie kicked gingerly at the ashes of the fire and soon rekindled it from its neglected remains with the help of Jake and Barny gathering dry wood. He soon had a good warming blaze to show for his careful efforts and a few smiles returned with the welcome warmth in the otherwise chill air.

"Summer at last," chirped Birdie, rubbing his hands in the warmth.

"Yes," replied Ely, who'd just joined them after tending to Little 'Un's hunger.

He'd found the pony a clearing, a little further into the woods where the grass grew thicker.

"It seems a long time since last summer," he added.

"I know, but don't forget though," chipped in Birdie, "we're further north here. The weather won't be as warm as we're used to in the Hamlet... and when we reach Icelar, it'll be cooler still."

"I suppose you're right," answered Ely, who was reminded of his previous journey. "We even had snow to deal with in October last year in the mountain passes to the south of here, and few of us have ever seen snow in Midvale at that time of year."

"Anyway," continued Barny, refusing to let the glimmer of optimism escape him, "if it's *that* cold, I'm sure we'll find an inn to thaw out in. As welcoming as the Blue Pig, I don't doubt."

The others submitted to his cheerful remarks, and smiling now went about preparing a breakfast.

For three days they did very little but rest, finding new strength for serious hunting and for repairing their vessel. Kelman showed little sign of improvement, even with the arduous attention of Abe, who stayed with him for much of the time. The Scar was now biting deeper. Henry and his companions had become accustomed to seeing Kelman's disfigurement, but had become rather more disturbed as it took hold of others around them. Amos was now showing worsening signs of affliction on his face and hands, as too were Samuel and Jake. Ely however, the only other among them who'd travelled on the earlier quest, showed no signs outwardly or inwardly. Even so, others who'd not travelled were now stricken with this thing that had brought them all these miles from home. To their despair Will, Kaleb and Abe all now knew the Scar first hand. Barny and Seth seemed to have escaped its attention, for the moment at least.

The three men of Fenny were more anxious than the others were, for they couldn't forget entirely that they'd been tricked into this business. Yet Henry Harding seemed resigned to two things, for he was a man of some principle. First, he'd decided on an adventure and, like all good seamen, knew the virtue in sticking with decisions, even when things seemed amiss. Second, he knew that these desperate men had become deep friends and any thought of deserting them grieved him such that he dismissed it. His two companions were less sure in their hearts, but as sure as ever in their loyalty to the captain. And they too had made dear friends.

At least they were all aided in one thing, in their will to forget the disease... Most now possessed beards, for shaving was difficult and pointless, and though some persevered, it was a tiresome affair. This at least hid much of the Scar, even on Kelman now.

They stayed in this place for several days, for although time was precious, the initial resting was needed and then much time was taken in hunting and preserving what they may for their further quest into the unsure colder territories of Icelar. All through this time, they effected repairs. A party of them had searched at length in the woods for suitable timber. They travelled a mile or more to pines for mast wood and, once found, a slender trunk was hauled to the beach and good use made of it. Waterproofing was difficult but with the skill of the sailors and the use of caulking stuffs, passable repairs were made with long hours of patience.

They'd moved their camp over the high dunes and a furlong or so into wooded reaches, after that first weary night. Here, in a quiet dell, they'd found shelter from wind and rain, for though fine at first, the full moon's passing had heralded a drizzle that stayed with them incessantly for two days and nights. The rain dowsed the fires but soon new ones were made, crackling into life under ash and oak. All around was a mass of fresh spring green. The floor of the woods was sparsely covered where the trees were thick and hazel brakes sprang up in profusion, matted with brambles. But where the trees overhead gave way to open sky, there spread a lush carpet below. The Northern Lady was now moored safely in waters of a depth more to her liking. Most of the repairs in waterproofing had been done where she lay at low tides and once re-floated finally, reloading was put in hand.

Kelman, although still unable to do much more than sit up, had made a gradual recovery. His fever had passed five days after they'd made camp and he looked much better for resting on dry land. His ribs were still dreadfully sore, but nothing seemed broken.

"You're a tough nut, Kelman," grinned Seth, as he offered a cup of gruel. "It's hare today... and gone tomorrow," he joked, but Kelman didn't grasp the jest. "Thanks for all your help out there," Seth went on, in more serious vein. "I'm sorry it meant you going through all this."

Seth grasped Kelman's shoulder in encouragement.

"You'll soon be back to normal now, and we'll soon be back in Icelar, even if it's by the rovers' route."

Kelman's wistful eyes glanced up at Seth.

"I happy to help you, Seth. You've helped me much since I came to you. You're a good friend to me."

As Seth met his glance, he knew Kelman's inner thoughts.

Laying a reassuring arm on his shoulder again, he answered them as if they'd been spoken.

We *shall* soon be in Icelar, Kelman. You and I and all the others. Kelman looked up again, his eyes less sad now.

"Thank *you* as well, Seth, for making me welcome. I love the Hamlet almost as Icelar now."

With this, he turned his attention to the hot bowl cradled in his hands and Seth made his way towards the shore to see how far preparations had progressed. Amos and Ely joined him and together they climbed the steep dunes until the sea came into view, heralded by a stiff breeze. To the north stretched the open waters. The day was clear, but there was no sign of Icelar. To the east and west, the woods ran for many miles, although in the distant east the sea broke into the land and beyond the breach could be made out another outcrop.

"Greylar," confirmed Ely to Seth.

"Greylar," repeated Amos. "I crossed those straights with Jamie and Sam on the raft last year. It was in these very woods, some way west of here, that we lost Sam. This coast holds sad memories for me. I'll be glad to bid it goodbye."

They turned their gaze to the south and here on the high sands above the trees they could see that the wooded land ran many miles inland. With eyes shaded from the westering sun, Seth could make out the dark misty shapes of high hills in the south-west.

"The tail of the mountains," decided Amos.

"Let's hope we don't need that route or any other this side of Fenny," said Ely, shaking his head, remembering poor Sam Rushey.

Afternoon was passing, but Henry assured them that preparations would be complete by nightfall, and an early start next day would be no problem.

Dawn followed a peaceful night and they soon lifted anchor and were away with the help of that same stiff breeze, sailing into the rising sun. The repaired mast did its duty, sporting the proud sail gracefully. The wind slackened a little during the day, but they still made fair progress. Soon they left Nording behind, passing the straights to starboard and skirting the western tip of Greylar. Here too, the land was quite heavily wooded, though here and there glimpses of the vast plains were revealed stretching inland beyond the wooded expanse.

The next day they sighted Icelar again. This time it was the extended tip that the earlier travellers had thought was a small island. The gulls were still there, visible as wheeling clouds from such a distance.

"We may reach Icelar tomorrow," Kelman enthused, as if he'd forgotten the hostility of his people. "We find the place I set out from, further north, around tip of land. It faces north itself. We leave the boat there, safe for long time."

The afternoon brought them to the Greymills. Here they moored and made ready for night.

When all was settled and all chores were done, Seth and Barny shared a pouch of tobacco and talked of the Hamlet.

"I wonder how things are, back there?" sighed Seth, drawing thoughtfully on his pipe. "I suppose the cattle should be coming on fine by now, with the new grass, though I don't suppose anyone will be paying them much notice with the Scar and all the trials it'll be bringing. I hope dear Sarah is managing. She's strong enough, but there's much for her to do, even with the promised help of others."

"I'm sure all's well. Or at least as well as it can be, Seth," Barny assured him. "The biggest worry our folks will have is whether the shoes will stay on the horses as long as they should. Young Tom's a fine lad and he'll make a good farrier one day, but he's green yet. I didn't really like leaving him on his own. Anyway, as for the pox... maybe it won't take too strong a hold there. Out here in the wild, with poor shelter and precious better food, no doubt *we're* more likely to come down with it."

His words were hollow, and he knew it.

"Maybe, Barny. But poor Kelman is an indication of how it could be soon. His fever returned this afternoon, although that may be due to his fall in the storm. We *must* find a cure... if there's one to be found. The Ice Wolf is all we can have hope in, or I fear most of Myre Hamlet is headed Kelman's way."

"Well," said Barny. "We've come this far. I'm sure we'll come to complete the task soon enough. There's only four legs to anything I know, and the longest one's well shod already. Besides, knowing you and Amos as I do, if the Ice Wolf is anywhere to be found, you'll catch hold of it and bring it back if you have to walk all the way."

"Maybe, but time eludes us, Barny. Time is so unsympathetic. It knows not our plight."

"But time *heals* too, Seth... and in more ways than one. *You'll* see. Anyway, I'm sure Kelman could use some company. He's over on the edge of camp, under the elm tree, where Little 'Un's tethered."

They made their way to the tree, but were surprised to find that Kelman wasn't there.

'He must have joined the others,' they both thought.

"Surely, he's not well enough, with this new fever," Seth said, half aloud.

On coming to their companions, they found that no one had seen or spoken with Kelman for some time.

"Where on earth could he have gone?" asked Seth, despairingly. "He shouldn't be up in the condition he's in."

Soon the company were all searching. Most of them scoured the woods, some to east and others to north and to south. Seth, Barny and Henry made for the shore, and for the boat.

"Kelman," cried Seth. "Kelman, where are you?"

He was answered only by echoing calls from the trees.

"Kelman, Kelman, where are you?"

Nowhere could they see or hear him. The three boarded the boat. Henry searched the well. Barny and Seth made for the hold, but stopped short in their tracks. There before them, in the fast fading light, propped against the foot of the mast, was Kelman, slumped motionless gazing down at the deck. In his left hand, he clasped the purse he'd been given in the Hamlet.

"Kelman! No!" cried Seth, as he knelt sobbing. "No! There was no need for you to be alone... not like this."

Henry joined them quietly. Barny knelt beside Seth, his eyes watering with emotion.

"No, Seth," he said softly, "don't you see... he's not *alone*. That's why he came here... to be *with* someone. Look!"

Seth lifted his head. His watery gaze followed the line of Barny's outstretched arm. There as the light failed he caught a dying glimpse of Icelar... Kelman's real home.

Seth turned his distant gaze from Icelar, and thought on tomorrow's trials.

"Raise the sail," cried Henry. "Lift the weight. All's secure and it's time we were away, while the wind favours us."

It was mid-morning, a fair day and blue skies watched white cushions of cloud rushing past, their fleeting shadows dappling the foaming waters. The Northern Lady, her sail borrowing the fresh wind, keeled and turned northwards taking the deeper waters.

Seth grieved heavily for Kelman. He knew it was the Scar that had eventually taken him despite his other pains and it was a great loss to all the companions. Not only had they lost his friendship but now they'd lost their only sure guide in Icelar too. They'd thought long on whether or not they should make for Ironmound, Kelman's home, for despite the threat of hostility there was the chance of more knowledge. But the whereabouts of the Ice Wolf, of which Kelman knew so little, would now be more difficult to learn. They also realised that if their search went north, as seemed inevitable, Ironmound may be the one chance of obtaining horses, not so much for the saving of time as for the saving of legs. Now the decision was made *for* them. They must risk a confrontation to learn what they may.

Despite mild protest from Henry, Seth and Barny had insisted that Kelman be taken with them to Icelar.

"Best be rid of the disease," Henry pointed out.

"Then leave us all here," Seth had said bitterly, for although Henry had meant well, he'd touched a deep wound.

"So be it," Henry had replied. "I know it means much to you. I understand."

That afternoon, they rounded the eastern tip of Icelar and now heading west along the rocky outcrop's coast, they came upon a small cove that they recognised from Kelman's earlier descriptions.

They moored the boat in sheltered waters and began the tiresome business of unloading the pony and what else they'd need for the journey. The shallows gave way willingly to a shingle beach. They discovered caves... one was that in which Kelman had found the boats, for here and there they found rotting planks... little else.

"Kelman must have been desperate," murmured Kaleb, "if his boat was little better than this pile of firewood. No wonder it fell apart."

Birdie and Kaleb had picked their way to the top of the sombre grey cliffs to spy out the land and, once on the tops, they'd seen that some hundred and fifty paces from the brink a pinewood stretched away inland. They'd now re-joined the others, who were looking in disbelief themselves at the wooden wreckage.

"The wood is there... a pinewood," explained Birdie. "Kelman told us aright... it seems to spread for miles."

The company decided that four of them should stay with the

Pulse

boat and wait for the return of the others. They knew this part of their journey might prove long, so the four... Simon, Peter, Jake and Samuel prepared for a lengthy stay. The caves would offer reasonable shelter, the woods ample firewood.

No one questioned aloud what was to be done if they didn't return to the cove, though they thought on it.

Jake and Samuel, though anxious for a cure to their ills, were tired... more tired than Amos and were happy to rest here and trust to the return of the others.

Before dusk, they carried Kelman to the cliff top, using the path that Kaleb and Birdie had found and they raised a mound in a peaceful glade, where the pines looked on and sighed mournfully. Each man dwelt upon his thoughts for some time and then they turned to the task still before them.

When the night was chased away by the dawn, those who were to travel said their brief farewells to the guardians of the boat and after an awkward climb with Little 'Un, they restarted their quest for the Ice Wolf.

"We could do without fangs this time," Amos bitterly recalled. "The wild dogs of the Greymills were more than enough for us, and *I* didn't meet a *live* one."

"This time we'll be ready," Ely resolved. "It's the Ice Wolf that will be surprised."

"If the weather there is any better than this, then I'll be surprised," added Barny opening an eye to the clouds which had now rolled in from the sea, blotting out the clear skies as they tumbled inland.

The sea below them looked uneasy. The Northern Lady, now like to a coracle, bobbed up and down on the swells, even in her sheltered mooring.

The four below them could be seen roping down and sheeting the hold as a precaution against the storm, though the brunt of any heavy seas would miss them sure enough.

The clouds now brought with them a chill drizzle that

sheeted down around them.

"What's so strange," said Seth, "is the bite of the wind. I know it's blowing from the north, but for this time of year it's cold, deathly cold. You're right Barny, and further north it'll be even colder. Ice Wolf may just be the right name."

They edged their way under the eaves of the pines. The undergrowth was sparse here, and offered a comfortable path, a little sheltered too.

They trekked mile after mile westwards in the dreary weather, caped against what reached them of the evil wind and rain. From the vantage point on top of the cliffs, they'd made out the distant reaches of mountains before the clouds came in. They knew from what Kelman had told them that if they followed the coast westwards, they'd reach the south-eastern tip of the mountains. These they must then skirt on their eastern flank until they reached Ironmound many miles to the north.

As they filed westwards, the wind shifted and the rain ceased. A warmer breeze blew from the west into their faces, soon dying to a whisper. All around them settled and a mist rose about them... a steaming mist, swirling in pools and patches, intertwining with the tall, silent pines.

At times, the mist engulfed them, leaving them for a few moments with no direction and no sight of the wood's edge. But the mist was restless, almost alive and the trailing wisps soon floated on, weaving living webs in the heavy, but restless air. The sentinel trees stood patiently, their lofty heads stirring above the travellers and sighing as if they breathed out the vapours that trailed down among their roots. The dank air seeped through their thick clothing, leaving them damp and chilled. No sound could be heard but for the whispering branches overhead and the shuffling footfalls on the thick bed of pine needles they now trod, built from ages past. The gulls that had wheeled above the cliffs and cried in defiance of the

Pulse

wind and rain had left with the coming of the warm breeze and an eerie silence closed about the travellers.

Then, the band of men from Myre Hamlet startled as one. They caught their breath. For that split second, and then once again some few seconds later, the air pulsed. It throbbed like a great heartbeat and the pressure made their own hearts skip a beat each time, leaving a ringing in their ears as the blood rushed to their heads. Little 'Un gave a stifled whiny. And then it was gone. The mists still wrapped themselves around the companions, but the pulses went as quick as they'd come.

The men looked at each other in disbelief. Most shook their heads and rubbed their ears.

"What in the world was that?" uttered Henry, as they stood bewildered, eyes still wide with apprehension of more to follow.

"No telling," Seth pondered. "It's nothing any of *us* has ever known. It felt so powerful, as if the heavens themselves were shifting.

The men, dwarfed beneath the tall trees, moved closer together and looked around them. The mist was clearing, and the wind shifted once again. The north wind returned and back came the rain.

"This place has an ill feeling about it. The throbbing aside, the whole atmosphere is unreal."

Seth spoke these thoughts aloud absently, not realising that he'd begun to speak.

"Sure enough," stuttered Ely, startling Seth from his trance. "The Ice Wolf will be a harder prize than even *we* may have thought. Let's hope the price is not too high."

With this, they resumed their shuffling through the trees, thankful at least that the mists had gone and the seagulls had returned. Even with this brief halt, and a later one to eat, by dusk they'd made good progress although the mountains, when they were to be seen through the trees, seemed to march along fleeing before them. The downpour ceased and they made camp dispiritedly, expecting a damp night and a dark one too, for the moon was young, clouds or no.

What fuel they could find was damp, but they were becoming expert with wet kindling.

"It's sure to raise smoke," protested Kaleb, "and if eyes are prying here, they won't come by to warm their hands, will they."

Kaleb, easily dispirited as he was, had become convinced that the throbbing heralded the immediate onset of doom at the hands of some unseen enemy. He felt the need to make his protest despite the prospect of welcome warmth.

"Perhaps it *will* raise smoke," conceded Seth, "but we've seen nothing to threaten us. And if there *is* danger, I fear it needs no fire smoke as a guide. If we *must* be ambushed, then let's at least have warm feet and full bellies."

"Maybe you're right," agreed Kaleb. "I'll lend a hand with the packs. Food will be welcome.

After they all had eaten and felt warmer, they set a watch in the darkness, two men to a stint. Those who were to watch later were asleep before the dampness crept back into their limbs but Seth and Henry, who took the first hours of vigil, stumped uncomfortably around the fire, keeping it kindled from a small stock. The chill was back in the air even though the wind had left them. They talked at length, drawing their minds from the discomfort. Seth learned much more of Fenny and its coastal waters. Henry was a native of Fenny and the sea town was a large part of him. Despite his superstitions he revealed to Seth, perhaps only half knowingly, that he'd always looked for far horizons. Despite the presence of the Scar, he was most grateful that this journey north had come his way.

"I fear Peter and Simon are more than reluctant in this quest," he confided, "for they've more ties than *I* back at Fenny. Peter has a mother who depends on him and Simon has a girl

Pulse

who perhaps will be his wife. Yet they're both good men. They'll stand by me in this, for they know that's how it should be.

"My only friends, until you all came along, were Peter and Simon... and the Lady. Now I have *you* all, for although you may feel I've given help with little return, it's given me a sense of purpose. Catching fish and ferrying folk locally is fine until you weary of it, day following day, year following year. You've given me a chance to help mend a great ill, and for that gift I'm grateful.

"And for all I know," he went on, "your need to pass through Fenny and even the coaches from the Hamlet may have brought this evil luck to my own home. Happen our quest is for Fenny too. Perhaps Simon, Peter and myself have as much need of travel as you do... we'll only know when and if we return."

Seth shrugged his shoulders in agreement with Henry's uncertainties, knowing that they too had thought uncomfortably on this, but he couldn't hide that his thoughts now were elsewhere.

"We shall all return, each to his home, Henry. Sarah means much to me. The Hamlet too. Like *your* labours, ours on the land can be tedious too but, with Sarah there, it's given all the more purpose. I'd rather be there, labouring forever, than to spend one more day travelling here, not knowing what lies behind us now. The Hamlet needs our help, but Sarah needs it more I fear. Yet I speak unfairly, for she's some way from the village. She may avoid the illness."

"Maybe you're right, Seth, but let's not talk so heavily. Fate chases *us* well enough, without *us* chasing *it*."

They talked on, until it was time to wake Will and Kaleb. Both Henry and Seth dwelt on what each had said, each thinking of the other's and his own home before they found an uneasy sleep. The night passed with no disturbances and even

Kaleb slept like a felled tree once his tiring watch was over.

And so they travelled on into thicker woods, cursing the mountains that walked before them seen from the forest's edge when they troubled to look, still hazy in the higher distances. Even when the wan sun brought a measure of warmth through the hazy cloud, it wasn't as warm as early summer should be. A dead, pallid air persisted. They saw little moving... a crow or two cawing high above, a rabbit here and there darting for cover at the click of a hoof on stone or the sharp snap of a dead branch underfoot. Even these seemed echoes of reality in the uncanny silence that hung like a curtain all around them. The fruits of hunting were poor despite their needs.

Early on the morning of the next day their march took them downhill and the coast took a turn for the north. Here, the cliffs had tapered away to nothing more than a low progression of hills, rolling in the distance behind sand dunes. The dunes held back a grey sea that stretched away to the north and east. Barny led the pony out from under the canopy of the forest to view the distant peaks. He almost fell over backwards at the sight that met his upturned face. The trees thinned away to nothing and there before him, less than a mile distant stood a spur of rock. Up it climbed. At its nearest it was, he guessed, as tall as the cliffs they'd climbed from the cave and as he cast his eye north-west along its nearer face it rose ever higher and beyond it were the mountains they'd seen earlier, still a misty blue in their furthest reaches.

"Look!" he called to the others, stumbling back to the path. "Look, the mountains."

His companions followed him as he returned to his vantage point and beheld in surprise and awe.

"A welcome sight," declared Will. "Though warning was lacking, we're here at last."

"But a harder path awaits us now, for we must follow the

eastern foothills," Seth reminded him. "There seems little prospect of shelter, by their barren aspect."

"Well, *I'm* glad for one to leave these woods," said Barny almost whispering, with a cautious glance over his shoulder at the trees, as if they might be listening. "The nearer the hills, the less travelling left, *I* say."

"Yet it concerns me still," continued Seth, gravely. "Our packs seem heavy, but we may wish them heavier, for if we're delayed at all, we'll be desperately short of food. And for all its silence, the forest perhaps had more to offer than the hills before us. We must move on without delay. A week at least I guess to Ironmound, and to have food still then gives us the chance of meeting Kelman's folk or no, as we may choose."

They set off around the spur and on to the foothills, hoping to put some distance behind them that day.

They crossed lush, grassy lowlands before they reached the hills. It was marshy in places but this didn't stop Little 'Un taking some of the grass with him, when Barny allowed. Kaleb lost a boot, straying into boggier ground.

"How you manage those fields I'll never know," sniggered Barny.

"Look here. This place is bad enough without your nonsense," snapped Kaleb, as he emptied his boot and placed it back on his sodden foot with a stamp.

The others laughed, endeavouring to restrain themselves for Kaleb's sake. Barny leaned back, fists on hips in laughter. Little 'Un saw the joke and nudged the farrier playfully. Barny struggled to balance himself but his feet were stuck fast in the mud and his hands grasped at thin air as he keeled helplessly backwards. His cries terminated in a squelch as he hit the soggy turf.

"Serves you right," scowled Kaleb, scarcely able to keep himself from smirking.

They moved on and as they did Kaleb burst into a fit of

laughter. Barny rubbed his soaking rump, grimaced painfully at the cold and wet sensation and joined in with the contagious laughter.

It was much as Seth had feared. They were forced to take a winding path strewn with boulders, which became larger and more numerous as they wove their way through a barren land. The weather at least was dry now and still cool, which suited travelling. By day they picked their way laboriously, sometimes on wide pathways, other times with no clear way at all. Always they flanked the ever-growing mountains. At nights, dusk came early, as the sun was lost behind the towering rocks.

When the waxing moon rose early, they used the half-light to as much advantage as they could, prolonging their trek into later evening, but the path was wearying to them and they welcomed the poor camps they made among the boulders. The pulses in the wood were fading from their minds and their guard was lessened and eventually dispensed with.

Their packs were lightening and the food was now rationed carefully. Water was no problem, for streams tumbled across their path, but lack of grass was becoming a problem for the pony.

CHAPTER EIGHT

Sentinel

On the third hill-bound night, they decided to halt quite early, for clouds covered the moon as dusk threatened. As they looked for a suitable camp, the wind rose and howled from the east through the boulders, whining and whistling with a thousand voices. They put on capes and cloaks as grit swirled into their faces as they searched for shelter now.

Amos, who'd taken the head of the march, called back to the others desperately at the top of his voice.

"Hi! There ahead, above us, to the left. I think it's a cave."

Sure enough, some fifty feet or more above them, a dark hole gaped in the rock face. South-east it faced, and might offer better shelter from this dreadful gale. The pony squealed and shied as the searching wind threw clouds of dust around them.

"Alright," called out Seth, as loudly as he could. "You and Ely go on ahead. See if you can find a way up. We'll follow as best we can."

They found that a path wound up from the boulder-strewn lowland, picking its way over the steep slopes that lay between them and the hole in the shear rock face that formed the foundation of the higher mountains. They approached with caution now, for this path perhaps was no natural path. It maybe the cave was occupied. Once the dark hole was reached, Amos called back to Abe Arden.

"Get the tinder box, Abe. We'll need to spark a flame to see anything at all, but we'll never start a fire out here. We must brave the shelter of the cave mouth first.

Abe fumbled with packs, the pony restlessly sidestepping as he did so. Despite Little 'Un's reluctance, the box was soon to hand and Abe made his way upwards. With the help of kindling wood they'd brought with them, a welcome flame spluttered into life. The companions looked on eager for its light and for some warmth, peering from their cape hoods, which were pulled down about their eyes to keep out the howling wind.

As the light flickered, frail though it was, capricious shadows fled from them across the rock walls, revealing more than just a small cave. Indeed, the light wasn't potent enough to reach the further wall or much of the vaulted roof. The floor about the three men was rough-hewn of the living rock... not a natural floor. Some delver had worked here to make a home, though they guessed it wasn't lived in now. The deserted ruin of a fire, long since dead, lay close by... old and black.

Abe added some charred, half-used fuel from the old fire to their own, hoping at least to keep it kindled until all were safely inside and organised for the night.

The gale outside rose ever higher, screaming and howling about the ears of those who it still embraced.

"Is it safe?" shouted Seth, heeding less the need for caution than the need to escape the biting weather.

"It seems to be," called back Ely. "Though someone has lived here. It's possible that they're still here," he shrilled.

"Then we must chance it," bellowed Seth, in reply. "It's impossible out here. Little 'Un's almost frantic. We're coming in."

"Wait," yelled Ely. "There are voices in here."

As he yelled, he and Abe scurried to the entrance side of the fire, backs to their companions. Amos followed, pacing backwards to the entrance. They peered into the depths, as the sinister discord of wailing voices rolled forward out of the darkness. Ely's heart pounded. He breathed heavily, but at length he laughed falteringly.

"It's alright," he stammered. "It's the wind. The wind plays deceiver in this devilish place."

"Devilish, maybe," laughed Seth, as they all entered at last,

Sentinel

"but a welcome shelter after all."

Yet they felt uneasy. It seemed less safe than outside in the open somehow, but there was little choice. And so they settled, timidly moving around the fire, putting it between them and the yawning mouth, while the alien voices persisted.

"If the cave was once occupied," pondered Seth, "we'd do well to explore its depths, to see that we're safe and alone. The fire won't last long, so let's use it while it does. Amos, you and I shall go a little deeper. A brand from the fire will help."

On exploring their shelter, they were surprised, for it extended back beyond all their expectations... some forty paces they went before they perceived the further wall. The sides were barely visible in the fitful torchlight. As they went, the roof and walls converged narrowly to a small inner cave, little taller than a man, tunnel like. And from it they sensed a creeping, foul stench.

"We must see if it leads on," shuddered Amos. "The smell may have an owner."

Carefully, they inched their way along the fissure, some hundred cautious paces, and there at the end of the way, now narrowing to some three feet or so in width and in height, was placed a large boulder. The air was dank... more dank and musty than the air they'd left with their friends. A reek of stagnant waters, putrid in their nostrils, hung like death about them, filling their reluctant lungs with every choking breath.

"Maybe it follows on from here," whispered Seth, carefully kneeling with the firebrand, hoping to see beyond the obstructing rock.

"It's no use, Amos. I can't see beyond the boulder. I think we can assume it's quite safe... for tonight at least. We must set a watch, just in case, though the dweller has surely deserted his home long since... it doesn't smell of life. Let's return to the others."

As they left the narrow way, breathing more easily as they

went, Amos tripped and stumbled in the half-light. His foot had unwittingly discovered a large cache of tree logs.

"Glory be!" exclaimed Seth. "Firewood. What a boon this will be tonight."

Seth held the torch aloft whilst Amos gathered an armful of logs and the two of them inched their way back towards the precious flames near the entrance of their rock-hewn shelter.

The fuel was warmly greeted by their companions and soon the blazing fire had the shadows dancing fearsome on the rough grey walls. But the depths remained in a darkness which threatened to smother the light like a blanket. The wind had died to a whisper and with it fears subsided too. The crackling heat helped too.

"The cellar at the Pig is dank and eerie enough," said Barny, "but at least the barrels keep you company there. My, oh my. Give me one of those barrels and a mug."

He sat back against the nearest wall, feet and hands outstretched in the fire's warmth.

"Best ale in all Midvale," he chuckled.

Henry handed him a flask.

"You'll have to make do with water for the time being Barny, my lad. But when we're back to the mainland you'll join me in a mug of ale at the Ferryboat... if *I've* a say in it. And then later we'll pop back to the Blue Pig and you can prove your point as soon as maybe."

"A pleasure," gargled Barny, downing a swig or two of the clear, sweet water which was welcome enough after the day's marching.

Seth smiled, but his face was grave despite it.

"I'll join you both," he added to their conjecture. "But first we must turn our thoughts to our plight. There's much to achieve, much to think on, for the reality of our quest is cold enough. We need some warmth of heart out here in Icelar. Here in this cave my heart is heavy and I've a sense of ill being. I

Sentinel

hope I'm wrong but evil has been here, I'm certain. We must be careful. We must watch this night through. The corridor behind us smells unwholesome and stale. The boulder at its further end speaks of something beyond. We must surely leave the stone unturned, but still we must eye it."

With this return to the reality of their situation, they prepared to sleep. They brought a good supply of wood to the fireside. Seth and Will set themselves to watch the brooding darkness of the innermost depths. The fire burned reassuringly to their right. The others were soon asleep and, with a careful ration, Seth lit his pipe and Will was soon learning much of what Henry had offered Seth regarding Fenny and the sea around it.

As they talked, they grew more tired. A drowsiness befell them. The glow of the fire swayed before them sleepily. Eyelids weighed heavily. The wind of the night still sighed among the rocks. Seth felt himself falling... falling into a slumber with the wind hissing in his ears.

"Aghh! What is it?" he called out as he lurched from his falling. Will too jolted upright at the cry, yet the others slept on unheeding. A cold chill took the two men.

"What?" answered Will, almost whispering.

"N... Nothing," stammered Seth. "I fell. I was falling asleep. The wind woke me. Just the wind."

Yet the chill sensation didn't leave them. They sat, not daring to move, straining their eyes unable to penetrate the darkness.

Little 'Un was restless, shuffling and pawing the rock floor in the half-light by the wall, his nostrils flared. He offered a whiny that echoed stonily.

"Wait! There it is again!" Seth shuddered, wide eyed with uncertainty. "There, a hissing above the noise of the wind."

"You're right," Will managed, huddling nearer the fire in a trance.

The hissing was shrill and undulating, like breath drawn

between sharp teeth... first in, then more softly out again. The two men crouched, petrified, unable to warn the others who slept on. The hair stood stiff on their necks and they felt a cold sweat rise in them. Something was there in shadows at the cave mouth. Seth forced himself, against the trance, inch by inch, to turn his head towards the entrance, straining his eyes to see what his senses had already unfolded.

"Aghh!" he screamed again in abhorrence as his eyes met the gaping hole in the rock. His scream and the volley of echoes it brought broke the trance. The others woke and, as one, startled and turned to see what Seth and Will now stared at. Little 'Un stood trembling.

There on the path, swaying to and fro, were two limpid yellow points of light... pale eyes in the dark backdrop of windy moonless night... swaying to and fro on a hideous body, thin and sinuous as a snake, dark, segmented and with many spidery legs. It swayed uncertainly, supported by its lower half ... some eight or nine feet long in all... an enormous centipede-like creature. The eyes were unblinking and, watching, it hissed as it breathed through yellow fangs in a flat, grotesque face, almost voicing whispered words as it did so.

They watched it and they trembled, half expecting it to venture in towards them. Yet it didn't. There it remained, watching, swaying, hissing.

"What're we to do? What're we to do?" echoed Abe at last, hysterical.

"Wait," answered Seth with cold certainty. "Wait, and be ready. It hesitates at the door. Perhaps it fears the fire. Be ready if it enters."

He manoeuvred with his foot, stretching to bring a burning brand close enough to seize at need. Others followed his example.

"Let's see if it makes a move. Let *it* decide, but be ready," Seth continued, his eyes still wide, fixed in stark resolve,

Sentinel

returning the spectral gaze of the sentinel at the door... the only door. *'Or was it?'* Seth thought. He recalled the boulder at the end of the tunnel and then dismissed it for the moment.

And so they waited, not daring to move more than a foot or hand cautiously to a more comfortable position. Not daring to approach this hideous thing nor turn away from it. The prepared brands had died and now a pale light waxed at the entrance behind the guarding creature.

Day had come and still the sentinel watched, swaying this way and that. And it continued to watch their every move as they became more adventurous, relighting and tending the fire, fetching more logs, tending Little 'Un and preparing a sparse, uneasy meal.

Though they now moved with some freedom, they were still terrified, and discussed how they might escape, for the loathsome thing seemed reluctant to make the move that Seth watched for.

So it was that they were confronted for all that day and the following night. The guard watched, never blinking or eating. There seemed no intention in it to attack, so they'd become easier, fewer men watching at a time as the others slept. Yet they'd become gradually uneasy again for they feared to challenge the creature with what few weapons they had... hunting knives, a hammer, rope... and fire.

'Yes. That's it... *it fears the fire, or it would attack us,*' Seth had thought on the second night in the cave, *'and now is the time for action.'*

Little 'Un was desperate for food by now and as for the other way?... Barny had persuaded them that *he* at least wouldn't leave Little 'Un behind.

With great resolve, Will and Kaleb had advanced upon the creature, a flaming branch each held, Will advancing from the left, Kaleb from the right. The thing hesitated in its ceaseless weaving, then continued, hissing ever louder as they approached. First it eyed one man, then the other. Kaleb took his chance and stabbed at the foul eyes with his torch. It turned upon him, mouth wide, and crashed its fangs upon the branch devouring the flames and spitting the smouldering remains to the floor. As it did so, Will lunged forward, drawing flames across the creature's body. It didn't flinch but turned and quenched the flames again, leaving Will holding the spent faggot.

Kaleb retreated, and as Will stood for that split second, bemused by the impotency of the fire, it struck. Like a snake it darted, in an instant its fangs finding Will's left arm. He felt sickly with a searing pain as the needle teeth sank into his flesh. He twitched and with sudden awareness of what was happening he brought the branch down behind the head on what might be its neck. Its jaws opened, its head twisted to attack this new threat and as Kaleb and Seth sprang forward to Will's aid, he fell reeling into their arms. They shuffled hurriedly back to their place around the fire, defeated.

So they sat again wondering what they should do. Rations ran shorter and they ate almost as sparingly as the pony who shared a few stale biscuits.

Will's arm became paralysed, deathly cold, with no feeling at all. Yet he'd no fever and there seemed no sign of poisoning. They sucked the wound but no fluid issued from the needle wounds. Nothing but the deathly cold sensation in his arm... the total numbness.

"It'll soon mend, Birdie," Seth assured him.

But Will's face was grim.

With days and nights wasting, Seth resolved, "We must brave the tunnel, for though its stench is foul, maybe *there* is our freedom."

"Or death, by the smell of it," Amos coughed, lungs stifled by the very thought of it.

"And I *still* say I won't leave Little 'Un," insisted Barny.

But he knew in his heart that he *must* if there was no other way. He bit his lip, half wishing that it would prove to be a dead-end.

And so it was that Seth, Amos and Ely fought their way through the stinking air, sweating with the lack of clean breath. They tore at the heavy boulder that blocked the way. All but exhausted, they rolled it clear and a wave of the foul air hit them, stronger than ever. Ely vomited and sprawled onto his hands and knees, clutching at his throat, gasping for air, yet wanting not to breathe. Seth grabbed at their torch, which lay neglected against the tunnel wall. It burned poorly in the rare air but thrusting it before him into the void he motioned the others to follow.

"Come on. We must see what lies beyond," he wheezed.

But his outstretched foot found no footing. He screamed out with surprise and as he lost his balance, lurching forwards, he let the faltering torch fall, flinging his arms wide, grasping instinctively for support. Quick as light, Amos grabbed an arm and fell to the ledge, clinging to Seth as his friend toppled over the brink.

Ely, recovering, lunged forward into the gap to help as the torch fell deep into the chasm.

The two men, grunting and choking, hauled Seth to safety, yet as they did so they saw the reason for the reek in the fading light of the falling torch... Corpses piled high... some animal, some human, many reduced to bones, some still rotting, staring up to meet the gaze of the living. Then the torch flickered and died and all was darkness. They coughed and retched and hurriedly rolled back the boulder in the total blackness.

Despairing, they felt their way back to the others and telling what they'd witnessed they trembled and wept, for they couldn't understand it. Once more, they were defeated. They must think again.

The pony was ever more restless, with little food, pawing the floor as if in search of grass. He was tethered to a rock to ensure his safety from their guard and this only served to make him more restless. Barny comforted him as best he could. They fell once more to staring at the fire, fuelled continually from their store of logs. They were utterly defeated... behind them a trap and before them a loathsome guard. Daylight came and went meaninglessly outside their prison, barely penetrating the darkness. When the light *did* come, they saw a barren land, brown and monotonous hills, file upon file. The days were ever overcast... dry, yet cloud filled and sombre.

The nights had been clearer and cold and seemed long for June. The moon, when they saw her climb across that patch of sky, was waxing to the full, showing grey, phantom shapes of the rolling hills below this high prison.

The presence of the Scar served to make them all the more forlorn. Amos battled with the thoughts of death, for he knew it might now come to him as it had to Kelman. They'd have been strong willed enough to disregard it but for this depressing prison where all time stood still and where they were lost in an eternity of thought.

Will, Abe and Kaleb too were anxious that their quest should go forward... for time insisted they move swiftly.

Seth wept at memories of Sarah and every one of them, including Henry, wept inwardly at the thought of home.

"Why does it wait there? Why?" Seth screeched uncharacteristically, his emotions overflowing. "It won't attack us. It won't leave us. We must force our way out. We *must*, for we'll die if we stay longer."

They'd perceived over the last night or so that, though the gruesome creature didn't sleep, late into the darkness it lulled as if resting, easing its swaying, lowering its hissing breath to a murmur.

"We shall attack... all of us...when it rests tonight," Seth whispered.

They whispered, for they suspected their captor could understand their words for it would seemingly become agitated when they spoke of escape.

"Barny. You and Henry take the watch," Seth continued, "and when it's time to wake us, if the creature is a rest, then we'll act. Some of us must escape at least."

So, as the others slept, Barny and Henry took their watch. They spoke little, for they were weary with this awful place. They each gazed at the cave's opening and Barny fell into a waking dream… of the forge and young Tom, of the Blue Pig and Myre Hamlet. The visions before him paralleled much of what was taking place back in Myre Hamlet, though he couldn't know the true plight the Hamlet faced… the plight of everyday struggles for survival in the distant homestead, lost in Midvale, all those miles to the south. The travellers here in Icelar thought often of what must be the way of things back home, yet their despair was far removed and was more a consequence of their journey. They'd despaired often at the obstacles they'd encountered… the wild men, the atmosphere in Fenny, at first quite hostile, the disaster at sea and the loss of poor Kelman. And now, upon Icelar at last, each day had become more daunting. Now they despaired all the more for their fate it seemed was beyond their own small control, unless they could break free of their evil captor.

'And,' thought Barny, *'that dreadful throbbing, the memory pounding in his head.'*

And as he dwelt on that ill experience in the mist, his heart skipped a beat, for at that moment Henry gripped his sleeve in terror… that self-same throbbing filled the air. Once, then once again it came, echoing more loudly by far than it had among the trees. The rock shook its roots. Little 'Un gave a stifled cry and the two men stood speechless, trembling, eyes wide in anticipation, as their friends awoke only half-conscious of the first pulse, but wide awake with fear at the second.

Their guard still swayed calmly to and fro at the entrance, silhouetted against a clear moon, a moon close to the full and rising early over the grey foothills.

As they watched, a new terror struck them, petrifying their already stony silence. A dark figure drifted into sight on the path behind their captor... drifted, almost as if carried by the breeze, for it didn't walk on feet. Draped it was in a black, hooded shroud that floated on the air, and the half-bowed hood revealed a deathly pale face. The skin, if it were in truth skin, stretched thinly over a bony countenance, the jaw square, the eyes pale slits, luminous like the beastly creature it now accompanied. And silhouetted though this figure was, the flickering firelight revealed teeth... long, flat, bared upper teeth. Set between dreadful bony cheeks and in thin drawn lips that showed the roots they were. Seth was reminded of the hooded figure in his dream in Fenny, yet back then he'd seen no face and hadn't imagined such a dreadful being beyond the curtain of the hood. There'd not been the same cold, deathly feeling... How could this be what he'd foreseen?

"We're lost!" cried Kaleb.

"No we're not," Seth whispered as sharply as he dared, glancing at the spectre as he laid a reassuring hand on Kaleb's shoulder. "Not if we bide our time, then attack together, at the right moment.

The spectre floated nearer and glided to a halt, just inside the cave doorway. The sentinel slithered forward, still reared up, swaying and hissing now all the more as if expecting some reward for its successful vigil. The ghostly figure motioned the creature to one side with a sideways sweep of its arm and at once was obeyed as a cowering dog might obey its master, having asked too much. There it cowered in the shadows, yet still it watched and guarded.

The hooded figure raised its head and spoke in a creaking,

thin voice... a voice like to a gate on ungreased hinges. And they understood the voice.

"Yes. You *are* lost. You were lost when you set foot on this island."

The companions stood aghast at this creaking, whistling statement of doom, for there was great weight in the words, yet thought Seth, *'it didn't hear my whisper it seems.'*

"I was aware of you when you were on the beach, in the cove," and sharpening to a shrill hiss it continued. "Your friends will await your return in vain, for you will never leave this cave."

Amos, who stood near Seth, moved forward at these words but Seth, restraining him, whispered, "Not yet."

"But I'm ill enough," Amos answered cautiously. "The Scar will take me before long. Let me help this way at least."

"Not yet," repeated Seth. "We must strike when it relaxes its guard, for one chance is all we're likely to get."

Amos stood his ground reluctantly and Seth thought for a moment.

"We must find its weaknesses, if indeed it has any," he mused, "and since it understands us, we must find out what we can of it."

At last Seth replied boldly to the creature.

"And why shouldn't we leave this cave?" he said, surprising his companions with what, to them, was a pointless attempt at bargaining for their lives.

The spectre, unmoved by Seth's attacking tone, continued only half acknowledging his question.

"I am Kaan, mightiest of the brethren of the Banefell, though I have been named the Prince of the Fallen by some. You will be offered to the Lord of the Icemere, for you have strayed into his kingdom... unbidden. You will die in the pit."

At this, they heard a dull rumbling behind them in the cave. It was the boulder at the end of the tunnel... rolled aside by unseen helpers, or perhaps some supernatural power.

A sickening chill gripped the companions. Seth gave the pit no thought, for he was absorbed in thinking how advantage may be made as he talked.

"And what right has Kaan of the Banefell to say whether we're to leave or to stay?" said Seth, with forced conviction, for he knew his threats were hollow.

Still ignoring Seth, the hooded figure continued, as if answering unasked questions.

"The Watcher was sent here when you entered this place... a place which once belonged to mindless men of Ironmound... until Kaan discovered them. The pit was their rubbish hole. Now it is their tomb, and so shall it be yours. You were destined to enter here, for you were lost when you set foot on Icelar," the shrill voice continued. "The Scar, as you call it, takes all mortals in the end, for so the Lord of the Icemere demands."

At the mention of the Scar, the Myre Hamlet men gasped, astonished that this evil being knew the very thing that brought them here. Seth, although still searching for some moment of attack saw this, cool-headed as he was, as a chance to find out something of the Ice Wolf and perhaps as a chance to explain that they meant no ill. The others looked on in awe as he continued.

"So you know of the Scar?" he said. "Then how can you say we were unbidden? Perhaps you'll realise that it's only the Scar that brings us hence to this evil place, for we've been afflicted with this awful thing by ill chance in our own country. We seek only a cure. We search for the Ice Wolf... that's all. And then we wish to return... to leave Icelar to itself."

"Then you have failed," hissed the spectre. "There *is* no cure. The Icewood holds no answer for you."

And with this almost protective sharpening of tone and with the direct answer, Seth knew he'd hit on something... 'The Icewood?' he thought. 'I didn't mention any Icewood, so this creature tells us where to search, without our asking.... and if there's no cure, why bother to threaten us with death here in the pit? And with this, Seth's heart lifted.

Returning to its normal waling voice, Kaan continued.

"Kaan has spoken. You will not leave here. I have moved the stone."

Beckoning the Watcher forward with another sweep of its mantled arm, the dread figure stood in the doorway, watching through its yellow slitted eyes. The Watcher moved out of the shadows, now erect again, swaying as it coiled towards the fire, moving this way and that, herding the companions back. Beyond the fire it took them, devouring flames as it advanced, disturbing the ashes and the logs as it slithered onwards.

The men retreated, Barny hanging on to the frightened pony. Kaleb, Ely and Henry held torches they'd taken from the fire as they went, but these guttered despairingly. Seth knew that they must attack or escape the advancing beast before they were trapped in the awful tunnel. The stench now drifted out to meet them. Kaan followed from the entrance as the Watcher swayed, checking any attempts to escape its advance.

Seth was now desperate. He'd hoped to attack their captor at the entrance. Now he was running out of time. He drew his hunting knife and lunged at the wriggling head, guided by the two points of light. He felt the hairy, spidery legs smothering him has he aimed his blow at the sickly eyes. But his strike went wide and as he toppled forwards, he felt the fangs sink into his shoulder. Deep they bit and with a cry of despair, he fell to the floor. And so the figure advanced over Seth's writhing body. The rest of the company were in a trance of submission.

Passing the fire, Kaan watched intently as the servant herded the men of Myre Hamlet to certain death... all that was except for Seth and Will, for Will had lain while all this was going on still stricken with a deadened arm. Despondently, he'd lain in the shadows by their gear, near the walls of their dire shelter. He'd woken when the throbbing came. His first thought was to struggle to his feet and join his friends near the fire yet he too, for that instant, had been petrified by this new sight. And in that split second he'd realised that he might remain undiscovered, so crouching he'd carefully retreated a step or two further into the darkness and had waited. Now, desperate to use his concealment to their advantage, he looked on in pain as the Watcher drove his friends towards the pit.

'The fire,' he thought wildly. 'The Watcher has no fear of it, for it treads it as if it were not there. Yet Kaan, the master of this thing, carefully avoids it, skirting the flames at a comfortable distance.'

And with sudden hope, Will acted. In an instant, he lifted himself and charging forward he stooped as he rushed past the fire, gathering a flaming branch with his good arm. He was on the spectre before it realised. Kaan perceived him now and turned to face the attacker, but too late the Watcher was called. Will thrust the flames at the hooded face and with a piercing scream the shrouded horror reeled backwards. Will brandished the fiery wand as if it were a sword and, bearing down on the cowering face, thrashed this way and that. And like dry hay in a summer field the veil like robes of Kaan were caught in the fanned flames. Another shriek of terror filled the air echoing and drumming around the cave.

"Will! Look out!" cried Kaleb. "The Watcher!"

Perceiving its master's danger, the Watcher had turned from the others and slithered hissing towards Will. Yet Will was heedless of the cry of warning, for he stared open-mouthed at his victim. As the robes burned, the spectral form melted into the air, the nothingness spreading from the skirts and body of the robe to the hood... and Kaan was gone.

"Will!" shouted Kaleb again.

And at this second cry, Will turned and was more amazed, for the Watcher too dissolved before his eyes. The master gone, it couldn't hold its form. It too disappeared. The echoes spent themselves and they all stood, suddenly aware of silence, and of freedom from their captors. Barny still had a hold of Little 'Un. The pony looked more at ease.

"Look to Seth," called Barny, reminding them that Seth had fallen to the Watcher. To their joy, he was moving. He raised himself, with help from Kaleb and Henry. Stiffly, he arched his back and rubbed at the wounded shoulder. The numbness wore off almost immediately and, shocked, he turned to Will.

"How's your arm, Will?" he asked. "The Watcher bit me deeply, yet my arm is recovered."

To Will's amazement, there was life in the fingers of both his hands.

"Thanks be... I feared I was stricken for life, if I had any life left, with a dead arm at best," he smiled, flexing the arm in disbelief.

"It can only be that our the Watcher was but a phantom... with a phantom sting," said Seth. "We were held here by a ghost... no more, no less. But what of Kaan? He too seemed ghostly enough."

"I don't know," said Henry, pensively. "He had some substance, for he burned. He felt the pain. Yet it was no human substance, surely."

"Yes," Seth went on. "He spoke of the Lord of the Icemere as a servant might of his master. As if he were enthralled. My heart is chilled to hear of this 'Lord', for it seems that if he's a reality we must search close to his dominion. The Icemere can only be to the north, as too must be the Icewood."

Though inwardly they rejoiced at their escape from immediate peril, their hearts sank at the thoughts conjured by Seth's words.

"Yet, the Hamlet needs our efforts. Indeed, more so as time passes," Seth continued. "We must press on, even though it be to our greater danger. I for one won't rest until I find the Ice

Wolf, for now I'm all the more sure it exists."

"But what if the Lord of the Icemere sets us a trap by Kaan's words?" said Henry, with a grimace, "for it seems even *he* knows of our presence."

"There is indeed a chance of that," said Seth, "but I hope not, for Kaan's words seemed hollow and full of vanity. Perhaps this Lord of the Icemere is yet unaware of us. And if I'm wrong, if it *is* a trap, if we go further into peril, still we must try... until the last. And remember also, Kelman told us of the Ice Wolf. *He* was no ghost. I believe in him and his legends. We must chase the Wolf, despite the chance of being chased ourselves.

"Come on now. We must be clear of this ill place. If Kaan *was* indeed Prince of the Fallen, then I don't wish to meet his followers. Who knows what evils *they* may command? Let's make ready and move on without delay. Look! Dawn greets us."

Sure enough, the complete darkness that the setting moon had left outside now yielded to grey morning. Soon shadows fled, as in the east a huge sun peered above the hills, shimmering golden-red in a clear, still sky. They didn't eat, for urgency to be away now filled them. The pony needed grass and the lower reaches of the foothills, the plain, offered that at least. Then they'd head north for Ironmound.

The fire was dying and they didn't tend it, but busied themselves packing gear, sharing their load with the pony.

Barny looked down at the embers. "We've the men of this island to thank for our escape, it seems," he said, kicking at the ashes. "Their pile of firewood was our salvation."

"Yet we've the men of this island to thank also for bringing us here in the first place," replied Will.

And so they left that dreadful shelter and looked to the new day.

CHAPTER NINE

Respite

Accompanied by fair weather, they made their way down from the path. They stumbled, for the hills were steep at first, strewn with loose rocks.

Here and there, streams ran down from the higher hills, bubbling over the rocks, hurrying on their way. The companions followed Little 'Un's example and drank their fill of clear, sweet water, cold and fresh. The water in the now empty bottles they'd relied on in the cave had become stale to the taste, and this new source was like nectar. The chatter of the water took Seth's mind to Puddlefork, to the Puddle Stream, and to much else.

Before long, they came upon clusters of trees, gathered around the streams now that the flow of water steadied as the hills receded. Old gnarled trees… hazel, willow and here and there an ash tree. Many more had stood there once. Many stumps told them this was where the wood stock had been gleaned.

Feeling safer now, they rested here and found food to aid their depleted stocks. Fish and rabbit they caught, and grass too was here for the ever-patient pony. He grazed with relish for a while under the clear sun. They camped here and continued on the following dawn much refreshed. Before long they found the ground more even and so they set their direction north, toward their goal. They trekked on with the rising sun to their right. Their hearts lifted for it was another fair morning, the fairest they'd seen in Icelar. Now they felt summer had not deserted them, though it was still colder than they might have expected. They soon perceived that the lowlands stretching away eastwards were indeed a vast grassy plain.

"Like Greylar," said Amos with enthusiasm. "Fine for Little

'Un, and better for us than caves and boulders. Yet I'd welcome a few more trees... if the weather breaks, we'll feel it."

But the weather didn't break and for six days they trekked north through unchanging landscape, with little to slow them and no sign of evil things. Little 'Un soon regained his fitness with the steady exercise of walking and the men too soon felt much better. At one point the pony went lame, but Barny soon set him right.

"Only a stone splinter," he'd assured the creature, removing the troublesome object from a sore foot with the ease of experience. "The soreness will soon go, my little fella."

Although they felt urgency they went at a steady pace. It was now mid-June. They'd been travelling for two months and had been much delayed. With this sort of progress they couldn't hope to be back home before September, even if they achieved their hopes and quickly.

"At least we still have a chance of missing the winter," Kaleb offered.

"*You'll* be back in time for ploughing then," Barny replied, "and *I'll* be back in time for drinking."

"We must continue to rebuild our strength," said Seth. "We'll need it again ere long, I'm convinced of that."

They'd all come to rely heavily on Seth's judgement, though they'd already respected it for many years. He showed wisdom, even with the strain of their task. Henry too, with all the discipline learned at sea, concluded that Seth was a man to trust in.

Though they'd seen no more evil these past few days, the feeling of evil persisted. Sometimes it weighed heavy around them, brooding maliciously in the silent air. Sometimes it left the silence feeling more peaceful and now and then birdsong would break the eerie quiet. At nights, they continued to set a guard, just to be sure of their safety.

Respite

Some days before, they'd noticed that the shadow of the mountains some miles to their left turned eastwards far before them and then, turning north again, merged into the unfathomable horizon. They'd also noticed, with surprise, that the peaks above the spur were snow-capped.

"Strange," Will had said. "They must be higher peaks than we might imagine... snow in June and all."

"Mmh," mused Seth. "Even down here, the days, though fine, are short and quite cool... like September in the Hamlet. The mountain spur will soon be at hand and then we'll need to make our decision. We'll be nearing Ironmound. From what Kelman told us, it's nestled in the hills beneath that turning. There we must decide... do we meet Kelman's folk, or do we avoid them?"

Next morning they woke to cloudy weather. The wind now blew from the east and with it a degree of warmth came. They headed north-west for the niche in the barrier before them, and re-entered depressing foothills, much like those they'd crossed further south. As they came nearer to the upper slopes, memories of the Watcher flooded back and with the closing in of the rock walls, apprehension came. Rain now threatened, but the tormented sky held. Now and then, as late afternoon turned to evening, the westering sun burst forth from the grey drear in golden glory as it sank towards the horizon. With the sun's last flickering effort, the men of Myre Hamlet beheld two things... before them on the undefined path, between boulders some hundred paces away, stood a dark figure, ill-defined but for a moment caught in the golden-red of the dying sun. Beyond this un-assuring sight a column of blue smoke that puthered skywards was caught by the wind and drifted dispersing into the higher reaches of the climbing terrain.

"Ironmound?" questioned Seth at the sight of the smoke. "And one of Kelman's folk no doubt.. *They've* found *us* without our searching. We've no choice after all, it seems."

They approached the silent figure, half expecting it to be Kaan, for the robe was like unto that belonging to their earlier encounter. Some fifteen paces now between them, they perceived the robe was of heavy cloth, earthy and warm, though the hood was drawn over a hidden face, and still they were apprehensive. The figure offered them no attention, remaining motionless, supported by a tall wooden staff. Seth, hand on dagger, noticed the head was bowed and once again his dream at Fenny came to his confused mind.

"The figure on the path!" he exclaimed absently.

He was relieved a little, for the lonely vision in his dream had at least shown no intention of harming him, but his dream had nonetheless been strange. The dream-figure had made scant effort to communicate with Seth, and had vanished when Seth himself had tried to utter words. Now in waking encounter, Seth expected no different. Dumbly, he turned to his fellow men and, as in his dream, they urged him to speak with the hooded being that confronted them.

They felt anxiety rather than fear at what stood before them, and Seth was as unsure as any. His dream had told him little. He made as if to ask who might stand before them, fully expecting disappearance, but as he opened his mouth, the man held forth an arm in friendship.

"Welcome."

A gentle voice, full of sympathy reached them over the dividing distance, and they were reassured. That voice was enough for them to know that this was a friend.

"I've expected your coming, Seth."

The whole company were shocked at this knowledge of Seth's name... not least Seth, who stepped back a pace and eyed the fellow with renewed caution.

"I dreamed, more than a month since, of a room ill lit, for I perceived you. A companion extinguished the lamp. 'Sleep well, Seth,' he said to you, and I perceived also that his

Respite

sentiments didn't help you that night. I watched you dreaming restlessly in the darkness, and you almost met my silent questions. But at the last, it was too much to ask and the vision faded. Yet I knew this dream meant we'd meet and I knew then that you'd come to these hills, yet I knew not why."

Seth, perhaps now reassured anew, was astonished that this fellow knew they'd come, and that he indeed knew his name.

"You must explain to us how this knowledge can be," Seth said, "for it's beyond our comprehension. I am..."

At that very moment, a chilling cry went up to the right of the companions and in an instant wild lumbering forms sprang out from behind rocks, screaming as they charged lurching towards the band of men.

It was a hunting party from Ironmound. They were much like Kelman in appearance. They carried clubs and sticks and looked all too ready to use them.

"Quickly," called the stranger. "You must fly. We shall be safe enough, but you must run, for I can't hold them long."

He waved his staff in the direction of the mountains.

"Follow the path," he instructed, "I'll be behind you. Don't fear, but go."

With this, Kaleb and Abe gave a cry and set off at a run up the path.

"Come on," cried Kaleb as he went. "What are you waiting for?"

The others followed now. Barny, who was holding Little 'Un, pulled at the pony's rope.

"Come on, you rascal. We'd better be out of here."

But the commotion unnerved the pony and the more the farrier pulled the more the little rascal resisted, now pawing at the air, fully laden though he was.

"Come *on*, you darned fool," insisted Barny. But with this angry shout of impatience, the pony reared once more and lurched free. Eyes rolling and ears back, he turned and galloped wildly down the path in the direction from which they'd come. Barny staggered after him.

"Come back Little 'Un," he called, but the pony, packs and all, was gone.

"Away! Away up the path," came words ringing in his ears.

He shook himself and turning saw that the wild men were almost upon the stranger. He ran now, up the path towards their hooded guardian, ready to help fend off the gruesome attackers, but as he neared again he was commanded, "Follow your friends. I shall be with you. *I* am safe... *you* are not."

Hesitantly, Barny passed by the robed figure and then turning, with a last glance, sped after his companions who were now far in front of him and had turned to wait. He muttered as her ran.

"Little 'Un... you stubborn little... Oh!"

The wild men bore down upon the guardian, screaming ever louder, wielding their crude weapons, intent on killing the one who dared stand in their path.

"Stay," commanded the hooded man, as they pounced, and he thrust the staff before him. A blinding flash of light burst forth, throwing back the deepening shadows of evening, and instantly his assailants fell back screaming, this time in terror. A score or more they numbered, and now they all stood hesitant, loping a few steps forward, and then falling back again.

The staff burst into flame again as a warning of its continued potency and then the man that held it turned and made off up the path towards the companions, ushering them on as he went.

"Come. I'll take you to safety, before they come to their senses... if senses they have. It's not far to go."

Bewildered, they submitted to his pleas.

"But, the pony," cried Barny, in lone protest.

"You must leave him," ordered the stranger. "They'll no doubt have him by now and that may be to his advantage, for

Respite

they use horses, and they value them. *He'll* be looked after well enough, but *you* would not be. Come now."

So they followed, like lost sheep, along the ascending path which soon reached the sheer face of the higher peaks. But on it ran through the ravine, still climbing, leading on to the heart of the mountains, smooth rock closing about them and towering high above. The shadows grew darker still.

"We should get there before full darkness. Not long now," said the stranger as he hurried them along, glancing back now and then and looking for pursuers.

"Get where?" asked Henry, in mild protest at the continued anonymity of their destination and of their saviour. "And who *are* you?" he added.

"To Sharfell," their guide replied. "That must suffice for now. Time presses. I'll explain when we reach there. I am Tavar. That too must suffice for now."

They were burdened by the packs they carried and, since they were unfit from their ordeal in the cave, this hurried flight up an ever-steepening path soon had them panting for breath. Though they'd fought on through pride, the men who were afflicted by the Scar showed ever-increasing signs of fatigue. Abe and Kaleb were almost on their knees by the time they'd climbed to the higher reaches. Will however, and even Amos who was worse afflicted if appearances were anything to go by, were better able to cope and they showed no signs of giving up, even with tiredness creeping upon them.

The others still showed no signs of affliction, yet of these remaining four, Ely seemed grave. Often on the journey, he slipped into trances... trances reminding Seth of how his friend had returned from Greylar, as if in some dreadful dream. Seth was deeply concerned for him, but the prospect of a decent shelter raised them all a little.

Tavar felt fatigued too, but didn't show it. The path forked and, without hesitation, he led them to the left. Downwards the path now went, almost as steeply as it had risen. They stumbled forward in what little light was left to them.

Seth glanced up at the sky. Daylight had fled. The clouds had cleared with the onset of night. The moon hadn't risen and stars were springing out above them... yet, suddenly the stars were gone, as if a blanket had been drawn across the heavens.

The footfalls of the companions echoed and Seth realised that they were scurrying down a corridor, a dark tunnel in the rock. Before them in the distance they could see lights flickering in the otherwise total darkness. Torches, a score or more, danced yellow and welcoming. Then the stars were alight again, as the huddled band issued from the tunnel. Tavar turned.

"Bar the gates," he called.

Unseen guards swung creaking gates across the doorway through which they'd come.

"That's good," said Tavar. "You're safe for the moment. Let's find shelter.

The travellers looked around them as they walked out into the open once more. The torches, ensconced in brackets upon the rock walls, formed a circle some hundred and fifty paces in diameter. The rocks formed a circle around a small, flat plateau. The lights were set in pairs, each pair marking the entrance to some cave like opening. As they passed clockwise around the perimeter, they saw that each of these openings had strong, heavy timber doors set on iron hooks and bands. Within the circle were what must be other dwellings of stone... squat, with small windows glowing with warm light. These buildings were huddled together, nearer to the centre than to the edge of the circle.

The travellers reached the far side of the circle, seeing no one, perceiving no one other than the hidden guards who'd closed the gates.

Tavar pushed upon a door, somewhat larger than others in the ring. It yielded, an inner light flooded out to greet them and they were inside.

Their host threw back his hood and shook his head, brushing back long, grey locks with both hands to reveal a proud face… a thickset, kind face with bushy brows and a mass of grey beard. Immediately, the whole company were asking questions.

Tavar laughed warmly and, holding forth his hands, gestured them to cease their questions.

"Enough. Enough. You're in safe hands for the moment. You're obviously in need of food and before that a wash. Then I'll tell you more of this land and you'll tell me more of your quest, for perhaps I as well as you have something to learn."

CHAPTER TEN

Dunbeck

Much of their stock of food had been lost with the pony, but they carried fresh clothes in their packs... if they could be called fresh, for though unworn, they'd suffered in the wrecking of the boat and though dry now, were creased and salt-ridden.

"We've robes for you here," said Tavar. "They'll suffice until your own can be freshened."

With this he disappeared outdoors.

"Just look at this place," said Barny, glancing around him in the lamplight. "It's hewn from the rock."

Sure enough, the room and others adjoining were some unnatural cave, or indeed a cave fashioned into a neat dwelling. A simple table of stone stood on the cold, matted floor. Four wooden chairs and a stool stood by. A sweet-scented wood fire burned in a natural grate, the smoke swirling above and disappearing up a guessed chimney. These things, and the lamp that lit it, were the only furniture in this main room.

Kaleb peered around a stone door jamb into an adjoining room. It was clothed in darkness, but he could make out a number of low pallets of straw that he assumed were beds.

'Comfortable enough,' he thought. *'If this is where we're to stay tonight.'*

Barny made his way to another doorway. Cautiously, he peered round it. Two sharp eyes met him in the darkness. He stepped back in surprise... he'd had enough of eyes in the dark. There was a flutter of wings and a disgruntled squawking. It was a hawk, perched comfortably until Barny had disturbed it. He breathed a sigh of relief and as he did so, the outer door opened and Tavar re-entered carrying a bundle.

They washed and re-clothed themselves. Tavar prepared

food for them from an adjoining pantry. At his bidding, they sat at a low table, some seated as was necessary on the floor.

Bread and cheese, with butter and honey were all that appeared, with a flagon of clear, cold water as sweet as that which they'd tasted in the hills. But these few things were plentiful and more wholesome than any they'd tasted. Perhaps recently jaded palates deceived them, but more likely the food was produced more skilfully than even the produce of the Hamlet.

"And now," announced Tavar at last, "for the answers to your questions. I see more clearly now what I glimpsed on the path back there. You've the Sign of Darkness upon you... the Pox of Icelar. Perhaps that answers in part the questions *I* would ask of *you*.

"Yes. We come in search of a cure," offered Barny. "For our homestead in Midvale, over the sea, is stricken by the Scar."

"A cure indeed? Then I'll tell you what I can to help you in your quest, though it make your search little easier, for I know little of any cure... only what, or who, we think to be its cause. I'll tell you of the Bane of Icelar... or Hilar as it once was called. We give this bane, or rather its owner, the name the 'Bane of Dunbeck'. Over a hundred and fifty years ago, there was a town not far north of here called Dunbeck. It was nestled in the lower mountains, as indeed this place is, though it was built on the higher slopes of the valley of the river Dun. There a simple folk dwelt... farmers as *we* are here."

And seeing the questioning look in their eyes, he continued.

"Beyond this stone circle, to the south, are hidden green valleys where our sheep and goats are pastured and where we grow enough cereal for our needs. Bees we keep there too in the apple orchards. We do the best we can, though the summers are not as they used to be."

He continued, returning to the history of Icelar.

"The summers were better in those days at Dunbeck. The

food we produced then was more wonderful than that we have here. They were wonderful days indeed."

He said this as if in a trance, remembering days that he'd known himself. The travellers were taken aback by this.

"*You* were there?" Seth questioned, eyes wide in astonishment, asking the question on all their lips.

"Er, oh, yes," said Tavar, returning from his trance. "Why, of course, you're wondering how... all that time ago. I must explain more," he smiled. "The men of Dunbeck had been content for many years with their way of life, but a few of us became restless. We journeyed many miles, all over Hilar and learned much. We delved deep into the lore of nature, and beyond it. We learned deep secrets and the mysteries of life. And a time came when those among us who retained the old ways grew tired of continual delvings, yet we learned many things that were of benefit to all. We learned of the body and of the mind. We learned the healing of many ills and *we* few learned longevity. A few of us survive today, all these years later, yet there's great regret in our hearts. Some learned to control the shape of things and to conjure up fire and wind at will, and perhaps there was nothing amiss, even then. But there were those among us who fell to evil ways... or else evil ensnared them for with some the knowledge of these things turned sour and it was used for malevolent purpose. I and others denounced them, but they persisted and soon they segregated themselves, hiding behind locked doors, and great evils they wrought.

"We who still strove for good rather than ill-use of our knowledge became fearful of what was happening, but we held no sway over those others and we didn't realise until it was too late what bane they were to let loose upon us all. We escaped with those of the other townsfolk who we could persuade. We fled to these parts and coming to Sharfell we settled, feeling great safety behind the rocks, some ancient settlement of our ancestors. We shaped it further and fortified it as best we could, for we sensed the impending evil would break.

"Yet we could never have realised how great an evil. And then we knew... even here, some miles from Dunbeck we heard a great explosion. The air throbbed, pulsing for many hours afterwards. It was dark night, yet the sky to the north erupted with intense light and flame belched high above the hills. We were angry and we were sad for the loss of Dunbeck. We soon found that many folk from the town fled mindless and wild southwards. They settled near here, at Ironmound. Their descendants are the wild men you almost met. They mean no ill, but are totally and innocently savage, hunters of men now, for their minds were turned by the evil thing that came out of Dunbeck."

"Yet *we* knew one who wasn't entirely savage," said Will.

Seth agreed, adding, "Kelman was his name. And though he caused us to be here, he did it unwittingly and he showed us friendship and compassion, doing all he could to make amends."

So, Seth explained all that had happened, from the expedition to Greylar to their arrival south of Ironmound, helped with the occasional comment from Will and the others.

"And so, here we are," he concluded, with a sigh, "in search of the Ice Wolf."

Tavar breathed a sigh of remorse and shook his head.

"It would seem that *you've* fallen foul of the recent outbreak of this disease... a consequence we fear of the evil from Dunbeck. When the evil first arose, this disease became rife and it killed many in Ironmound. It's said that some of the people of Ironmound found a cure in the Ice Wolf from the Icewood in those early days. Certainly some travelled north and certainly the disease died out and was forgotten. Then it returned and seemingly disappeared again, but now it's returned once more. Only unwritten legend remains from that first time. We ourselves never needed to look for this Ice Wolf. In those early days, we avoided all contact and this perhaps spared us the disease. Then, when it came the second time, it seems we'd become immune, perhaps through our use of the controls of mind and body. Feeling safer, we made contact enough with these wild men, with no ill effect. We tried to cure them with our medicines but our potions availed nothing. They became more apathetic and more hostile towards us and to each other. Soon it was impossible even to try to help them. The cure, if ever there'd been one, was already distant legend to them and they didn't even search as their ancestors had done for a cure. We ourselves wouldn't leave this area through fear of evil abroad and these days we still venture forth little from Sharfell... it's safer that way. Today is the first time I've left the lower hills for some months. This I'd not have done, but last night I dreamed again, this time of your coming. I saw you on the path upon which we met, and so I came to meet you... for dreams mean much here and are very often visions of truth."

"And what of Kaan and the Watcher?" said Henry. "Were they a product of this evil that was created."

"Yes, and no," answered Tavar. The Watcher, I fear, was a product of Kaan, and Kaan as he appeared to you was a product of the brooding evil, for Kaan was once a friend of mine."

As Tavar spoke, his tone was grave, but now it was coloured with sadness and regret.

"He was one that fell into evil delving. He perhaps more than others engineered much, unaware of how close he trod to the terrifying abyss into which his mind was eventually lured. He and his fellow dabblers fled the evil they'd unleashed and heading south they passed close to here. In fact, they tried to enter, evil still in their hearts. From what they said, we feared to allow them in. They'd have tried to change what we'd found, so we reluctantly resisted them. Our power by then was great enough to withstand them, for *their* power had been lessened by that terrible confrontation in Dunbeck. They fled then, down onto the eastern plain and by all accounts went south, finding eventual refuge in the hills... that would be the Banefell he mentioned, and his fellows would be the brethren.

"But as for the 'Lord of the Icemere'... let it be said that Kaan had no dealings with any 'Lord of the Icemere.' This title is new to me, but I think I know of its origin... the Bane of Dunbeck. No dealings with the Bane could be controlled by Kaan. Many years after the dreadful day, we came across Kaan and some of his followers, nearby. They were becoming adventurous, though still they brooded in minor evils.

"In our brief encounter, we told them of what little we'd learned from the Ironmounders... that the dreadful evil of Dunbeck seemed to have shifted, by all accounts breeding its malevolence upon a northern plateau of the Icemere within the Icewood. And indeed the name 'Lord of the Icemere' might be fitting, for its evil bred a cold breath that spread around it and the woods and the lake became icebound for much of the year. Even in summer, ice and snow are rumoured to linger still under grey skies. There are rumours too of wild dogs roaming the frozen forests, hunting the smaller animals that adapted to the new cold.

"Yes, the dogs are no doubt the Ice Wolves of the legends of that earlier time when some men searched for answers to the Sign of Darkness.

"Unless things have changed, Kaan held no allegiance to 'him', for he's no 'person'. 'It' has no slaves. It merely broods and bubbles with evil. They're unwittingly enslaved by their early dabbling... by a sinister thing they unleashed on our world.

"And as for Kaan," Tavar went on. "Even in this day it seems he didn't rest, for he and his followers had become wightish shadows of evil. They roamed half real, half illusion. The fire that you put upon him appears indeed to have *finally* destroyed him, or maybe only the illusion he presented... For myself, I'd guess that he *is* destroyed utterly since the Watcher, you say, dissolved with no attack upon it and so too the creating force must surely have perished. Kaan, it would seem, is no more. The fallen have lost their prince."

"And how much do you know of the Icewood?" asked Seth.

"I travelled there many years ago," said Tavar, "but it wasn't the Icewood then, for it was in the days before the evil, when life abounded there, when even in winter it could be easily travelled. It was a fair, wild land of hills and trees, much as here, but the trees were numerous and magnificent... more so than any I had seen in Hilar, majestic pines rising fold upon fold. The Hiwood, as it was then called, was a wonderful sight though many of its trees must have perished now. The plateau can be looked down upon from the paths approaching it and mile upon mile of trees stretched over it. It's as flat as this table, quite unbelievable, in the heart of all those peaks. Yet it *can* be reached with a climb of some effort from the south, over the hills that protect it from this direction. And there may be less lofty ways of reaching the plain too. Rocky precipices boasted waterfalls beyond number and beyond beauty. There were deer too... the stags were as proud as any you would see. The great eagles and hawks with silken plumage were prouder still."

At this, renewed fluttering and squawking arose from Barny's recent acquaintance. The farrier glanced doubtfully over his shoulder.

"That's Heg. He's friendly... even to strangers," Tavar assured. "He's tame, and doesn't hunt. He's content with berries and fruit since he was tamed. He will eat no meat, dead or alive. He will only eat what I share with him. He's full of such surprises. He flutters now through jealousy. Yet he's more dear to me than all the eagles of the Hiwood and he's luckier, for most are long since gone, I fear.

"If you must continue your quest, and no doubt you must, I'll tell you all I remember of the shape of that land, and of the routes you may take to and from it. But you must make due allowance for ages passed, and for the ice, and no doubt for the evil itself for I fear it may lurk even stronger the nearer you come to your goal. But at least the time of year is as you would wish it. You would perish ere you reached it in winter. To come to it from the south, you must travel on the western side of the mountains. There's a pass from here to that far side. Tomorrow, when you've rested, I'll tell you more."

Tavar showed them to the pallets of straw, their beds. He himself returned to join Heg in the other, darkened room, snuffing out the lamp as he went.

The travellers, weary as they were, and with contented bellies, were soon asleep, in more comfort than they'd enjoyed for what seemed an age. Seth dwelt for a short while on how fine it would be to rest here for some days, but he knew they must soon be away and he drifted into slumber in a vague and uncertain hope that Tavar might be persuaded to travel with them.

They were awakened next morning late by Tavar. Little light penetrated into these rooms, for the only window was a narrow slit in the rock to the side of the heavy door and it still seemed that dawn struggled to overcome the darkness.

Breakfast was already prepared and they ate eagerly, feeling the reality of their rocky refuge more than they had in the heavy blackness of the night. They all shared Seth's feelings, wishing dearly to stay here for a while. It made them sad, when otherwise they'd have enjoyed the tranquillity of this peaceful place.

"No doubt you'll wish, or at least find it necessary to be away quite soon," said Tavar, as he joined them at the stone table, as if reading their very thoughts.

"Time brooks no delay it's true," answered Seth with

resignation, "though we're all weary. There will be time enough for rest when we return to Myre Hamlet," and with this, he sighed. "We must be away tomorrow, if at all possible, for every day we delay may bring the loss of more lives. We've lost enough days already."

Amos touched his face, and shuddered at these words, gritting his teeth, knowing only too well that Seth was right.

"Do you have horses that you might spare, Tavar?" Seth went on. "If the terrain would allow, they'd prove valuable in saving time."

"We've ponies, that's all, for hills wouldn't suit long-legged horses. These, you're welcome to borrow. They're much like the pony you brought with you… sturdy and surefooted in this terrain, though you'll find them more use for carrying you burdens than carrying you yourselves. That in itself will speed your progress. If you travel west of the mountains the way, if it's not changed, should allow the ponies a path."

Though they all longed to, even Seth daren't ask Tavar if he might travel with them, for they remembered his words of reluctance at leaving Sharfell.

"I'll make sure you have ponies," Tavar continued. "You'll leave fully provisioned for the journey. You'll need heavier clothing for the climate, though you could do without its extra weight. Now, if time is your master, you'll be wise to think of limiting your number… eight will slow you down. I think that four would be better. Amos, Kaleb, Will and Abe. Afflicted as they are, will only slow you down. Ely too will benefit from a longer stay here."

A clamour of protest from the men named greeted these suggestions, but all but Amos realised that Tavar was right, and their proud objections were overwhelmed by the state they were in.

"I *shall* go with you," cried Amos, thumping the table. "Or indeed *without* you, following if I must. I've not passed through the trials of Greylar and Icelar to be left here at the last. I'll stick to you like a leech, be sure of that."

He raised himself from his seat and folded his arms in defiance.

"And, besides," he added, more calmly. "If there *is* a cure to be found, the sooner I receive a potion, the better."

He sat down again, still ill at ease.

"But Amos," said Tavar. "Do you not feel that for us to avoid the presence of the Scar on this journey might help the cause?"

"If there are those among us who are free of it after all our journey so far, then surely they'll be none the worse for its company a while longer," Amos insisted.

Tavar smiled. "With Seth's agreement, five it is then," he laughed.

"Five indeed," Seth beamed, clapping his hands hard together, realising fully what Tavar was suggesting.

Their eyes met, and Tavar grinned. "Yes. You've perceived my intention. *I'll* travel with you. I've thought long this night, on the past *and* on the future. We at Sharfell owe it to the people of Ironmound and indeed to the people of Myre Hamlet for, as you've no doubt perceived, it was we as well as the fallen ones who encouraged delving all those years ago. Though we chose the clearer path, *we* are in some ways to blame for evil befalling this land and yours... perhaps, even the face of the evil that lives in the Icewood. We may together bring back the Ice Wolf's cure...we here to help Ironmound and you to help Myre Hamlet. Who knows, the legend may live in reality, yet shall we *find* the Ice Wolf? If we find it in the wild dogs then what's the nature of the cure... the meat? The blood? We can't say. We seem to go forward on a quest with a great uncertainty. After all, a fire won't light without knowledge of the tindering."

"Yet, with *your* help and guidance, we've more help than we could have dreamed of... or rather, wished for ere we started,"

Seth said, smiling at his initial choice of words. "We had dear Kelman, who would have been help enough, yet he knew little of the land north of here. In fact, he gave us little hint of the evil that lurks here. No doubt he'd learned to live with it, taking it for normal through the years of his life."

"But remember, Tavar replied, "it's many years since I travelled that way, before the ice, and I perhaps fear the evil more than you, for I've come to know over long years the dreadful malevolence it spreads. And still I don't know its real nature, though I've pondered *that* long enough."

"Then if there's any more you know of our paths, and of the evils they may take us to, you must tell us before we set out," said Seth. "For who knows, we may yet lose you, leaving us needing lost knowledge."

Tavar looked at the travellers. He clasped his hands and shook his head, smiling.

"You've a wise leader in Seth," he said.

The visitors to Sharfell spent the morning of that day relaxing in the peace of those hills, talking at leisure with the inhabitants of the hilly encampment.

Later, they ventured south with Tavar and beheld the sheltered pastures and orchards of which he'd spoken and *they* were a sight indeed. Beneath a clear and lazy sky, they marvelled at what they saw. Winding away from them were green fields, their lushness beyond compare and further off, the fields held corn. Through the pastures gurgled a clear stream, chattering over its stony bed and running away down the valley, skirted by grassy overhangs. The fields climbed to hazy, barren slopes above which was a band of tall trees. Though here and there oak and ash occurred, most were fir trees, stood like armies guarding a secret place. The orchards had young fruit and on the grass fresh flowerlets abounded… white and yellow-golden. The bees went here and there about their business. Despite what Tavar had said, this place seemed untouched by the cold hand of evil. Skylarks sang above them in the sun-drenched sky, and those who beheld the valley now for the first time were comforted beyond measure. The afternoon seemed to last far longer than the days had allowed recently.

Meanwhile, all was made ready for the impending departure of the five. Tavar had entrusted Heg to one of his close friends. He knew that the hawk would be well cared for in his absence.

In the early chill of the next morning, they stood beside two ponies who now carried the larger part of their load. They took with them, in addition to the freshened clothes they now had put on, heavy cloaks similar to the one that Tavar always wore. They expected cold, very cold, conditions before long and this necessity, together with other essentials for their journey increased their load. They were well provisioned with food from Sharfell, though this was restricted to those things that would travel well, that wouldn't become stale and unwholesome, such as oat biscuits and dried fruits.

Seth and his fellow voyagers were reminded of that day back home in April when they'd said their all too brief farewells. They moved now towards the eastern gates by which they'd entered on the night before last. It might as well have been pouring with rain as it had been when they'd left the Hamlet, for they were as reluctant to leave. At the gates they said their fresh goodbyes.

"We'll be back with all speed, and with our return we'll bring you aid," Seth assured the troubled men they left behind.

They were cheerless, yet they had no will to go further with the five, for all an early cure might hold. Among the five, Tavar alone didn't appear downcast.

CHAPTER ELEVEN

Blizzard

Henry and Barny led the two ponies into the tunnel and through the guarded gates while Seth, Amos and then Tavar followed into the cold shadows. The iron gates clanged shut behind them, the echo running up and escaping before them into the daylight beyond the rocky passage. As they re-entered the vast openness of this clear day a friendly sun, yet unseen within the circle of rock, greeted them warmly as it rose over the eastern lowlands, melting away the lingering chill of what had been a starry night.

Soon they'd reached the fork in the path. Before and below them in the east rose the pall of smoke that marked Ironmound. It wavered in the breeze. Yet were it not for the smoke, the breeze would scarcely be perceived.

They hurried to take the more northern route that wound north-west into the upper hills, and the shelter of Sharfell was lost.

They trekked through the pass, which took them into the heart of a gaping ravine. The sun was lost to them and on either side towered stark grey rocks. Below them, to their left, the rocks slid down into shadowy half-guessed depths, for they followed a precarious path on the northern flank of the huge rock fault. It was barely wide enough for a pony and a leader at his side.

Barny felt the height more than any of his companions did and had to hand his charge to Seth.

"I thought *you* could lead a pony anywhere," laughed Seth.

"Oh! Sure I can," said Barny giddily, "but there's not much call for taking them up the side of a house in the Hamlet."

"This is the scar that *we* are more familiar with," said Tavar. "Sharfell finds its name from this rift. Yet we all know that the

Scar *you've* come across before today is of greater concern... for its perils are less avoidable and certainly less predictable."

On they went. Henry's pony, bringing up the rear, stumbled on a boulder. Sure footed though the creature was, it needed all its skill in balance. Scrambling to recover under its load it sent a shower of loose rocks and stones cascading out into the chasm below them.

Barny, looking over his shoulder at the noise, leaned back onto the face of the rock to his right and closed his eyes. He was unnerved afresh. As they strained to hear the landing of the plummeting stones, the men of the Hamlet perceived the deep echoing murmur of water below them. If the shower of rocks ever reached the water they didn't hear rumour of it.

"And you think this is more predictable?" Barny said.

"Have heart, Barny," said Tavar, "for we leave the ravine soon now. It turns more to the southwest and we'll find a way through in our present direction. This much of our path, I know for sure."

The next few days' travelling took them through less hostile country. Soon they'd reached the western extremes of the range of mountains. They'd made their way to the foot of the high slopes and, unlike in the east, there was an absence of foothills.

Having followed a winding path down onto the plain, they'd found in turning north that the rocks to their right had sharpened again to high cliffs with very little feature. The level they were now on was of sparse grasses that ran to the very feet of the cliffs. Here and there streams issued from rocky ravines similar to, yet much smaller than, the Sharfell ravine. Most of these streams were little wider than three or four strides and all but a few ran at a depth easily waded. One or two however turned out to be deeper and, though they flowed the slower for it, they caused some small delays and more than small discomfort.

As they moved on northwards, even with the sun, they

found the cold grew, and still the darkness came early. Night shelter was hard to come by, but the weather had stayed fine. The heavy cloaks offered more than enough to keep them from the chill grip of the crisp nights.

The moon offered less light as she waned and they were soon unable to use it to any great advantage in night travelling. By the evening of the fifth day, they'd travelled what Tavar guessed to be two thirds of the way to the Icewood. They'd made progress beyond their expectations, but here, even in summer on these low levels, they were surprised to find the streams on the verge of icing over. Where the water cascaded over stepping-stones, icicles formed. The sun now appeared wan behind them in the south in the clear midday skies and offered the palest excuse for warmth. Their warm breath hung on the crisp air.

"Soon we'll reach the river," said Tavar. "That will be our first great test, for though there were stepping-stones when I crossed it many years ago, I recall that they were treacherous, half covered by the rushing waters. Maybe we'll be lucky enough to find the water to be lower. We must hope there's been little rain or snow in the mountains. If we pass the obstacle that is the river, there are yet more to come. But let's not put our bridges under our feet too soon."

The hint of further dangers worried them, yet also it hardened their resolve. They didn't trouble to ask for more details from Tavar.

As dusk enveloped them, the distant rush of water came to their ears, even louder as they marched on. They rounded a corner and there before them was the river, a restless torrent swirling and eddying in its uncomfortable rocky bed. They approached it, leaving the cliff corner where it turned eastwards. Now they could hear a distant pounding, like continuous thunder many miles away. They turned their gaze upstream and there, only a furlong or so away beyond clustered trees, they beheld an eye-opening sight.

"The falls," said Tavar. "I remember them now in all their fury, but this other sight holds greater concerned for us," he said, leading them under the trees.

They stared after Tavar's outstretched arm. The stepping-stones were there, close together but covered by two feet of swirling water. And worse, beyond the flat and slippery stones, the water was deeper than a man might tread.

"So here we are," went on Tavar, "and here on this side we must stay… at least for tonight. The light fails now. We must think of a way to cross, for our path is, by need, across these treacherous waters. We'll make camp back there in the cliff fold and tomorrow we may see more clearly what's to be done."

With thoughts approaching despair again, they followed Tavar's advice. With a fire fuelled from the trees upstream they settled quite comfortably, lulled by the constant roar of the heady falls.

They ate of their rations, but by now they'd exhausted their supplies of tobacco and those among them who used it were missing the solace of a pipe.

Soon they slept, the falls ever churning into the night. All except Tavar, who pondered upon their crossing and beyond into the deeper darkness he knew would comfort them should they cross safely.

The morrow brought rumour of storm, for clouds had engulfed the blue reaches of the day before. From the north the clouds piled, wave upon wave… a grey brooding mass. The travellers stood now, stiff with the lingering cold.

"Looks like we're in for a soaking again," said Barny, casting a suspicious eye aloft. "Still we can't get any wetter than we did crossing from Greylar, and there's the river first anyway. While my feet are on land it can rain all day if it has a mind."

He re-joined Henry in loading up the ponies. He stroked the muzzle of the two patient beasts and wished that Little 'Un was with them.

"Rain all day, it will not," said Tavar, "for these clouds are heralds of snow. The Icewood is ever nearer, for it sends envoys to meet us."

"Snow in June?" cried Seth in disbelief. It's cold for sure in these parts... but snow in June?"

"You saw the ice in the streams back there," answered Tavar. "It's colder than you imagine. I fear the waters are colder still. They flow from higher places, more unsettled by evil at a guess and the clouds too come from such places. This threatening weather troubles me, for perhaps it's already broken in the hills. We must cross before the torrents reach us."

"And how are we to cross?" asked Henry. "*We* shall find it perilous enough, but what of the ponies?"

"We shall cross with great care," answered Tavar, "and with rope. There's a length that will suffice in the pack. See the trees... they meet the waters on both banks... where the stones are. We must secure the rope this end and *I'll* venture to cross first. Once the rope is tied on the far side, it should be an easier crossing for the rest."

"A fair suggestion," said Henry, "but would it not be safer to leave our guide on this side until the rope is secured. *I'll* go first."

"And would it not be safer to leave the sea captain on this side also," replied Tavar. "Unless you all intend to put at greater risk your return to your homeland."

"*I'll* go," said Amos, as resolved as any, "for if *I'm* lost, then little will it matter."

"No... it's for me to cross," said Seth, thoughtfully. "Henry and Tavar are both right for *their* part. And you Amos... we need you more than we'd thought, though we *had* planned to leave you behind. If we find this Ice Wolf, you'll be the trial of its virtue. Without you, we'd learn little of its potency immediately. We may find out before our return is made

Blizzard

complete whether indeed it's worth our returning."

"Too right, Seth," said Barny. "It's you or I. And if I thought I'd not lose myself in the rapids, I'd be in there now, but you'd be safer crossing than finding the need to fish *me* out."

So, despite the cold, Seth removed his boots, his heavy robe and much of his clothing, for he knew they'd be needed dry. Indeed wet, even the rope would have weighed heavy on this difficult crossing. More than once, Seth slipped and slithered. Once he nearly disappeared into the waters, teetering on the edge of balance, slimy stone his only foothold. With the uncoiling rope on one shoulder, he dropped to his knees and breathlessly faced the relentless battering flow of icy water, paddling desperately against it. Carefully, he rose again and went on. Though only twenty or thirty paces in all, he welcomed the outstretched branches of an alder tree with great relief. His legs numb with cold, he clambered from the water. Chattering and shaking, he tied the rope securely and beckoned the others to make their crossing. They too took off much of their clothing. It was bundled for the most part on the ponies, but some, Henry shouldered.

First, Barny and Amos inched their way across without mishap and with one pony... Barny leading, Amos behind. As they went, the two men clung to the rope on their left, using it as a support against the seething waters, but near the middle of the flow they had to rely on balance more, for the rope was slack enough to take them perilously near the edge of the flat tables of stone. The watching men at either end daren't untie the rope to tighten it whilst their companions were crossing. Now they were across safely and after the rope had been retied, Henry and Tavar followed in like manner with the other pony. In midstream they felt the first flakes of snow. Once all were safely across, Seth made to return to untie the rope so as to take it with them, but Tavar advised that they leave it in place for the return journey. And now, the storm was upon them.

Whirling shapes filled the sky in a blustering wind. Then, as they made to move on, their ears throbbed. Yet the booms that accompanied the throbbing seemed less harsh than before, swallowed by the continuous pounding of the waterfall.

They dressed hurriedly before making for the thicker shelter in the heart of the clump of trees. Seth's heart sank, for as Barny donned his robe, he saw that the sign of the Scar was there on his chest. Barny caught Seth's glance and forced a smile, knowing that Seth now shared his secret.

The throbbing came twice, and then was gone.

"The 'Lord of the Icemere' won't let us forget him it seems," shouted Tavar. "Even close to his territory he beats out a warning though over long years I've become used to his incessant reminders. Every few days they greet us in Sharfell, a constant reminder of that fateful day. Yet nothing that we know of has ever come of these noises, except for the shadow... the grave shadow over what would be a peaceful place.

The trees here by the river grew close up to the rock face of the cliffs and this combination offered good shelter from the blizzard. They found fuel and lit a fire to dry what needed drying, and to warm their bones, for the cold was becoming one of their greatest enemies.

For most of that morning, the snows fell with what seemed like malicious intent. They stayed put throughout the hateful storm, knowing that to move from shelter would be folly. Prompted by Barny, they sang snatches of songs from the Hamlet. Tavar listened with interest, for being a farmer of sorts, the words held much for him. They also learned sea rhymes of Fenny and Tavar, seeing virtue in this light-heartedness, recounted stories of the earlier days in Dunbeck. They were merry in that grey clearing for these few hours and the fire burned warmly. For a time, they were heedless of the snows beyond the canopy of the branches.

Seth glanced at Amos now and then. The songs and laughter

lifted him for a while, but there was no mistaking an underlying torment now. Amos looked distant much of the time. The hideous scaring of his face grew worse, yet the strange thing was that little physical pain afflicted him.

Seth cried inwardly. He knew that Amos was heading Kelman's way. He hesitated to think how many more would be suffering in the Hamlet and he hoped above hope that the Scar might be held in check there. Yet secretly he quailed at the possibility, the likelihood even, that they might never find the boon for which they searched.

"We must achieve it," he said quietly to himself with fresh resolve. *"We must... and quickly."*

He glanced skywards and saw that the storm was passing. The pale blue sky returned. Looking north, beyond their leafy shelter the landscape dazzled them. A carpet of white spread over their route, but on they must go.

They soon found that by travelling close to the cliffs, they trod in but an inch or two of snow. Luckily it had drifted in only a few places, so the snow, crisp with the cold air, proved easily trodden.

"Another three or four days should see us on the plateau of the Icewood," said Tavar. "It's likely that we'll see more snow before then though, so perhaps more time will steal away. The path I know of, the path I travelled before, offers shelter for much of the way, yet it shall I fear offer certain perils also."

And more he could not, or would not, say. His brief hints left the others uneasy and even suspicious if suspicion were any use now, for they'd committed themselves to Tavar's care.

They trekked on for the remainder of daylight and all next day. They covered much ground despite the lingering carpet of white. The throbbing came twice more that day, and louder than ever before. They couldn't be sure if it were coming more often now, or whether it was that, further south, some of the lesser occurrences hadn't reached them. Either way, its increasing presence heightened their dread of what they approached.

In the distance before them they could see that the snowy mountainous reaches turned west and seemed to bar their way.

Seth began to wonder at the supposed ease of their path. With snow about them already, surely in the hills it would be a treacherous climb. They were well protected against the cold, but their gear wouldn't help the uncomfortable and dangerous difficulties of wading through any great depth of snow.

Tavar was merely thoughtful. He was the only one who might begin to perceive what the real nature of the evil was and he seemed to be battling to comprehend it further. Despite this, he was anxious that they should avoid any confrontation, for he was unsure away from the shelter of Sharfell.

They made camp again close to the hills but were colder than before. Here there were no trees for fuel. The next day brought a renewed threat of snow. Over breakfast, Tavar explained what now lay before them.

"Remember I told you of the plateau of the Icewood and of the path down onto its vast plain. No doubt you're wondering how we should come *down* onto a plateau, when here we are almost at the level of the sea. Well, before us not far off now, as can be seen, the hills turn to bar our way. They meet the coast and wouldn't be passable in these conditions, though I found a way through them in better days… when June was summer here, and still it was difficult. But we now go a different way."

Tavar looked up, aware of a darkening sky… darkening despite the new day.

"Snow threatens again," he went on. "And perhaps it's well that we've reached this point before more snow reaches *us*. A mile or so into the lower hills lies a cave. I'm almost sure of its whereabouts. But this cave is *more* than a cave for, coming from the north, it is linked by a chain of caverns with roofs unguessable. Natural tunnels join these caverns and this chain descends from the plateau to a point where it issues into the hills before us... from the cave which must be our entry. The feel of the tunnels was strange. It smelled of ancient waters long since dried, yet leaving dampness in the air. Its higher reaches had been worked and shaped. Altered to give access to the plateau from the darkness. Whoever had dwelt there had long since left."

"How will the ponies fare?" put in Henry.

"Yes. Don't forget the ponies," added Barny. "Little 'Un, bless him, found *one* cave bearable, but this sounds a task indeed... tunnels and caves and all."

"Don't worry," Tavar assured them. "The way is steep in places, but not too smooth and the ponies are surefooted. *They* will manage it if we do. I've hesitated to mention it before now, for if the climate had been kinder, we might have chosen the daylit way, despite the rougher climb. The darkness below ground may prove daunting, though shelter from snow and wind can't be ignored. Our problem will be the loss of our eyes. I'll be able to help with light from my staff here and there, but that light is precious. I recall few false tunnels and no difficult passages. I remember eleven caves in all, some larger, some smaller, and the far end will be heralded by a long upward sloping shaft. When I entered before, from the north, I watched the daylight fading more each time I glanced over my shoulder."

"And how long must we travel underground?" said Seth, apparently undaunted at the prospect of a dark shelter.

"It took me four days, nigh on," Tavar explained. "But I was in no hurry then, and I went with great care, for I didn't know what to expect. I wondered at the caverns with interest for as long as my staff allowed, and didn't just pass through them regardless. It should take no more than two days this time. Is it agreed then that we try it?"

Seth had already decided, but he turned to the others. "What do we say then? I for one am willing to avoid the snows."

"It seems the only way, from what Tavar says," said Henry. "And it sounds safe enough by his account." Amos was resolved to follow any path that needed following.

"Could we take torches with us?" said Barny, unsure of venturing into caves again. "I don't like the thought of meeting another Watcher, especially without a light to see it."

"There's no fuel," answered Seth.

"Fair enough," said Barny, accepting the futility of his suggestion and resigning himself to a choiceless choice. "On we go then," he offered, with a shrug of his shoulders. "But what of the ponies? They'll find little comfort and no food there and though they're full *now*, what prospect have they of food on the plateau?"

The ponies pawed the ground and found grass as they'd done since the first snows at the river crossing. It would be their last real forage for some days and Barny's words were of importance for he'd little wish to subject them to an ordeal such as Little 'Un's.

"They should find grass enough once we reach the plateau," said Tavar. "And if not, the trees will provide something. With luck we should be back here within the week."

As they climbed the hills towards their underground path led by Tavar, the sky darkened still further. Their ears and noses and the tips of their fingers were aching with the cold, though they were growing used to this mounting discomfort. They rubbed their hands together to keep as warm as they could. Then, as they progressed higher, the snows started again. The winds in the desolate hills howled and sent the flakes swirling this way and that.

"Look," called out Tavar, pointing skywards. "The hawks are still here, despite this foul climate."

Above them, a lone hawk emerged from the greyness and swooped as if diving for prey. The party stood transfixed as its dark shadow plummeted towards them. A shudder of fear ran through all but Tavar, who was used to such birds of prey, for he'd tamed Heg. All but *he* thought perhaps that this might be some messenger of evil. Maybe some evil illusion sent to spy on them. Tavar remembered only the birds of old and his heart rose to think that they were still here. As the bird neared, it spread its wings and lurched awkwardly in the buffeting wind.

"Heg!" cried Tavar in surprise. "Heg, why are you here?"

The man of Sharfell was happy to see his companion, but he was disappointed also, for now he thought he was right after all to fear that the hawks and eagles of old hadn't endured the coming of the ice.

The others sighed with relief at Tavar's recognition. Heg squawked with approval at having found his master and, alighting on Tavar's shoulder, he fluttered to repel the falling snow. Settling, he took to preening his ruffled feathers.

"It looks as if we've another companion," said Henry, "but will he abide the dark caverns?"

"I'm sure he will," said Tavar. "He's used to being indoors for much of the time at Sharfell, for though he's free to come and go there at his will, he seems to delight in the company of man. He too will be glad of shelter from this awful deluge."

By midday, they'd reached the area of the cave as Tavar remembered it but in the relentless snows they could see very little before them. Yet there it was... a dark tear in the black curtain that hung before them. Heads bowed and hooded they entered willingly, first Tavar, then Henry and Barny with the ponies, then Amos aided by Seth, for the Scar weakened him if it didn't pain him too greatly. Amos would normally have been the strongest among them, but he groaned and shuddered under the tightening grip of his illness. They stumbled forwards over the threshold thankful for the shelter and as they did so, Amos, head half-turned against the wind, out of the corner of his eye, caught sight of someone or something watching some distance away in the snow. He called out, but Seth thought this was at his stumbling. The others turned and as Amos sat recovering his breath, he gave another cry of disbelief at what he'd seen, pointing to the cave mouth as the others gathered around him.

"There, outside," he said. "We're being watched. A figure in the snow. A man? An animal? I'm not sure."

This was all he could manage for the moment. Tavar sprang to the entrance with Heg clinging to his shoulder and fluttering to maintain his balance.

Tavar looked first in the direction that Amos had indicated, then all around, but there was nothing to be seen. He returned to the group inside, who huddled together from the cold of the storm.

"There's nothing," he reported, thoughtfully.

Amos, recovering, explained what thought he'd seen.

"It was hideous. No... strange rather than hideous. First, I thought it was a man, for it stood upright, clothed in tight garb... boots, breeches and short coat. No cloak. But its head... its face was that of a dog."

"A dog?" the listeners gasped.

"Yes, of a dog," he went on. "A short stub face, with screwed up features and small, twisted ears. And worse, the face glimmered pale blue in the dull light. The creature had a long, curved knife at its belt, I think, and it stood upright, motionless, gazing in our direction."

"If that's not hideous," said Barny, in fright, "then the Watcher was as fair as a rabbit in spring."

"But I could see nothing," repeated Tavar, guessing that Amos had seen what he himself had dreamed of some nights earlier, still trusting that each encounter had been no *more* than dreaming.

"I tell you, I saw it," insisted Amos. "Whether it was real or illusion, the dog-man was there. I may be ill, but I'm not mistaken."

The air pulsed heavily three times, shaking the very roots of the rock beneath them and they were reminded yet again of the evil thing that they were approaching. This, and Barny's reminder of the Watcher, had them thinking Amos was all too right.

"The figure must have been some manifestation of the Lord of the Icemere," said Seth. "Let's hope it's no more than an illusion."

"I fear that may be true, Seth," Tavar agreed, coming to the conclusion that Amos was right. "And illusions can prove as dangerous as material things, for if we're not careful, they'll deceive and torment us all too easily. As for the 'Lord of the Icemere', it's ill that we must give the evil an image, for I'm sure that the evil is abstract, with no real form. It relies on such as we to give it substance, to give it reality in our minds. We must, if we can, deny its very existence. Yet even *I* find it hard not to submit to this trap. We must be wary, yet of course travel on. If Amos *is* right, let's hope these illusions stay above ground."

After resting briefly and uneasily they moved on, damp and uncomfortable. The first cave was small and dank and in the light borrowed from the entrance they perceived their first tunnel. Tavar led the way, Seth bringing up the rear.

The floor was quite level, though here and there it twisted unexpectedly, seemingly shaped by the steady erosion of running water in some long forgotten past.

Seth and Tavar called cautiously to each other now and then to ensure that the party was still intact and thus they trekked on for what seemed like miles, virtually blind in the darkness, when suddenly Tavar realised in the darkness that the walls fled… to the left and right.

"Here's the first cavern," he called to Seth and the others, not troubling to turn. His voice was soaked up by the darkness and by the absence of echoes, Seth knew that it was a vast cavern indeed.

Amos had managed well enough so far with Seth's occasional help, though he imagined shapes leering at him in the darkness. The faces of dogs in his mind left him wide-eyed with fright.

Without warning, a searing light filled the cavern and then died down to a soft glow, barely reaching the nearer walls. It was light from Tavar's staff. Their leader had seen enough to guide them now, with the help of the pale glimmer that remained, to a tunnel on the far side of the cavern.

The others had seen little in their surprise, half-blinded by the flash.

In like manner, they continued, now climbing steadily as they went. Through four more caverns they passed, some larger, some smaller, linked by the threading corridor, which Tavar found anew with sudden bursts of flame at each new cavern entrance. One tunnel they'd taken led to a dead-end some half a mile or so from its beginning, and they were forced to return, otherwise things went well.

Now, the men of the south took the brief moments of light from the staff to glance around them at the wondrous rocky roofs that teased them in the vaulted shadows above… sand textured roofs they were, with weird rock formations thrusting down, sometimes touching the floor as if resting after centuries of stretching to reach it. Random boulders were strewn in places around the rough walls. The bright light momentarily flashed back at them from veins of ore running through the silent rock. At times the rumour of running water reached them from some unguessed source.

Heg has remained unruffled, even at the first flash of light. He was used to it no doubt. The ponies too were not disturbed, obediently carrying their loads into the unseeing night of the mountain roots. Once or twice Heg, bright eyed and alert, took

Blizzard

to the air, launching himself from Tavar's shoulder in a swift, rippling of wings, soaring almost beyond their perception. Tavar recalled him...

"Not so flighty, Heg! Amos may have seen more than a daydream back there. Let's go with some caution at least."

In the narrow passages they nearly always travelled in darkness, conserving light for the caverns where they were in greatest need of guidance. But something was amiss. Tavar had become less sure of the path they were taking. They halted inside the entrance to the next cave.

"The earlier caverns were quite familiar to me," he said pensively. "Yet now I'm unsure. The last cave and this one feel quite alien to my senses, and they lead on downwards. We should rise steadily until we reach daylight, for I descended continually on my southward journey. We'll travel on a little further, but I fear we need to turn again and find the true route, or else we might be lost."

They entered one more cave and Tavar was at last convinced, for this smaller cavity showed no major exits... mere cracks in the rock walls were all.

"We must return, but first we must sleep. We'll need more energy, for we still must climb all the way, steadily but relentlessly."

They ate and settled. The ponies were impatient now. Tavar didn't heed his own advice. He comforted the animals while the others slept and he kept an eye out for any intruders.

When they restarted, they were anxious, for time was so precious. Amos was despairing of reaching their destination at all, let alone returning.

They retraced their way, ascending again where they'd come down in error. They soon came to the largest cavern.

"I know this one is right," said Tavar. "I remember its magnificence. There must be some other tunnel."

At the end of the passage, Tavar held his staff aloft and

summoned light. And he held it longer this time, as he surveyed the nearer walls for the exit they'd missed.

Amos gave a cry, pointing to the hole by which they'd first entered. There in the brilliant light shielding their eyes stood a dozen or more figures.

"The dog-men," he shrieked. "I told you, they *are* real."

"Dog-men is an apt name," cried Seth, for even at this distance they could make out the pale faces of these half-human forms. "And they look ready enough to fight. See, they draw their knives. They must have followed us. The one you saw, Amos must have raised the alarm. They come in pursuit."

"I fear you're right, Seth," said Tavar. "Dog-men indeed. They're, no doubt, products of evil, sentries posted to protect the northern realm. They belong to the 'Lord of the Icemere' sure enough. Illusions, but *fell* illusions. We were fortunate, if fortunate is the word, to pass them so easily. But they advance now. We must hurry. Look! There's the exit we want."

He pointed to their right and, with the staff still blazing, he leapt off in the direction of the new exit. Heg flurried into flight, squawking and screeching. The others stood dazed for a moment and then were following, the ponies led at a fast trot. But the distance was little further for the dog-men who'd spotted the intention of the intruders. They too hurried towards the escape route.

Tavar reached the gaping tunnel and turned. He could see that his companions would reach him too late. Sweeping forward towards the oncoming ogres, now he stood menacingly. Seth and the others noticed and sped ever more urgently towards the salvation offered by their exit. Footfalls sounded everywhere. Tavar's staff burst into brighter light. The dog-men checked, shielding their eyes again. It seemed they could travel in the darkness of the caverns with ease. The bright light of the staff only served to blind their sensitive night-eyes.

Now, the light of the wand dwindled again, flickering

hesitantly. Tavar's power was waning, but at last his companions had reached the tunnel mouth. He began to back away from their pursuers who now advanced again warily.

"No! Get back!" came Seth's cry.

A commotion broke out and Seth and the others retreated from their tunnel, back into the cavern. Tavar turned to see half-a-dozen dog-men issue from their intended path, curved knives brandished above their heads. From both sides now the dreadful creatures bore down on the man who they saw to be the leader of the travellers. Tavar was desperate, for the staff-light was at a low ebb and threatened to die. The leader of the main band, from the southern entrance was upon him. Those at the rear were closing. He thrust his staff forward, and a shower of burning sparks met the dog-man's face. It fell squealing horribly, then was gone. In the same instant, the foremost of the other party fell crying in agony. Some dark squawking thing clung to its face.

"Heg!" cried Tavar, and suddenly he was aware of what was needed. "They *are* illusions, of course, but the staff is spent. We must fight them with their own kind, and with this he held both arms aloft and called out in a speech unknown to his fellow travellers.

"*Hailé, Hailé, Valkanata Sil Tavar!*"

And with this, the air was full of wings. Seth and the others cowered against the rocky walls. In the shadows, Henry and Barny hung on to the frightened ponies and they all looked on, dumbstruck. In the dying light of the staff they could see shapes wheeling and turning, diving and flapping, clinging and tearing at the luminous dog-faces. The vast cavern echoed now with fluttering and wailing. Then mere echoes the commotion became, for the source had gone. The dog-men, illusions that they were, melted into the rock, as their false being was mortally extinguished. Their unexpected attackers too were gone, all except for one... Heg, who returned to his master fluttering with pride.

"We're safe, for the time being," sighed Tavar. "Our winged allies have seen to that. They're gone and we've found the right path again, though we must needs go carefully now, for we've no light to aid us. And we may yet find more of these vile apparitions."

"But if they're not real, then why fear them?" asked Barny as they entered the tunnel. "For illusions can't harm us."

You're wrong, Barny," said Tavar. "We must take them seriously, for the illusion is so strong, that even knowing them for what they are does not banish them from our minds. And, as you found out with the watch, such things can inflict a wound that to all intents is real, and remains so unless the deception itself is utterly destroyed. If these soldiers were to wound us and escape, we'd be inflicted with no hope of cure and that illness, however false, would be the end of us for we'd be unfit to overcome the difficulties of our journey."

Seth thought deeply on these words.

"Then could the Scar itself be such an illness?" he said at last. Is our quest simply to destroy the source... the evil source that's spread it so far?"

"Perhaps you're right, Seth," replied Tavar. "But I fear you're wrong, for it spreads from one to another without the presence of an individual manifestation. And remember Kelman. He died like many of his villagers of the disease. It has a deeper malevolence than any apparition *I've* ever encountered. Perhaps if the source itself were destroyed it would fail, but don't be misled. Have no doubt that it's deadly, for it creeps and festers ever increasing its grip. I fear the only hope is to place trust in the Ice Wolf and in the legends of the people who once travelled as we do now. We must take forward our search for the Ice Wolf, on the plateau."

"Then could these soldiers not be the Ice Wolves, for dogs they are?" insisted Seth, not entirely convinced by the words of the mage.

"And, if they *were*," said Tavar, "how would you put them to your use?... for once any wound be inflicted, they'd disappear before your eyes, and with them, your cure. No, this Ice Wolf, he'll be a reality, not a deception, of that I'm convinced, and we must hunt him accordingly."

They followed Tavar into the new darkness, still confused by this strange world of contrasts, of stark realities and scarcely believable happenings conjured from nowhere.

Seth wondered if it wasn't all a peculiar dream... Kelman, the Scar, the journey, Tavar and all. But it was all too real, he knew that in his aching heart, and the journey was all too necessary.

Tavar said little now in the monotonous darkness. Still he called now and then to Seth at the rear, but he said no more, seeming deep in thought. From his earlier words, Seth knew that Tavar had been reluctant to leave the comparative shelter of Sharfell, for he and his kinsmen there had always avoided contact with the evil that Kaan and others had unleashed. Seth now wondered if Tavar was trying to avoid a confrontation with the Ice Lord, preferring to think that the Ice Wolf had nothing to do with such a bane... avoiding confrontation through old habit rather than through wisdom maybe. Yet even with this seed of doubt, Seth trusted Tavar. After all, without him could they have come this far?

If any other dog-men had infested the caves ahead of them, then they'd fled or disappeared into thin air. But the Ice Lord reminded them of his presence with repeated poundings that even the travellers were beginning to accept as normal. Amos alone was badly troubled, but they passed without further incident through the remaining chain of caves. It still proved to be some distance however and they rested for sleep once more before they passed through the last remaining cave. Upwards they climbed until they reached the slanting shaft that Tavar had told of… but there was no light. They'd lost all sense of time underground. Amos had slowed them and with the wrong turn that they'd taken, they'd been underground for nearly three days.

"Stars," said Tavar, pointing to the upper end of the dark shaft before them. "No snow storms for the present, but we'd do well to wait for daylight. It'll be cold enough, even then."

"Anyone would think it was warm down here to hear *him* talk," Barny whispered to his pony, nudging him playfully. "Still, I guess he's right, but you'll be looking for food as soon as were up and in the open, eh."

So there they settled, eating what they dared. Still without fire, they put on the thickest clothes they had, hoping to keep in the body heats of their trek through the catacombs. They were all too aware that the snowy terrain awaiting them could prove deadly should they need to travel it for long. They hoped to reach the trees as soon as may be for fire fuel, for shelter and for more food too.

Mercifully, daylight soon crept into the shaft. Anxious to be out in the open, they made their way steadily along its length until they reached a platform at the mouth of the rocks. As they'd climbed, the light in their eyes had increased, pace by pace, and so they avoided being stung by the brightness of the new day.

CHAPTER TWELVE

Icemere

A fresh, icy cold morning greeted them and they stood on the platform beneath the outcropped roof of rock that formed a canopy over their heads.

The sight before them was breath-taking. Even Tavar, who'd seen it before the snows came long ages ago, sighed with disbelief at the stark beauty of the scene below.

Everywhere under the pale, distant blue sky was white and silent. No birds sang, no water ran. Before them, the snow had drifted waste deep in a wide arc. The land fell away gently onto a winding, downward path which passed between gnarled bushes clumped here and there. Down and down the path wandered, merging into the carpet of whiteness. Their eyes lost the path on a vast flat plain, for the most part tree covered and everywhere snow covered. Beyond the plain, on all three sides, the land dropped again. This was the plateau of the Icewood. Their hearts froze as they came to this realisation.

As they stood in wonder, the hint of wind that reached them from below carried the smell of evil… a sweet smell, vague yet sickly.

Thankful at least for daylight, they crossed the drift and silently began to file uncomfortably down towards the plain at Tavar's bidding.

"We're here," he said at length. "The plateau. It's bleak, but things could be worse. We may yet see more snow fall, for how long we must search, time alone may tell, and what weather time will bring we shall see."

"This quiet. This stillness is unnerving," Seth mumbled, as if struggling to come to grips with a new challenge.

"There are no creatures living here, surely," he said. "No sign even of the dog-men. It'll be a long search and with food as low as it is we'll be hard pushed to achieve anything at all. We'll pine more gravely than the ponies unless we find something to hunt.

"It's disheartening indeed, Seth," said Tavar with a sigh. "But the wolves wouldn't be out here in the open. They'd use the shelter of the trees and they'd need water. Up here everything is frozen. In the lower, sheltered places there would be less ice. The lake that is now called the Icemere is amid the trees down there, though I don't doubt that it too is frozen. We shall see."

There was a hint of reluctance in these words, for Tavar knew that a quest to the lake would bring them to the threshold of evil.

"If there's any prey at all," he went on, "it'll be down among the trees and that's where we must search for ours. As for the dog-men… if there are none here, all the better, but don't be taken in, for illusions leave no footprints, even in this *snow*. They could be near for all we know."

The others glanced suspiciously about them as if expecting to see enemies on all sides, but the silence and desolation persisted. On they trekked, unsure of their final destination. They'd completed the journey, yet they'd only just begun it. The smell of evil had lessened and that at least was welcome. They'd reached the plain now and the tall frosty shapes of trees floated silently past as they made their way into the shadowy heart of the woods. Some of the trees were mere dead shells, long since mortified by the cold. Others lived, apparently thriving on the cold, others clinging to life desperately in the hope of summer, but all of them were still and snowclad.

No wind stirred now. The footfalls of the companions were crisp, hardly audible even in the silence and cold breath hung on the cold air. As they went on past midday they were deep in darkening woodland. Paths were still easy to find and the fresh snow underfoot was thinner, yielding to sparse undergrowth.

"About time too," said Barny. "Now we can rest and give the ponies a chance to eat. They've had precious little and we don't deserve their patience."

The vegetation was of grasses and ferns. The ponies shunned the ferns but relished the tufts of grass, icy though they were.

When the tremors came now, the trees shuddered into life for a few seconds, shaking off much of their snowy mantle and then all was still and silent again.

As they travelled on and evening drew near, a wind sprang up from the north-east and the sky clouded over, promising a little warmth. A mist began to drift about them, and soon it was a dense fog, clinging dank to eyebrows and beards.

The trees, looming unexpectedly now, appeared white again. Sparkling frost was thickening upon them. The sun was sinking fast, hidden by the cloud. The light was fading and a westering red disc appeared through the trees to their left for a fleeting moment. For that instant, the woods were tinged blood red, then shadows fell.

Tavar had sent Heg aloft in search of wolves, hoping he may find some sign of life more easily than they who were earthbound. He'd winged on high for much of the day and now swooped earthwards with the dying of the sun, eyeing out the travellers and settling on Tavar's shoulder, screeching shrilly for a moment.

"He's seen nothing," declared Tavar to the eager faces around him.

"We must make camp then," said Seth, downcast. "And a fire if we may."

They chose the relative shelter of a brake of bushes akin to hazel, but evergreen it seemed for they still bore leaves in this wintery clime. The bushes afforded drier ground too. A fire was kindled with much patience from Henry and was promptly extinguished by a fall of snow from lofty branches somewhere above them. The resultant hiss was accompanied by enthusiastic curses from Barny, who'd just begun to feel warmth returning to his numbed limbs. Tavar saved Henry from expending further efforts with a reluctant burst of flame from his staff, replenished now as it was. Barny jumped back in surprise, eyebrows near to singeing.

Amos slumped dejectedly beside the fire. The ponies grazed nearby, oblivious to the thoughts that enveloped the men. Tavar kept first watch and carefully tended the fire, drying fuel as he could. Heg accompanied him, settling in the lower, dead branches of a nearby fir. Soft tremors punctuated the silences often.

The fog dissolved and when the cold dawn came, they saw that the sky was clearing again. The wind had shifted to the north and it brought with it an icy blast. The fire fell to embers and they were anxious to move on and to stir aching limbs into warmth again.

The cold bit ever more cruelly. They shivered and chattered and they despaired. On they must go into oblivion. The spirit of the mainlanders was all but broken at the lessening prospect of finding what they'd come for.

Tavar grieved also, for even *he* in truth held fading hopes of finding the Wolf now.

"We near the Icemere. I sense it," he called as he helped load the ponies. "The tremors feel deeply rooted here, as we're standing on their source. And listen… there's a faint thrumming behind it."

Sure enough, an undulating drone could be made out on the edge of hearing. They quailed at this realisation of the nearness of evil.

Seth had never thought that he'd be glad to hear the dreadful cry of a wolf, but now he wished with all his heart for a hundred such voices to fill his ears. He palmed his fist in fresh resolve and, gritting his teeth, he shouldered a pack and called to the others.

"Let's be away," he shouted as cheerily as he could. "Today we shall find the wolves."

But his words fell cold and hollow. Amos was weakening ever more and he struggled to keep up the pace, soon forcing them to slow down. Henry and Seth supported him, whilst Barny took charge of both the ponies. Tavar marched in front, still hoping for some sign, some clue. Heg flew aloft now and then in renewed searching.

Amos began to call out at times, eyes wide, clawing at the air... at unseen attackers.

"Get away," he'd scream. "Leave me be, you cursed things."

Then he'd fall silent again as if in a deep trance as he stumbled on. He was suffering more than Kelman had by far. They'd progressed little that day, but they'd reached the Icemere by dusk. A flat expanse of snow-laden ice lay before them in the deepening night. The trees failed close to its shores, condescending to leave a wide path skirting its bleak edges.

To the north side lay a hilly terrain, tree clad, black and brooding in the darkening gloom... the only hilly place in all the plateau. Tavar was ill at ease.

"I don't remember this landscape," he insisted, shaking his head wistfully. "And the droning... it's louder now."

They camped again in the shelter of the trees close to bushes. Tavar did what he could to ease the fever for Amos. He brewed a potion with herbs from a pouch that he'd brought from Sharfell. Amos drank, and soon fell to uneasy sleep by the fire.

"And where now, Tavar?" enquired Seth, warming his hands in the glow of the fire.

"We'll skirt the Mere," answered Tavar. "Perhaps we'll find something now we're near the lake."

"I hope so," said Seth. "Amos will go little further, I fear, and the cold bites us so. Our food's desperately low and there's nothing here to hunt. Nothing but the prospect of Ice Wolf, and *they* lead us a merry chase, sure enough."

"But there *are* things here to eat, if we're desperate enough, Seth. Food is the least of our worries, for the smell of evil has returned, stronger than before... sweeter and more sickly. Don't you perceive its reek?"

Seth nodded, nostrils flared.

The cold had gripped them deeper as the day had worn on and they were suffering gravely.

Something told Tavar that the lighting of a fire may be dangerous, but they'd perish without it. If they stayed much longer here they'd likely perish, even *with* it. And now, the frost bit their fingers and toes to the point of agony as they gleaned what they could from the fire.

Tavar didn't sleep that night. With Heg upon his shoulder, he sat staring thoughtfully into the darkness, his back to the fire which cast his long shadow towards the hill that lay beyond the ice.

By the following night, they'd travelled around the west side of the lake to its northern extreme. As they travelled, they'd perceived that the hilly mass, which appeared to watch their progress, was in fact an island... far nearer to the northern shores of the lake than to the south. It had also appeared much larger in the brittle daylight, though it *was* indeed at least two miles or more across. And now it was behind them. Here it was only a hundred paces from the shore.

Tavar agreed reluctantly that they should make camp, for the sake of Amos. The mage was even more uneasy now. He insisted that two watched and that *he* would be one of those at all times.

"No. *You* need rest," Seth insisted. "Henry and I shall take first turn."

"You are thoughtful, Seth," answered Tavar, wearily, yet doggedly. "I need sleep rather less than you. Let Barny watch with *me* first. He will be grateful for an uninterrupted sleep afterwards. *You* can follow Henry in the early hours."

Seth submitted to this demand, for demand he knew it was and nothing would change Tavar's mind.

The droning continued as Seth drifted into sleep. Yet he didn't drift contented, for he knew that their quest was failing. Exhaustion was all that found *him* sleeping deep.

Amos slept fitfully under shelter of bushes, feverish, crying out often.

Seth was woken by Henry and took his shift with Tavar. The night dragged on ever more endlessly, Tavar still deep in thought, Seth grieving as he tended Amos in his fits of fever.

"The wolves!" cried Seth's stricken companion. "I hear them! Listen! Listen!"

But Seth, tears in his eyes for his friend's pathetic state, as much as he longed to hear the wolves, could hear nothing but the terrible droning. He turned to Tavar, bereft of hope.

"There *is* no Wolf," he cried. "There *is* no cure."

And he wept openly.

"That, I do not know," said Tavar. "But think, Seth... there's something else. There have been no tremors since we camped here. This night has been free of *that* rumour of evil at least. Yet it means something... something ill I fear. There's evil closer than ever. The stench of it is all about us."

And as he said this, Heg flapped skywards, squawking and squealing. The ponies took flight, breaking their tethers, but in the wood they checked. Henry and Barny shambled into wakefulness and all except Amos, who laid delirious, cried out in one voice.

There on the nearest shore of the island stood a man in the half-light of the crescent moon. But it was no natural man. A glimmering, purple halo surrounded the figure. It approached them and as it came they saw that the glow was from its flowing robe. The head was bone, flesh, straggling hair and little more, lurid and deathly. The men of the south heaved as they caught a new, deathly smell and as the figure glided over the snow covered ice with a ghostly swishing sound it grew in their eyes until it towered almost ten feet tall. The humming was all around them now. They all cowered, backing to the fire... *all* that is except Tavar, who stood staff in hand, resolved to face this thing he'd hoped to avoid. Heg bravely re-joined him from the blackness of the night.

"So, *you* are the 'Lord of the Icemere'," Tavar mocked.

Seth and the others stood amazed at his composure, for they knew that he'd no wish to meet with the thing that came out of Dunbeck. Yet it was his fate. There was no turning away.

"I *am* the Lord of this place," it sighed, its thin voice almost floating away before it reached them. "And the Lord of other places I shall become in time. The ice will spread, my friend, and all shall be mine."

Tavar flinched at this reply but continued.

"And why are you not content with your own kingdom. Why must you seek to destroy those who don't concern themselves with you?"

The creature breathed its response.

"For many years you've hidden from me, man of Dunbeck. But long ago you *did* concern yourself with me. Before you knew my strength. Before I showed myself..."

"Before I knew the evil that you are," insisted Tavar, interrupting. "And if you have quarrel with *me*, then you've none with these others here, yet they and their fellows of the southlands are dying... dying because of your foul probings. They're stricken with disease which surely stems from you."

"Does it not then also stem from *you*?"

The voice now mocked Tavar. The fell being paused as if thinking for a moment and then went on, in a suspicious tone.

"But the pestilence spreads further than I intended if it has escaped the land of Icelar. Yet why do you come here? Are you intent on seeking your revenge?"

"Some do not dwell on revenge, Lord of Death. Some merely

look to their own wellbeing. We're here to seek a cure and nothing more."

Tavar's mind was swimming now, he battling to keep his wits, for the being before him was all evil itself, yet now it talked almost musically, enchanting those who listened.

"And what is the nature of this cure you seek?" the evil being crooned.

"The Ice Wolf is all we ask," cried Seth, rushing forward willingly to Tavar's side, encouraged by the prospect of some clue as to finding it. "But we can't find it, if we don't hear..."

Tavar seized his arm and checked him.

"Don't speak with it," he whispered.

Seth stood bewildered.

"The Ice Wolf?" droned the Ice Lord. "I doubt if it will deal you any good, for *I* know no virtue in it. But should you crave no more than that, then we are well met for I can lead you to it. It lives upon this very island and you're welcome to take it for what you will, for I have no quarrel with the southlands. Come now, I shall show you."

Seth had submitted and moved to follow the Ice Lord willingly, for he was overjoyed to hear these words. Henry and Barny moved to follow him.

"No! No!" screamed Tavar. "He tricks you."

For a moment the spell was broken. Tavar, to the surprise of the others, burst into a loud commanding chant in some strange tongue akin to that which he'd used to thwart the dog-men in the caverns.

"*Hailé, Hailé, Elnataia! Hen Selnar. Hailé, Elnataia Sil Tavar Belador.*"

Heg perched restlessly now, having shifted to the forearm that held the staff. At the word *'Belador'*, Tavar flung his arms wide unaware of Heg who flew upwards into the nearby trees. The staff burst with blinding light, more bright than before and the air filled with a ringing. But it was the ring of evil's laughter.

Seth looked on in disbelief.

'Surely Tavar will throw away the only real hope we have,' Seth thought, looking on in disbelief.

"You play with fire, master mage," roared the Ice Lord contemptuously. "But there's no fire to melt *this* ice. And your words are empty too."

The evil thing taunted Tavar thus then, turning to Seth and the others, resumed its melodic tones and the spell was woven afresh. Tavar's three friends were lost to its calls. Amos lay suffering by the fire.

"Let my servants show you the way, men of the southlands. This Tavar would have it otherwise, to your undoing."

Tavar glanced behind him. In the shadows of the trees he saw them... dog-men. They'd appeared from thin air and were drifting eerily towards them. Tavar was desperate now. He'd summoned his incantation from the depths of his memory... from those days when he'd use the words without thinking. And he'd shaped them now, or so he thought, to combat the dark cloud that had overshadowed him all these years. But all seemed lost. Here was the end of their road, for he'd failed. His mind raced as the dog-men moved in. He glimpsed the Ice Lord turning and the three men were following. The droning grew again and among all this the voice of Amos reached him, screaming out.

"The Wolf! The Ice Wolf! It's here. Listen! Look!"

Tavar turned to see Amos clawing desperately at the bushes, trying to rise.

'Even Amos would follow,' thought Tavar.

But Amos didn't follow. Wide eyed, and laughing madly now, he stumbled back into the snows around him. The frail, brittle branches of the bushes snapped as he clutched at them. He fell, and was dead.

Tavar's mind returned to its panic and then he remembered.

"Metal. I need metal," he whispered to himself. His eyes darted here and there. Then he spied a hoof-pick at Barny's belt and, as the farrier passed him following Seth and Henry, he snatched the hoof-pick free of the belt and again he chanted.

"Hailé, Hailé, Elnataia! Hen Selnar..."

Now, the dog-men were clawing at him from behind and Tavar felt hot pangs of deadly pain in his shoulders.

"Hailé, Elnataia Sil Tavar! Belador," he continued in agony and this time, as the staff in his left hand burst once more into flame, he sent the hoof-pick winging. It found its mark and a searing flash of light stung Tavar and his companions. They were flung to the ground violently.

Recovering, Tavar stood up and looked around him. Where the Ice Lord had stood, there was nothing. Nothing but a wide circle of steaming water where ice and snow had been. The droning had died. The dog-men were gone without trace and with their disappearance Tavar knew the pains would go. He dropped to his knees, taking support from his staff and he wept, exhausted. The cloud had gone from his mind.

Seth, Barny and Henry got to their feet and stood reeling from the shock and recovering from the spell. Seth saw Amos, still and cold, the twigs still tight in his grasp.

"You fool," he sobbed angrily. "You fool, Tavar. You've *destroyed* our only chance. We're lost and you're to blame."

Seth knelt beside Amos and taking the twigs threw them to the ground. He clasped the hand that had held them.

Tavar now knelt beside them both. He too was stricken with grief, despite the failing of his false wounds and the riddance of the 'Lord of the Icemere'.

"No, Seth. We had no chance with him. He was evil to the core and he had no heart for you or Myre Hamlet. We must search on."

He spoke with sensitivity, for he knew that Seth was blinded by despair. He bowed his head and then as if some change came over him, he smiled.

"Seth!" he called out in joy. "We've been *given* our only chance… look!"

As he spoke, he gathered the scattered twigs and handed them eagerly to Seth.

"Amos was right. The Ice Wolf *is* here. See, he's found it for us."

Sure enough, as Seth looked at the bundle of leafy twigs, he saw what Amos, and then Tavar, had seen.

"The leaves! Their shape! The head of a wolf!" Seth called out.

He wept again, with joy at their find, but with grief for Amos and for a moment a hope welled in him that Amos might even now recover from the Scar and from his deathly sleep. But it wasn't to be. Amos was gone and the Scar was real. Barny too was still in its grip.

"The Scar is no illusion, then," he said, gravely. "We'll need the Ice Wolf, shall we not? All except those who've perished."

They were confused now, between joy and grief, and Barny tried to lift them.

"And I'll need a new hoof-pick, thank you very much."

They smiled at his gesture.

"Then let's find you one… in Sharfell," mused Tavar. "Let's be away from this dreadful place. It may be many a day before this starving cold will depart, I fear. The ice is still our enemy. Look… the sky broods with the threat of more snow. Let's make all haste back to the shelter of the caves in the mountains. With speed, we'll be there by tomorrow night."

"But, Tavar," protested Seth. "You forget that we must say farewell to Amos."

He faltered, holding back his emotions.

"And more important, we must gather the leaves of the Wolf."

"What of Barny," said Henry. "Shouldn't we try a potion as

soon as may be?"

"Forgive me," Tavar offered. "I'm forgetting all dignity in my haste, but the place still smells of evil. I'm not sure we're rid of all its ills, even now."

Seth smiled wistfully, plucking more leafy branches from the bushes at hand.

"*This* is the smell of evil," he laughed. "The Wolf has an ill breath, for sure."

"You're right. It was under our noses all the time," Barny quipped.

"Very well, Barny. See if you can strike fresh fire," instructed Tavar, now more at ease. "I'll prepare a potion for you, but I'll need hot water before I can do much."

Barny was unsure which may prove worse, the Scar or the attempting of a cure, but on reflection decided the fire would be necessary.

"Don't worry," Tavar assured him. "I can tell a poison plant easily enough by now, and so can the ponies. Look… they seem happy enough with this one."

Sure enough, the ponies were eating mouthfuls of the Wolf leaves with good appetite.

They couldn't dig a proper grave for Amos, for the icy ground was solid, and they had no proper tools to aid them. Assured now that the source of evil was gone, they took him across the ice to the hilly island. There, they raised a mound of loose stones and said what they found in their hearts in farewell to their friend.

They returned to the camp downcast, but soon the warmth of Barny's fire and the smell of a cooking pot raised them. The southerners had found a small ration of dried and salted meat in the packs to add to a brew of leaves and roots hacked from their icy beds. Their meal though hot was meagre and rather tasteless, yet it was welcome enough.

A potion was soon prepared from the now odourless Wolf

leaves and given to Barny who grimaced at the acrid taste, much to the amusement of his companions.

Soon after noon, they broke camp and made ready to return south. They'd gathered a plentiful supply of the Ice Wolf, tearing leaves from branches and packing them safely. Seth was still reluctant to leave... the cure had not been proved, for Barny showed no early sign of change, but Tavar convinced him that he would with certainty in time, saying...

"Surely, there's no other Ice Wolf, and if this one fails then you're lost, even if we wait here through all the season."

So Seth conceded, and by nightfall they were clear of the southern shore of the Mere and they camped once more on the ice plain.

The next day dawned clear and still. The threatening snow clouds had disappeared and soon the sun greeted them, peering over the mountains before them. But they hardly noticed its friendly face, for as they walked, they glanced about them, perceiving a wonderful thing. The snow that had shrouded this place for so many years was melting. Spring was unfolding before their eyes. They could feel warmth flowing back to their bodies, as it was to the earth about them.

Tavar, more than Henry and the men of Myre Hamlet, was overwhelmed by the change. Too overjoyed at first to speak, he stood and watched the picture before him filling with the rich colours of a season that had lain trapped so long. The dream, the memory of things long since passed was turning to reality.

"The spell is clearly broken," he said at last, arms spread to welcome the new dawn. "Surely, all Icelar is freed of its ice, and its evil."

Heg was already high aloft, wheeling and circling excitedly in the clear upper airs.

Only now, with these word from Tavar did Seth, Barny and Henry fully realise what weight had been lifted from Tavar's mind after these many years of sharing the guilt for the malevolent oppression which the Bane of Dunbeck had spread over the land... a land which Tavar remembered as fair, a land which now lived again.

As they travelled on through the day, the clear welcome trickle of icy waters around them grew to chattering that reminded Seth at once of the Puddle Stream and his mind raced away to summer in the Hamlet... Sarah dressed in breezy garments, with flowers laced in her hair and Ruffles, playful in the Puddle Stream, loping here and there, concerned with some elusive scent. But the Scar was there too. Icelar was rid of evil now, but not so the Hamlet... not yet, for the distance between Myre Hamlet and the Ice Wolf was great, the evil-smelling Ice Wolf still had its job to do.

They were climbing now, towards the mountain caves and Seth thought on the Ice Wolf... on the uncertainty of its survival on the homeward journey, and on concern that there be enough for their needs.

The sickly smell drifted strong again.

"Of course," said Tavar. "The smell of evil we sensed when we came by here... it was in truth the Ice Wolf... so near to the caves."

"Then we could have avoided the Mere and it's foul Lord," said Barny.

"Just so," agreed Seth. "But it's good that we didn't recognise it here, for the spring we now see might never have been."

"But Amos might have lived," added Barny, dejectedly. "Without these extra days of cold and with a draught or so of Tavar's potion."

Perhaps," agreed Seth, "but I fear Amos was too far taken to have survived, even with that aid. It's ironic that the Ice Wolf may never have been found without the final suffering of Amos. Anyway, I've been thinking, and I feel sure we're in luck at last. We may need more of the plant and here we find it in plenty."

And so they gathered more sprigs and leaves. But Seth, thinking yet further ahead, took a dagger and dug out several young plants complete with their roots and clods of soil. These he carefully wrapped in moss, plucked from the banks of a nearby thawing stream then in skins from the packs. These in turn he also packed with the leaves.

'They have a chance of surviving at least,' he thought. *'If we can keep them moist now.'*

The sun was westering and, before it sank beyond view, it settled in a long, distant streak of cloud, its dying fiery rays flooding across the western lowlands in a promise of return.

"We must say goodbye to this newfound sun for a day or so," Tavar reminded them.

They'd reached the mouth of the caves. The threshold was now clear of snow, but all of them wondered if the labyrinth really would be clear of dog-men.

Seth turned to gaze for one final time at the plateau of the Icewood. The snows were rapidly yielding to patches of vegetation, strangely green despite being deprived of the light for so long. The trees were showing more of their natural form in the gathering gloom. His companions glance too, with conflicting emotions.

"Farewell, Amos," called Seth. "Perhaps your new home will at least now be cheerier than it might have been."

With heads bowed, they left the open airs.

CHAPTER THIRTEEN

Sharfell

It was the afternoon of the twelfth of July when they emerged from the tunnel of Sharfell on their return from the Icemere. The tunnel had sheltered them for a few moments from the blistering attentions of the summer sun. The four weary travellers welcomed the gate guard, the doleful creaking and the bell-like clanging of the iron gates echoing deeply down the tunnel behind them. They were back in the refuge of the mountain stronghold. Though weary, they were in high spirits for they'd had a fair journey back south.

Perhaps 'refuge' was no longer necessary for the great burden of evil had gone. Fears of dog-men in the caves had been dispelled, though Tavar's staff had been fully spent... the destruction of the evil had taken most all of its potency and they'd laboured in long spells of darkness in returning. But Tavar's memory had been refreshed, and he'd led them well.

When they'd emerged from the caves, all sign of the snows had gone, and though the ground was boggy, their progress was much easier. The skies had been overcast for a while, but summer had returned.

"All Icelar is released," Tavar had declared joyously. "I feel the heat of the sun, even though he hides his face."

Their only real difficulty as they'd returned was a consequence of the coming of summer. The snows in the upper reaches too were melting and the river they'd crossed below the waterfall was rising to a deeper torrent again, as the wealth of water raced to find the sea. Thankfully, they'd left their rope across the waters and this proved good fortune for they'd not have crossed by the stones without it unless they'd waited for the waters to subside. Indeed, the waters had still been rising when they'd fought their way across. Much of the gear was saturated and the ponies of course were a problem, for they took to swimming rather than stepping and more than once they were on the brink of being swept away. But with great resolve and newfound strength in their triumph, they'd all finally clambered onto the southern bank.

The food had been sparse, even before they'd left the plateau, but soon the wild had offered them enough, and their goal of a trusted place had served to steel them on their way. When they'd surfaced from the caves, the sun had brought a new hope and hunting came good with it. The ponies were a worry and had to be watched, for the last thing they wanted was colic from the new grasses.

Barny had persisted with the medicine and by the end of the first week the signs of the Scar were retreating. The depression that had been building in him lifted, yet Seth more than anyone was elated by the abatement, for *he* saw its import to the Hamlet more than anyone did.

"We've done it!" he'd shouted jubilantly. "The Hamlet will be safe. There's no more evil now..."

But with these last words, his voice had faltered as he remembered Amos. For Amos wouldn't hear his voice. And Kelman... Kelman couldn't know the lifting of the curse.

'How many others?' thought Seth, *'before we can bring aid.'*

Yet he'd come, with the passing of days, to accept their losses, for at least they'd not been in vain.

The weather too had lifted their spirits high again for when eventually they'd re-joined the hilly lands the sullen clouds, which had shed heavy rains more than once, had drifted away inland.

Now, they knew it was summer, like to the better summers of the Hamlet... summer such that Tavar had seen beyond Sharfell only in the distant past. And with smiles they were all spurred on to the needed rest ahead.

Now that they'd reached Sharfell, Barny had little of the

disfigurement on him.

Henry was happy for his friends of Midvale, for they'd shaken off a great burden, and he was happy to have aided them. Despite their initial trickery, he'd come to love and respect them dearly.

Tavar, after affording himself great joy, had adopted once again his austere manner, though his companions still perceived the relief. He'd carried the weight of his early part in the spawning of the evil for long ages. His spirit had slowly failed in years of hiding... hiding from his destiny. But now, full dignity could return for he'd fought against his apathy and vanquished the internal foe. He'd achieved that which he'd thought upon for many years... the destruction of the evil of Dunbeck.

Heg flew to greet Tavar, a mass of feathers and talons. He'd left the men when they journeyed underground, re-joining them in the hills near the southern mouth. He'd then travelled with them until they'd reached the ravine. Then, at Tavar's bidding, he'd flown ahead to tell of their return and so they were expected, though the joyous news was still to tell to Tavar's gathering kinsmen. One such, Elmar, greeted them inside the gates as they entered the rocky circle.

"We'd guessed great things were afoot with the ceasing of the throbbing and the changing of the weather," he enthused, after listening to Tavar's hurried account of the recent events. "We were all hopeful, yet we daren't think for sure that the evil had passed. And now we must celebrate the destruction of the Ice Lord. The thwarting of the evil thing that's seized those of Ironmound and you others."

"But for now, we must rest," said Tavar.

And so it was that the small band of pilgrims found themselves back in the haven of Sharfell.

The ponies were relieved of their burdens at Elmar's bidding by some of the mysterious folk here in the mountains. The travellers took the packs to Tavar's dwelling on the far side of the settlement. Once over the threshold, Seth laid carefully to one side those packs which held their precious pickings. The wood fire no longer burned in the grate.

"Kaleb! Abe! Ely!" called out Seth, for there by the fire-hole were the men they'd left behind.

They'd preferred to meet those returning here, rather than in the light of day, for they feared discouraging news. And in one respect, they were right for Amos wasn't with them.

"We found it! We found the Ice Wolf," Seth went on.

And they embraced, happy for this, yet Seth with heavy heart for Amos.

"And where's Will?" said Seth, for a moment fearing ill news.

"Don't fear," said Elmar, who'd followed them in with Tavar. "He's at the stable-house. He insisted on being there, even though he heard you coming. He seems to have found interest there these last few weeks."

"But Will never was one for horses?" grinned Barny. "And now he prefers them to us? After we've been travelling too. Bless me! Folk are odd, for sure. He'll want to be a farrier next, I'll be bound."

They all shared his joke, not least Elmar who added, "I fear you're right, Barny Hensman, for he insisted that you join him there straightway."

Barny scratched his head, still beaming and clapping his hands on his thighs. He went eagerly to find his absent friend. But those present who'd stayed in Sharfell returned to their quiet, apprehensive mood.

"And what of Amos?" asked Ely, sensing enough to expect an ill reply.

"He's gone," Seth said, spelling out the news that he'd carried back from the Icewood. "He died in the end of the Scar, before the Ice Wolf could help him. And yet it was *he* who found it for us… a plant of all things, growing amid the northern snows."

"Yet we can be sure now that this plant has virtue, for Barny was showing signs on the northbound trek, yet is almost cured now. The potion that Tavar produced from the leaves has seen to that. Henry and I haven't suffered its attentions. How are you faring here?"

"Its progress has been checked but little, despite the attentions of the learned healers here in Sharfell," explained Kaleb who, out here away from the Hamlet, seemed less taciturn of mood.

"Yes," added Abe Arden. "*I've* learned much of medicines of all kinds here, yet this thing holds a secret even from Tavar's kinsmen. But at least now it seems we can be rid of its evil.

"Well," said Henry, trying to break the sombre mood, "we've much to tell you of our journey north and you, no doubt, have much to tell *us* too. But first I fear we need rest. Perhaps this evening, when we've bathed away some of our aches and pains."

"I know just how you feel," said Ely, dejectedly, for the news of the death of his dear friend had hit him badly. He recalled his return from the shores of Greylar… a return without some of the friends who'd started out with him. Now, friends come back here without his own companion on that first trip. He bitterly regretted not travelling on to Icelar this time with Amos and the others, but he'd needed rest badly and he knew, despite his sadness, he was better for it.

"Yes. You travellers must all rest," said Elmar. "There are tubs prepared all ready for you and when you've rested here the afternoon, you'll surely feel more able to talk of your northern deeds. I wait eagerly, for *I* myself am anxious to learn more of the destruction of the Ice Lord."

"Look," cried Kaleb, in a fit of laughter, unusual for him. The company turned to see Tavar, exhausted, spread-eagled and snoring in one of the wooden chairs against the further wall.

Barny leapt at Will Sparrow and with one gesture slapped him on the back. He hugged the pony which Will was tending.

"Birdie! it's Little 'Un," he cried. holding back tears of joy.

"Well, I'll be... How on earth...?"

Beyond this, he was lost for words. Will smiled and explained.

"He turned up at the gate after you'd left with Tavar. The Ironmounders never found him, or if they did, they certainly didn't catch him. But how he found his way up here, I'll never know. Perhaps he sensed the other ponies here. Anyway, he was well enough when he turned up. He still had the full packs on his back too, though the contents had suffered in his freedom."

Barny rubbed the pony's neck and flank, and fed him a handful of oats from the nearby tub.

"Well, I'll be..." he repeated.

When early evening came they ate an ample, yet simple, meal of bread and cheese, oatcakes, early fruits and stored nuts, and fresh milk from the goats. This was followed by mead as sweet and fresh as the milk. They wished that the potions Tavar had prepared for them earlier had been as inviting. They were gladdened too to find that Elmar had produced tobacco despite their understanding that there was none to be had in Sharfell. Then the stories were told... of the caves and the dog-men, of the snow and ice, of the trickery of the 'Lord of the Icemere', and of the desperate throwing of the hoof-hook, of the finding of the Ice Wolf and the return through empty caves and across swollen waters... the heartbreak and the joy.

Those who'd stayed, told of the delight of resting in Sharfell, of the beauty the others has merely sampled in the valley nearby, and of the sudden uplifting of the weather even in this fair clime.

Elmar insisted upon his earlier suggestion, "You must all stay longer and shake off well your weariness, and we'll arrange a celebration the like that Sharfell has never seen, such that we might have seen in the days of Dunbeck, before our fleeing."

Seth was prevented from expressing his concern at the suggestion of such a delay.

Tavar voiced his sentiments for him, "Though your intention is well founded Elmar, my friend, I fear you forget that our visitors from the southlands are still upon their quest. Even now, they think to make haste back to their ailing families and friends. Urgency must still plague them until they've returned home and rid their homeland of the Scar of the Icewood… the Bane of Dunbeck. And as for celebrations? I'm not sure what you have in mind, but if I guess aright, then I'm doubting of its wisdom. With the 'Lord of the Icemere' destroyed, I feel a great joy and perhaps one day we may even return to Dunbeck and Icelar will be known as Hilar once more. But before that time, we must meet with the men of Ironmound and do all we can to rid *them* of illness, for was it not we who brought the Bane upon them? A small share of Seth's treasured leaves and plants should be enough to put things right."

"You're welcome," assured Seth. "We owed a lot to Kelman in the end and he'd have wished his people well, despite their cruelty to him. And all we'd ask in return is knowledge of your herb-lore, for we'll need it."

"Abe has already learned much," Elmar assured them, "and Tavar will ensure he knows what more he needs to know."

"We've learned much of healing and bodily preservation," continued Tavar, acknowledging Seth's gesture with a smile and a raised hand. "And that's good, but even with that knowledge, it's taken ordinary men, with faith in their hearts to find it in us to help cure our terrible error all those years ago."

He paused, deep in thought.

"Yes," he went on, "the knowledge of healing is good, but much of our magic must stay unused for, even guarded, it would surely trick us again. Evil would blossom afresh behind our backs. And so, Elmar, we must allow no shapeshifting here, no illusions as of old, for our friends have seen enough of them."

"You're wise indeed, Tavar," Elmar answered after a thoughtful silence. "Though magic may have good intent, it's seemingly too strong even for those well versed in its practice. The spells of old must lie unused and buried forever. But the mage-light of the staffs? This we use even today. Surely a celebration of light after darkness would be both safe and fitting."

"Very well," smiled Tavar. "There's little harm in *that*, for it's a simple deception, not akin to those of the body. So be it. A celebration of light. But it must be soon, for time brooks no delay."

"Tomorrow then," said Elmar. "When the sun has fallen. And the day after, all will be free to depart as need demands.

"Elmar will accompany you when you leave us," said Tavar, "and you'll have ponies to ride to the coast... not over-swift, but they'll save your feet and time enough for the mainland."

"Yes," agreed Seth, at last able to speak his thoughts. "Tomorrow is precious, yet I concede we need to recover our breath before going on. You've made us welcome here and we're indebted overmuch to you, Tavar, but we'll be away then, for what hope has the Hamlet without our return?"

Seth's thoughts, of course, were for all those left in Myre Hamlet, but Sarah was his truest concern. She was strong, but if illness had taken her, she'd little hope of managing. Help from other farms would fail with the spreading of the Scar. The winter would be bleak, for even good crops would go unharvested if the worst had prevailed.

Sharfell

"I too must return to the coast of Fenny. To familiar moorings and to the Ferryboat," said Henry. "But don't forget our first concern, Seth. We must re-join the Northern Lady, and who's to tell what might have befallen her. Simon and Peter are good men, and would wait through years, though a month and more in that bay will have seemed longer than *our* trials. And the throbbing, the pounding of the Ice Lord... let's hope their hearts have stood the test."

"Don't fear," Seth reassured him. "Your men are stout enough. The bay is sheltered and unless the likes of Kaan had meddled with them, and by his words he'd not, there's no danger of their having deserted us. Besides, Samuel and Jake wouldn't allow it, for they know the thwarting of our dilemma rests on our safe return. The four won't let us down."

"But remember, Seth," said Kaleb, frowning. "Jake and Samuel were also ill. Perhaps not as badly as Amos but they were troubled enough. Let's hope they're not in dire condition now, and that the Ice Wolf is in time for them as it is for Barny."

"All the more reason for our swift departure," agreed Seth. "But first, a day's rest, then onward."

"So it will be," enthused Tavar. "And I shall join Elmar and the others in their little game."

Their day in Sharfell was a fine one. Seth, Barny and Henry recalled the time spent there earlier, before the new summer, and fair though it had been, now it was more fair. The fierce sun beamed down all day. The fields and valleys were still, almost lost to time, for the day seemed longer than any they'd known. They rested in the pasture. The cornfields and the distant mountain vistas shimmered in the buzzing heat of midday and they feasted on the provender their hosts had produced. The orchards, whose fruit was swelling ready for an early ripening, sheltered their heads and shaded their eyes as the heat grew stronger still past noon. And they bathed in the crystal streams and lay down among the flowerlets that bloomed stronger and more profusely than before. A woodpecker could be heard, busy pecking for insects in the nearby pines. Coloured finches darted here and there between the orchards and the forest trees.

Seth knew now that this day wasn't wasted, for it seemed like a week of gentle recovery from the strain of marching. With more ahead, this was valuable indeed and the ponies that Tavar had promised would no doubt regain them this day at least.

When nightfall came at last, the waning moon was already high in the sky. The visitors to Sharfell were ushered in torchlight from Tavar's rooms to the buildings in the centre of the settlement. Here they climbed stone steps and came at last onto a floor sheltered by a lofty roof which was supported by four stout pillars at its corners. The walls were open to the night except for a low rail. This was the tallest building. It occupied the dead centre of the circle and this upper platform was a watching tower, built of old before the place was made secure. Tonight it would be used for watching once more, but this time for the watching of a celebration. Elmar and Tavar were elsewhere, making ready. The men of the Hamlet were accompanied only by one of Tavar's people... a young friend of Elmar's by the name of Gilimar. The lad was dressed in a simple skirted garment of grey cloth, quite unlike the heavier robes of the elders. He snuffed out the torch and placed it in a vacant bracket on the nearest post.

Below them, all around the central cluster of buildings, there gathered a throng... most of the inhabitants of Sharfell in fact. The womenfolk, the children and some of the elders. Their excited clamour died to a murmuring and then all was silent, and in one accord, a number of the doors of the outer dwellings opened.

Tavar and a score or more others, becloaked and hooded, now stood in the doorways, each with a staff held aloft in both hands. The doors closed behind them and the torches on the rocky walls were extinguished as if by some host of hidden hands, and in an instant all was reduced to the silvery shadows of the moonlight.

A clear voice broke the silence, echoing words akin to those used by Tavar in confronting the 'Lord of the Icemere'. And it *was* the voice of Tavar. Yet now, though solemn, the voice was calm. Though sharp and clear it was gentle and though the words were meaningless to those who knew not this high tongue, the tones spoke clearly enough of love and light, of wisdom and of caring.

"Hailé, Hailé, Kalnatori!"

"Hailé, Finis Belador Nori Pelamiri," the words went on and, as Tavar spoke, the others who were assembled called out chants that were similar. Yet each chant was different and they echoed all about, interlacing in a sympathetic theme, a music of high voices. Then, of a sudden, it ceased. Clouds drifted in, covering the moon and stars. All was totally dark and quiet. The onlookers waited with bated breath and wide eyes. Points of blue-white light now grew in the darkness.

"Twenty-three in all," whispered Will, hardly daring to speak.

As they watched, the lights showed the dim shapes of the staffs that sparked them, and the staff bearers' faces peering from hoods showed pallid. Then, the lights rose, leaving their source, changing colours and growing in intensity. Bluish-whites became fiery reds and emerald greens, crystal blues and golden yellows and ambers, and scintillating whites. And each globe of light produced a shimmering halo.

The light hovered, hesitant for a moment and then, with one shout of "Libitar!" from many voices, the globes spun free and together they danced around the outer walls in like direction, some falling, some rising, each returning to its former level. Faster and faster they went, now pulsing brighter and dimmer.

Then some among them turned and followed the opposite direction, weaving to avoid those that continued on their original paths.

And so they danced, interlaced as the chanting had done, each one seeming to know the other's path, looping, rising, falling, pirouetting and some now soaring high over the roof in an arc, meeting their outer path again on the far side of the rock circle. As their speed increased, a swishing and swirling of wind accompanied them on their merry dance, sounding like a confused sea breaking on a windswept strand.

Then rose another shout… "Limitar!", this time the solitary voice of Tavar.

In unison, the globes raised skyward to a single point above the roof so that those watching lost sight of them and with a silent splintering of light they met, showering brilliant sparks down on Sharfell… and the lights were gone. The clouds passed and the moon shone out once more. The torches were rekindled spontaneously and with the opening and closing of the doors in the rock, the elders had departed the celebration.

Breakfast was a solemn affair, for the seven who now must travel on had little enthusiasm for the journey before them. Though they longed to be home again, they wished they were already there. The distance between was a nuisance, but to travel it was necessary.

Tavar had left them to ensure that the ponies and provisions were made ready. He intended to travel with them to the point where he'd first encountered them, but Elmar would be their only companion from there. As they ate, they brooded, and Seth tried to lift them.

"It was a fine display last night," he said.

But though all of them had been awestruck, at first no one spoke. Silently they continued eating, then Henry agreed.

"So it *was*. Like harbour lights swinging in a frantic gale."

"Huh," grunted Kaleb. "Give me the Hamlet with a field to plough, and lights to come home to that stand still. It don't make sense, messing with staffs and things."

"Maybe so," replied Seth, "but Tavar and his friends know by now enough to treat such things with respect. We were grateful enough for the lights underground. And where would we have been if Tavar hadn't used the staff when we all first met him, and then again in destroying the Evil One? With care, their craft has its virtues. Like all of us, you're feeling reluctant to travel on, Kaleb. Perhaps if his staff could carry you home in an instant, you'd believe in its merit. Have strength, for we'll soon be back there."

With these words, they knew at least that they all shared the same thoughts, and this in itself lifted them. The weather too was still fine and that was something to look forward to on the way.

"All's ready," Tavar said, smiling as he peered round the door. "You'll be clear of Ironmound before noon and with flat terrain after that you'll soon be at the coast. We shall miss you."

"Elmar insists on renaming the Ice Wolf 'The Myre Plant'," he went on. "That will be a reminder of the gallant farmers of the south at least. And maybe one day *we* might travel south, as *you* have travelled here, but without the same need for urgency."

And so they left the rock rooms and were gone from Sharfell. Tavar bid them farewell on the path where they'd met, this time with Heg upon his shoulder. Seth was last to turn away and with his last glance he was reminded of his dream when first he was aware of Tavar. It seemed to him that the dream had only now ended, or could it be that it continued? Was he in truth still in Fenny? He dismissed the thoughts with a smile and a last salutary wave, and on they rode with Elmar.

The weather was kinder than they'd expected, for a high bank of hazy cloud had covered the sun and they were all the cooler for it in their hasty progress. Once into the lowlands they alternated canter with trot and by late evening they'd made heartening progress.

There was little to slow them down. The ponies, fit enough to start with for they'd earned their keep in Sharfell, became fitter and they went on tirelessly. Seth found his mount rather uncomfortable, for the pony was narrow and his gait fast. How he longed for Tag's slow, rhythmic paces and his comfortable, wide back. The weather held fair and by the morning of their fourth day after setting out they were skirting the pinewoods above the cliffs not far from where they'd left their friends and the Northern Lady… their only sure way home. They'd passed close by the cave of Kaan, but keeping more to the lowlands where they could, for the fair weather allowed it. Indeed, had the weather been as foul as the snows of the north, they'd still have avoided those dread hills, even though their evil must surely now be gone.

A cool breeze blew from the north now. Henry had made his way to the front of the procession, for he was anxious to see his boat. The sight of the silver-speckled sea from atop these heady cliffs was more than enough to set his heart racing. The prospect of hoisting the sail and setting course out into the open waters tugged at his heart.

"Look!" he called back, for he was now a good distance ahead, and first to leave the shelter of the trees. "She's still there… the Lady. Just as if we'd been gone for no more than a day."

Sure enough, there she was, looking no worse for waiting in the bay.

"Hi there!" came a call from the pines on their right. The commotion of hooves and Henry's call had brought Peter from deep in the woods.

"Peter!" called Henry. "It's a glad sight to see you and the Lady still here. We have what we came for. We'll be on our way today. Where's Simon?"

"He's with the boat, Henry," said Peter, thoughtfully.

The others drew to a halt as Henry dismounted and slapped Peter on the back in high spirits.

"We made it, though until now we weren't sure we'd find you. Nearly two months have passed since we left you. It must have been awful waiting."

"We'd have waited an age longer," Peter assured him.

Seth dismounted and shook him by the hand.

"It's good to see you, right enough," he smiled. "And what of Jake and Samuel?"

Peter looked more grim and a silence gripped him. The others dismounted as Peter struggled to find words.

"The Scar?" offered Abe, gravely, breaking the silence.

"Then we're too late to help them?"

"I'm afraid you are," said Peter, able to speak at last. "We lost Jake less than two weeks ago. It was ill to see him suffering so. Samuel grieved more for him than we. Then Samuel went too, though he didn't suffer the same pain. We found him last week in the woods. He'd been hunting. We'd no idea he was so badly gripped. He must have fought it boldly, for he died up here without calling us. I think he knew he'd not see you again."

They fell silent, but it seemed they were hardened to such tidings by now. Yet it was also a bitter thing that men were dying, even though the cure was found. They knew that perhaps they should have taken Jake and Samuel north with them after all, yet their two companions had seemed so tired already with their illness.

"Don't you grieve, Peter," said Seth, "for you've done all you could. We forced you here and you've helped us to save as many as we may. Though it seems so unkind, some were destined to die. We're paying dearly for the cattle of Greylar. *We've* lost Amos too, though it was he who showed us the Ice

Wolf at the last."

"But Simon and I have lost good friends as well, Seth," said Peter. "We'd come to know each other well and they were good men. We did all we could. They're laid close by Kelman in the woods. We've found it much harder this last week, without their hunting skills, yet they taught us enough to survive. We've had more fish though than meat these last few days."

And so it was a sad meeting after all. The men of Myre Hamlet said their farewells to Jake and Samuel, and indeed to Kelman. They made ready to descend the cliffs. They must leave Icelar that day, and if they were to reach a landing on Greylar by nightfall, they must be away with all haste.

Elmar, who'd been quiet since their meeting with Peter, for the sad news had dulled his usual exuberance, now stepped forward to talk with Seth.

"I've prepared the ponies for the return to Sharfell, Seth. Your packs are unloaded. I'll hinder you but a few moments longer. Tavar bade me say farewell here, where you leave Icelar. And though he said farewell himself he wishes you to know that we of Sharfell... we of Dunbeck, will be forever in your debt, for you made us see the folly of our reticence... our apathy. Through your encounter with the evil Scar of the Ice Lord, you've helped destroy his creeping shadow for ever. We're as sad as you at all the grief it's caused you and we dearly hope that you return safely with your precious load, for that now has a part to play in the final routing of evil."

"And *we* are equally in *your* debt, Elmar," replied Seth, feeling great remorse at the parting of Sharfell and Myre Hamlet. "Though it's been ill chance that's brought us together, we perhaps more innocent to evil than yourselves, our parting is a hopeful one. Icelar will become Hilar again and Myre Hamlet will become Myre Hamlet once more. We've all paid dearly for our gains, but perhaps we've all learned something in the paying. Farewell, Elmar. We'll remember the lights of

Sharfell always."

"Farewell, Seth. And farewell you men of Myre Hamlet. We too shall remember. We'll remember the stout hearts of Midvale and of Nording."

With this, Elmar mounted his pony and turned to the north. At a call of their names, the other ponies followed him out of sight. All except a restless Little 'Un.

The companions stood, as Elmar disappeared along the shadowy edge of the woods and with little ado they descended the cliffs, boarded the Northern Lady and were away into the summer breeze.

CHAPTER FOURTEEN

Boy

Sarah's raised hand dropped to her side as Seth and the others, leaving now on their desperate quest, disappeared into the grey shadow of the Westwood. Rain dripped from her hood into her face, helping to hide the tears that now were flowing freely.

She turned, with a reassuring arm from Helen Blackmore, and followed the subdued crowd into the hall to shelter from the rain before returning to the farm.

"Come along, Sarah," said Helen. "They'll be back before we know it. Have no fear. All will soon be well again."

Sarah felt disappointed that she'd not been able to control her emotions while she was in company. But she couldn't raise her mood. She thought of the perils that those who'd been on that northern trek before had gone through and knew that, as before, not all were guaranteed safe return. Indeed *this* journey was likely to be more perilous. After all, they were journeying to a land more remote and by all accounts more hostile than Greylar. Yet in that earlier journey lay Helen's strength, for Ely had travelled it and returned safely enough. Though she was well aware of the dangers, she held in her mind the day when Ely and Amos had returned to the throng outside the Blue Pig.

"Hello, Sarah," called a familiar voice. "I was just saying to Josiah... I'll be over tomorrow to lend a hand with the stock. I know you can manage the dairy herd well enough, but there's much to do besides the milking."

"Alright, Hal," replied Sarah, somewhat absently, not really wanting to think about tomorrow in her present mood.

It had been arranged for those who were now left without their menfolk to be aided in working the farms and other occupations before the party had set out.

"After dawn then," he added and returned to his

conversation with Josiah Cavey. Hal was the youngest son of Martin Wileman. Although the family were now without the help of Martin, there were three sons and a daughter, all old enough to work, so Hal could be spared for some of the time. Hal was seventeen years old. His brothers were considerably older, but his sister was a year his junior. Kaleb Moody, who'd gone north with Seth had also offered occasional help from his two farmhands should Sarah be unable to manage.

After a warming drink with Helen, Sarah left the hall. She collected Meg, the roan pony, from the forge stables and bidding Tom good day, made for Puddlefork despondently through the pouring rain.

Once home, her spirits rose, for the farm itself held no fears for her. She was greeted by Ruffles who didn't yet realise that Seth wouldn't be home. She soon lost herself in the work she had to do and before long it was nightfall. The drizzle ceased. She came indoors and tended the fire she'd lit earlier, finding it almost spent. Later, she sat down more tired than usual but warm at last in front of the blazing log fire. Ruffles curled up at her feet, gnawing comfortably on a bone... the meat had long since gone but he busied himself with cracking it open to find the marrow.

The logs crackled and the fire roared as the flames flickered in the ingle. Sarah's face felt the warmth as she gazed into the flames and beyond them to the red stars in the soot... red starlets that told of journeys.

'What will tomorrow and the days ahead bring?' she thought.

She slept well that night. She was not contented, but she was weary. Ruffles slept in the house, which wasn't his usual place, though in the weeks to come he did so more often, for Sarah was glad of his company.

The cockerel woke *them* for a change and Sarah rose late to greet Hal, who'd already made ready for a day's work in the yard.

"It's a fair morning," he said, smiling and looking to the clear sky.

"It *is* Hal," replied Sarah. "But not as fair as the morning Seth will return on."

Hal perceived her mood and wasted few words in finding out what was to be done.

As the days passed, Sarah became more and more resolved to the prospect of the coming months without Seth. Even Ruffles seemed to accept his absence.

By early May, Sarah was feeling much brighter. The weather had been quite fair since the drizzle of the departure and so had made her work easier. Then one morning Hal called.

"Morning, Sarah. There's a fence almost down in the field beyond the stables. I'll see to it for you this morning. I noticed it last time I was over. You'll have the stock in among the corn like as not if we don't get it put right before long."

"No. Leave it, Hal," said Sarah, unexpectedly. "Another time will do. There's nothing wanting today. I'll let you know…" she ended, absently.

"Sarah?" Hal said in surprise. "The fence needs attention, or you'll have problems."

"No!" she repeated, more sternly, almost angrily. "Go away. I don't need you here," she shouted.

Hal made to protest again, but seeing that Sarah meant what she said, turned to go.

"You'll be sorry, Sarah Linden," he called back. "If those cattle *do* get through."

She ran into the house and, rushing upstairs, flung herself onto the bed in tears. She couldn't tell Hal that she'd seen the Scar that very morning when she'd woken.

From that day on, she shunned help from anyone. Her visits to the village became infrequent and then stopped. Even the milk went to waste on several occasions to the consternation of the grocer who collected it regularly. The fence remained unmended and many other tasks went begging. She looked to the winter already, thinking that she may not see it out and thinking she may not see Seth again. Perhaps she could have taken the blow more easily had Seth been with her. But he wasn't, and his absence and the disease together proved too much for her to bear at first.

On the night following her discovery, she'd had an uneasy dream. She saw Seth and Kelman in a dark and dismal room. Boards creaked, yet no one walked them. The only light was from the flickering of a fire somewhere unseen. They were talking, but she couldn't make out what they said. She imagined she'd heard Kelman whispering, 'Sarah has it too you know. Sarah has it too,'... and Seth repeating, 'Sarah has it too... Sarah has it... Sarah... Sarah...' And as the words faded, the flickering died and so did the dream. She woke sweating, fearing that Seth too had been caught by the Scar. In the dream Seth's face was in the shadows and, like the words, she couldn't really make it out clearly.

Later, towards the end of May, she overcame much of her nagging grief. News had reached her one morning that men from Fenny had come to the Hamlet to return horses left behind by Seth and his companions, when their boat had left the bay... the grocer had come to the farm with Tag when collecting the milk. News too he brought that, though delayed, the men were well.

Sarah's Scar had advanced but little and she thought now there was hope of Seth returning in time for her. And so she hardened and regained her confidence. Once again she found the strength to work and to travel to the village. She called to see John Arden to see if the apothecary might have something to soothe the Scar, though she didn't reveal the true nature of her need. She was surprised to see Josiah Cavey, the cobbler, in the dingy shop.

"Take this Sarah," said John, dismissively. "It's a balm that will relieve itching and inflammations of the skin."

She detected a coldness in his tone that she'd not known in him before.

Returning to his conversation with Josiah, John said, as if Sarah wasn't there, "It's the likes of Seth Linden who cause trouble like this."

At this, Sarah wondered if her condition was obvious to the pair and would understand such acrimony if it were so.

"Yes," said Josiah, who'd been eyeing Sarah silently, brooding at her intrusion. "Those as meddle where they're not needed always bring ill times... and those as help when it *is* needed get no thanks for it."

Sarah knew now why they were both so hostile. Hal had no doubt spread the word of his abrupt dismissal.

"I'm sorry," she offered. "I'm sorry if..."

But she couldn't find the words and desperately she turned and left the shop.

"Be away and look after you own chores," called the apothecary.

Perhaps their attitude was understandable. Quite apart any revelations from Hal, John Arden was under great pressure with the presence of the Scar in the Hamlet. He and the cobbler both had shown little interest in the prospect of cattle in the first place. After all, the herds needed no improvement as far as *they* were concerned. And they, like others, had first put their present misfortunes down to Kelman. Kelman had become a friend of Seth and Barny and the three of them had now left, seemingly deserting the threat of illness in the Hamlet. For all this, it seemed that many in the village had become hostile towards Sarah. The way she'd dealt with Hal hadn't helped... she'd avoided the village after rebuffing him, though now she would avoid it for a different reason... for the illness that was taking hold of her.

However, one day in mid-June, Sarah resolved to go to the

Boy

village again. Meg needed attention at the forge and there were one or two things that she needed. She decided to take Ruffles along for company.

'Perhaps I'll have a word with Helen, too,' she thought.

Deftly, she backed the pony between the cart shafts and hitched them to the harness. Ruffles, tail wagging, bounded into the cart, and the cart rolled across the cobbles. A brief halt to close the gate behind her and then across the bridge and along the lane they went.

'Today was a day for renewed hope,' she thought.

Meg trotted lightly over the dry lane. The Westwood was in full leaf, highlighted by a summer sun. Ruffles was in high spirits and Sarah smiled to see him darting about. One moment he was in the cart and the next he was in among the undergrowth, sniffing and snuffling as he ran. Sarah laughed, and called him back when he went too far. Here and there, deep in the woods, the sun pierced the canopy of leaves and sent shafts of golden light into the shadowy depths. The light shifted gently with the breeze giving a fresh green to the hazel which thrived around the clearings. The Puddle Stream sparkled in the sunlight ahead of her and finches and flycatchers darted to and fro.

"A day for hope," she called aloud and Ruffles agreed, with much barking and tail wagging.

Tom Greeted her cheerily, fussing the dog who leapt with enthusiasm on seeing the young smith.

"She'll be ready within the hour, Sarah. I've shoes made ready. I expected you before now. Where have you been these past few weeks?"

"I've been busy," she offered hesitantly, reminded of her earlier trip to the village, as she unfastened the traces and harness.

She detected a knowing glance from Tom as he led the pony from the cart.

"I suppose you know," she continued, "that Hal isn't helping now."

"That I *do*," he replied, "but I didn't like to mention it. And it's impossible not to know why. Folk are weird. They don't see your plight as well as they should. But folk are folk and ill feeling shows itself where it shouldn't at times."

Sarah was encouraged by his kind words, but she'd not known that the ill feeling was so very strong. Tom too had taken Barny's share of it, but folk were rather more careful with *him*, for they needed shoes and smithing.

"And how are *you* managing with Barny away?" said Sarah. "You look well enough on it."

"*I'm* fine," he said, smiling. "Plenty of work here as well you can imagine. I must get on, or I won't finish before dark."

"I'll be away then," she said. "I've one or two things to pick up before I go. I'll get them sent here to the cart. I'm off to see Helen as well. Will Ruffles be alright left here with you?"

"Oh, yes, of course. Helen, eh? You may find *her* less than friendly too."

'A day for hope?' thought Sarah, as she walked to the wainwright's yard.

Helen greeted Sarah with a casual hello, looking up briefly from her washing.

"Hello, Helen," Sarah returned. "It's a fine morning for drying."

"It *is*. But a fine morning for little else," she snapped. She wasn't in the mood for talking it seemed and wringing out the last of the wash, carried the basket to the cluttered yard. Sarah followed her with trepidation, not knowing what to say next.

"Look at all these carts and wheels," continued Helen. "There's little can be done with them before Ely's return. The lad knows a little, but he's not strong enough yet to work on his own. Still, they'll manage without attention, for they have the choice of the fallen."

Boy

Sarah knew that Helen's words were forced and there was little to be said between them. Living in the village itself as she did, she'd obviously encountered the ill feeling towards Sarah and she seemed embarrassed by the unexpected arrival of her friend. Throughout their strained conversation in the yard, Helen darted glances this way and that in fear of someone seeing them together. Once indoors again, little was said and Sarah knew she wasn't welcome. She'd hoped to confide in Helen her earlier fears and the reason for her sharp dismissal of Hal. But she found she couldn't.

Sarah left dejected to make her way back to Meg and Ruffles. As she stepped into the road she was greeted with a commotion. The coach from Fenny came clattering into sight and, with hardly a moment to stop, a lone passenger was dispatched to the road. He staggered as he hit the ground, thanks to an overenthusiastic push from others inside.

"The Hamlet," called the coachman as he cracked his whip over the heads of the horses, "though why you'd want to come here I can't see for the life of me. You're welcome to it," he called back over his shoulder as the coach sped off through the village onwards to the south.

The coaches had recently taken to driving on through the village without stopping, for the Scar had now become known to the coachmen. Few people in the village now cared who might know of their plight. They'd thought perhaps that outsiders may even help, but all that openness had brought was a terror of the thing. The news was in Ambleton and Fenny by now, and in the south as well. The coaches wouldn't pick up anyone from the locality of the Hamlet. Indeed, it was unusual to find anyone wanting to alight here this last few weeks. But this one had insisted. The Hamlet he wanted and the Hamlet he got.

The newcomer picked himself up and dusted down his ragged clothes. He scratched at his matted mop of brown hair and looked around bewildered. The brief stop, unusual as it now was, caused people to turn their attentions on the new arrival. People came out from nearby workshops and cottages to make what they could of the commotion. Felix, who'd come out of the Pig, stood at the front of the small crowd that gathered.

"And what business might you have here, young master?" he asked, abrasively. "We don't get many visitors from northern parts these days."

"The Hamlet," offered the boy, for he *was* a boy, of no more than thirteen years of age.

"That's right," said Felix. "The Hamlet it is, but what do you *want* here? Is it a fine room you'll be wanting?" he added, mockingly. "And a bath no doubt?"

The crowd laughed, and fell to jeering.

Sarah looked on exasperated at Felix taunting the lad and she felt her temper rising.

'Has the whole village gone mad?' she thought.

"The Hamlet," the lad repeated. "The Hamlet."

"Well," shouted Felix, now playing to the crowd, "you've got the Hamlet, and if that's all you want, be off and find your own lodgings. We've had enough of northerners here already."

The crowd, shouting now in agreement, looked ugly and Sarah ran forward, desperately placing herself between the boy and the hostile villagers.

"Look you here, Felix Cavey. If you've nothing better to do than minding your own business, then go and mind it. It's nearly noon anyway and your queues will be waiting. And as for lodgings, then the boy has found them."

"Oh, I see," retorted Felix, though beyond that, he was lost for word at Sarah's brave intervention.

"You all seem blind to our dilemma," continued Sarah. "The Scar may soon be with all of us, Felix. And if it's not with *you* already, perhaps it soon will be. And then *you* will look in hope for Seth's return even more than *I* do. Don't you forget... *there* lies our only hope... yours and everyone else's."

And with that, she turned and ushered the lad away to the forge.

The jeers lingered, then died away as some dwelt on what had been said.

"Let's be away from all this nonsense," said Sarah to the boy, as a bewildered Tom watched them leave the forge. "We'll be on the farm before long and then you can tell me all about yourself and why you *do* want to be in Myre Hamlet.

The boy smiled, but said nothing. When they reached the farm, Ruffles was through the fence and into the yard, yapping for all he was worth. The boy looked around him with a quiet interest. Such a farmyard was a new sight for him.

"First," said Sarah, "you must be hungry, if the coach made no better stops on the way than that in the Hamlet."

But still there was no reply, though the lad looked on eagerly as she prepared cold meat, bread and cheese.

"Lost your tongue then, have you?" she continued. "Well, there's no need for you to fear speaking here. I won't be sending you away, unless that's what you want, of course."

She knew by the look in his eyes that he was hungry, and perhaps more at ease at last. His eyes had shifted restlessly before the mention of food.

"Come along," she persisted. "What's your name, at least?"

"The Hamlet," he said again, in a bewildered tone, as if trying to communicate but knowing nothing else to say. And he retreated once more behind cautious glances.

So it was that Sarah was sure he was virtually dumb, yet he could hear her well enough. She took to calling him Ham. He would turn when she called him and when at times she gained his confidence he dropped his guard. Smiling, he'd help in carrying water or fetching logs for the cooking fires and even in preparing the food. But still she could get no other reply to her questions save "The Hamlet."

"The Hamlet," she said pensively. "Why do you know this name and no other? And why should you have this place in your head? And where are you from in the north, I wonder? And what *is* your name... if indeed you have one?"

She'd learned over the last week or two not to expect answers to her questions, but she continued to ask them. The lad was company to her. With Ruffles her only companion, it had been lonely. Even the grocer, when he came for the milk, said little and she avoided him when possible. The boy was tough for his age. He'd lived roughly... that much was obvious by the way he ate his food impatiently, but his heart was in the right place and he was learning much on the farm. Between them they mended the fence, after a fashion, and Sarah had laughed until she cried at his first attempts to milk the cows. He learned to ride, but found driving the cart more difficult. He enjoyed being with the horses... even plough horses held no fear for him. He and Ruffles became the best of friends and would often walk in the woods together and follow the Puddle Stream beyond the fork, deep into the heart of the woodland.

"You mind you don't get lost," Sarah had warned, but there was no danger of that... his instincts were almost as keen as the dog's.

In mid-July, Kaleb's two promised hands came, somewhat reluctantly, to help out with the hay. Between the four of them, the stacking was managed. The weather had looked on them with favour. These last two weeks, after indifferent weather, clouds had yielded to blue skies and the hay, a little late though it was, after much labourious turning was dry and crisp... something to be thankful for.

"The longest spell of good weather we've had for a long while," Sarah had said as they'd pitched the hay. "And just when we needed it too. Seth would be pleased to see it."

But her words were not the first reminder of Seth's absence and the presence of the Scar. Despite the cheering company of the boy, she dwelt on these things constantly. Her own condition was still of no immediate grave concern to her, but in haymaking, Kaleb's men had told her of the village and how it fared. More and more were stricken and, to Sarah's horror, two had now died... first Jack Marsh and then Martin Wileman... towards the end of June.

'What would Hal be thinking now?' she pondered. "And Kelman?" she said aloud as the boy played with Ruffles on the rug before the hearth. "He among the others must have suffered the same fate by now. And what of Seth?"

Always her thoughts turned to Seth. Here she was, lost in grief, with no one to help her in all her confusion.

"Seth, oh, Seth. Where are you?" she cried out and she fell to weeping bitterly.

"Seth," said the boy, turning from his play to look at Sarah. "Men of the Hamlet."

Sarah looked at him, astonished. Surely she'd talked of Seth so many times, yet now the boy spoke his name as if in sudden recognition.

"Then you *can* say more," she smiled, wiping dry her tears. "But 'Seth'?... do you remember the name from before you came here? Perhaps you met him? Then tell me. Tell me Ham, did you meet Seth?"

She gripped him eagerly by the shoulders. At first he was silent again but then, hesitantly, he spoke.

"Yes, I met him. He was with the other men you speak of sometimes. Amos was one of them. It was in Fenny."

And presently, Sarah heard the story... how he'd stolen the purse, for that was how he survived. How his uncle and another man had used him to steal for them. He told her haltingly that he'd not spoken for many years, since his mother had died and then in turn his father had been drowned at sea.

His uncle was a brute and his accomplice was no better and words wouldn't come then, even if he'd wanted them to.

And he told how, when Seth had given him the coin, and the two men lay unconscious, he'd run and run from the slums. For more than a month he'd hidden in the town. Still he used his skills to live, stealing food, for that he was well accustomed to. But he hung onto his coin. One day he'd heard a coachman talking of 'The Hamlet' to the passengers bound for the south. 'We won't be stopping there,' the coachman had said. But the boy remembered Seth's words when he'd given him his coin... 'From the men of the Hamlet,' and he resolved there and then to travel to the Hamlet for safety... perhaps he'd find friends there, for Seth had been kind, as no one had been for many a year. And the coin... *that* he'd use to pay the coachman.

"This is a glad tale indeed," said Sarah. "To hear of their progress from someone who's seen them. And more so that it comes from lips so long silent. Let's celebrate. But first what's your name, lad?"

"Tim," said the boy, bashfully.

"Tim? Tim!" she laughed. "Ham wasn't far wrong. Come, let's celebrate."

And with this, she hustled him to the stables and Meg and Tag were soon saddled and bridled and together they rode the fields, returning only as dusk descended.

In the weeks that followed, the farm was an industrious place. The weather stayed fine and Ham, for that name stuck, soon learned yet more of farming and of the Hamlet vale itself. Sarah tried to explain the problems that Kelman had brought and why the coachman and the villagers had shunned him and indeed Sarah herself. But he wasn't concerned overmuch with these troubles. His new life here couldn't be compared with the awful existence he'd had in Fenny.

As August came, despite Ham's help, Sarah was becoming concerned, for the fullness of harvest would soon be on them and there was yet no news of Seth. But then she thought, if Seth doesn't return, and I'm here alone, stricken, then what matter the harvest?"

The milk wasn't collected these days... a sign that things were even worse perhaps with the villagers, so the milk would go to waste.

Then, Sarah had a visit from young Tom. He seemed on edge, as if he didn't wish to be at Puddlefork but he told her briefly that Seth and the others should soon be back, for Barny had returned ahead of them and brought back tidings of the cure they'd found in Icelar.

"Glory be, Tom," Sarah had said, for she was relieved beyond all joy.

"In two or three days, Seth should be with us," he'd said.

But he also told of growing uneasiness. By day, men and women were taking to shouting and cursing at their ill fortunes and violence had broken out several times. By night, the Pig had become the scene of drunken brawls and poor Felix was having a difficult time. Chaos seemed never far off. 'People have left what sense they have behind.' Felix would mutter. 'They'll be gathering nuts next May frost the way they're going.'

"Hurry on back, Seth. *You'll* know how to help us to sanity," Tom has said to himself on more than one occasion, with growing concern.

Five days went by with no sign of Seth and his companions and at night Sarah became uneasy thinking of the hostile mood of which Tom had spoken. Ruffles stayed in the house every night with Sarah. Ham slept close at hand too, for the silence of the village road seemed threatening when night fell.

The weather was becoming unsettled and the wind turned to

the west. The moon was full and a restless night came. Sarah peered out from the kitchen and across the yard, but as she did so, mounting clouds took the moonlight. The wind was rising and, though she could see the woods now, the trees howled in protest of its fitful grip. Outside, a gate had loosed its latch and rattled to and fro on creaking hinges. The horses were uneasy too. Ham had long since gone to bed and slumbered peacefully. Ruffles lay beside him, content on the blankets.

Sarah shuddered and, drawing closed the thick curtains, checked the bolt on the door and made ready for bed herself. She once would have gone outside to see to the gate but now, she thought it too short a road from the Hamlet to Puddlefork. She took the lamp upstairs and, once in bed, extinguished the friendly flame and snuggled under blankets. Soon she was warm and after restless hours fell into a troubled sleep, lulled at last by the ceaseless rattling of the gate and the howling wind.

She dreamed that she and Seth were dancing in the Hall alone by the light of a single lamp and, as they swung round and round, faces appeared one by one, each leering in the light of its own lamp. At first she and Seth danced in silence but, as the faces appeared, strains of music could be heard, now loud, now soft, now sweet and now discordant. And hands belonging to the leering faces pointed to their own Scar-ridden faces and then to Seth and Sarah. She called out and the dream faded, but it was replaced by others. Then at last these other dreams left her in peace and she slept deeply.

Sarah's eyes opened, wide with fear. A yell from Ham had woken her suddenly. She could hear Ruffles downstairs yapping... yapping and growling deeply. Without hesitation, she flew from the bedroom, down to the kitchen and through it, grabbing the wood-axe from the wall as she went. She calmed Ruffles to whining and subdued growling yet still he bared his teeth. Now, she stood watching the kitchen door, knuckles white on the axe shaft. Ham was close on her heels and armed

Boy

with a staff he'd cut for walking. He stood in front of her, as she'd stood before him in the village, and they waited.

They thought they heard the whinny of horses, out in the yard, but if they had it was swallowed by the wind still howling and the gate that clattered on and on.

Sarah caught her breath as the latch lifted and someone shook the bolted door.

CHAPTER FIFTEEN

Bright Messengers

The summer weather bode well for the nine. Once clear of the cove and the eastern tip, they were favoured with a stiffening of the breeze which blew from the east.

They navigated the shallows at high tide. Henry saw to that, for he remembered the treacherous waters there on that northern coast more clearly than the rest of them.

With little change in the wind or weather their confidence grew and, after the shallows, Henry insisted on sailing on blind through most of the clear nights though they made brief stops for the sake of the pony and for water.

On the calmer nights, reflections of the stars glinted in the rolling waters and as they travelled on, and the old moon was taken by the new, the stars were as bright as Seth had ever known them. Some, far in the north, were strange to him... he'd not noticed them in Icelar, yet here in the vast waters of the night he marvelled at the sights he saw. Blue stars and orange stars blinked near the watery horizon and a myriad of bright messengers of the sky darted earthward, each flaring valiant then fading into dark oblivion. The Evening Star, diamond bright, cast clear shadows on the deck of the Northern Lady.

Little 'un travelled well and patiently, though this was more than could be said for Kaleb, who still found it harder than anyone to enjoy the sea, even with it quiet.

"Keep your blinking stars," he said to Seth. "Let's be back to Fenny and firm ground."

Food from Sharfell kept them well and Fenny, it was hoped, would soon refill their packs.

"They'll have sent the horses back, I hope," said Seth, "but we shouldn't find it hard to buy or borrow more."

"I'll need one too," said Henry. "I intend to come with you, if you'll have me. The sea can wait a while for me."

"But what of the Lady?" asked Barny.

"I've spoken with Peter and Simon," explained Henry. "They know how to use her well, and to look after her. Besides, nothing would drag them away south from the coast. She'll be in good hands with them.

"Myre Hamlet it is then," declared Seth. "We must make good speed for the sake of Abe, Will and Kaleb... they seem no better yet. It'll take some time perhaps, but better in the hands of John."

"I can't understand it," said Abe. "The potion seems to have *halted* the Scar, but it's slow to move away. Slower than it's been with Barny. It's true, John's lore may be of great import now."

They made Fenny harbour just more than a week after leaving Icelar, and with the help of Jack Roper they were lucky enough to find horses and tack for the urgent road home. They learned that their own horses *had* been returned, which was news they welcomed. They also learned with no surprise that the Hamlet's problems were no secret here now. Jack Roper was the only sympathetic one they found, though they were reassured when he told them that no one had been stricken here in Fenny, to his knowledge.

"They say that the Hamlet is the only place affected," Jack said. "But fear grows. The coaches refuse to stop there now. It's even said that only fools travel through, but the south itself still has its appeal for some. Trips aren't as regular now but one coach *did* leave only two days ago."

"A pity," sighed Seth. "We'd hoped to send news of our return ahead of us."

"Then I'll go ahead to announce the rest of you," offered Ely.

"But not alone," insisted Seth.

"*I'll* go too then, if you'll find us horses," said Barny. "So long as you look after Little 'Un. He deserves to see the Hamlet more than any of us."

"Very well," laughed Seth. "You know we'll treat him well. But you two beware at Weatherford. There may yet be danger there."

Horsed and provisioned, Ely and Barny were away without delay. They took what they could carry easily of the Ice Wolf. The others stayed the night on board the Northern Lady, for not even Jack Roper would put them in a room. Alan Wooley wasn't so grateful now, but harvests were near and he sold them what they needed.

Simon and Peter now took charge of the boat as quietly as could be, for local folk were none too happy to have them stay in Fenny... after all, they'd been with Midvalers and that didn't bode well now. They were not diseased, but maybe they carried it.

The other five rode out soon after dawn, Henry, not least among them, waved a grateful farewell to Peter and Simon.

Nine days they travelled hard, but by night they rested for if they were willing they were weary of the road already and they daren't overtax the horses. Several times, feet needed attention and they regretted Barny's absence. They did their poor best, but they were slowing.

They passed through Ambleton quietly on the second night using the derelict house once more for shelter. Home seemed not so far off now.

On the sixth day they rode their fastest, by the grey boulders and on past Weatherford. They shuddered at the thought of their previous encounter.

Now, with the Bucklebank close by again, they could make out the Westwood in the distance to the right of the road and their hearts rose high as dusk came down on the ninth night after leaving the seaport.

They looked forward to the shelter of the Westwood, for

they'd camped in open lands so far There'd been little fuel for fires at many of the camps they made. August though it was, with clear skies, the nights were chill. They'd eaten well this night. Seth leaned against the lone tree that sited their camp west of the road. He took a long draught from a leather water flask and after filling his pipe he took a stray smouldering twig from the hot ashes of the dying pot fire and sparked the tobacco.

"This Fenny tobacco's better than naught, he laughed," but there's better where we're going."

"Ely and Barny should be there by now," said Will, leaning back on his upturned saddle and wrapping his blanket tightly around him. "Let's hope the news is not too ill," he continued. "Surely they're not too taken by the Scar?"

Seth was gazing at the waxing moon as she climbed the eastern sky from warm amber into pale yellow.

"They'll be well, I'm sure of it," he answered Will, shivering. "After all, there are those among us who are hale yet and *were* so before we found the Wolf."

"And there are those who are not," said Will, dejectedly. "This potion takes its time. I for one feel little better yet."

"Never fear, Will. Given time and rest you'll mend. Just think on and remember that chair by the fire in the Pig."

Will was encouraged but Seth looked forward more to his *own* chair, by the fire at Puddlefork. He took a deep fill of tobacco smoke and dwelt on it.

"We'll be there ourselves in but a few days from now," he said after blowing the smoke skyward.

They set a watch as they'd done all this last week, for the wild men were still in their minds. The next evening saw them reach the Westwood. They found a scattering of gorse bushes and busied themselves with a good fire in a sheltered hollow just off the road. A shout from Kaleb, who was tending the horses, brought them running.

"Listen," he called in a force whisper. "Horses on the road, or a horse at least, and travelling at a fair pace too."

"It's from the south. No wild man, I'll be bound," said Abe.

As the hoof beats drew near, they checked into a trot and a voice called from the gloom.

"Seth! Will!" was the cry.

"Ely!" they called, running to the road as their friend dismounted.

"Seth. Seth," he gasped, for he'd been riding hard. "The Hamlet. They've gone crazy."

Seth felt a lump rise in this throat, fearing what this unexpected return of Ely may portend.

"Where's Barny? What's happened?" Seth asked, urgently.

"It's alright. He's well, or at least was when I left him."

Kaleb took Ely's horse and Ely was led to the hollow. After regaining his breath, he explained.

"We rode into the Hamlet three nights since. Perhaps we should've been more careful, but we went straight to the Pig. We were greeted well enough at first, but Felix seemed to be having problems. The ale had been flowing well that night. They were glad that we'd returned, with the Ice Wolf but when they clapped eyes on the little we had, they went mad. They fought over it like animals. Those who have the Scar were not the only ones."

"This is grave news, Ely," said Seth. "Then the village is overtaken with frenzy and panic."

"Not quite as bad as that I think, Seth. The drink had much to do with the welcome we received. Barny, bruised from the scuffling, stood up before them and explained that there would be plenty more of the leaf when you others arrived. It calmed them a little, but there were threats to take what more you brought, by violence if need be. 'Don't be fools,' I cried. 'We need sense and calm'. But they were too far gone for reasoning. I urged Barny to one side while they fought over what they'd taken and suggested I came back to warn you, if *he'd* do his best with them. I left the inn and after brief words with Helen I turned back and rode north again."

The travellers were disturbed greatly by this news and Seth thought long before he spoke.

"It would be folly to walk straight into such feelings, with this treasure we carry."

"We could hide it out here on the road, Seth, when we're nearer and come back for it when they're in a more sober mood," Henry suggested.

"No, Henry," said Seth. "It's too valuable to leave unguarded. And if we travel much further, are we not in danger of them coming north to meet us? For our own good and for the good of the Hamlet, we'll go a different way. The woods will offer us secrecy. Though they'll delay us, it'll be worth it."

"But surely, those who have this madness can't be *so* many in the whole village?" suggested Henry. "There must be many more who'll help to deal with them until they can be brought to see sense."

"It'll take very few to lay waste our plans for curing all," replied Seth. "It's worth the delay."

And so they agreed to travel a wooded path. They'd keep close to the road for as long as they dared, then head southwest to find the Puddle Stream to guide them to Puddlefork.

They travelled the daylight hours of the next day on the road, hoping to cover some distance before they committed themselves to the forest, but they went with caution nonetheless, ready to fly into the cloak of the trees should they hear rumour of approach. But no one came to greet them. At dusk they knew it best to be well off the road and they decided that the next day they should travel under the trees. The woods afforded passage for the horses and travelling on they soon lost sight of the road. The sun, above and before them, still offered a direction and the paths were rarely devious. Still they travelled with caution lest they be found. They went on foot now at times, for the boughs above them closed in and sometimes caught them out as they rode. They were reduced to a walk, but made good progress all the same. The light, still brightest before them, dimmed for here they were deeper into the bowels of the forest. Yet where it *did* break through in sharp shafts, all before them was highlighted in vivid colours. The trees, mostly birch, marched into the distance, their diamond trunks bathed in blue light. Their leaves, speckled green and gold, waved gently above the silent walkers, fanned by a warm breeze.

The path they followed began to rise gently and without warning they were in a rocky place. To the right, the ground rose ever more steeply and they were now shadowed by a sheer face of stone that ran southwards. Moss-grown granite littered the stony path which now fell again. The cliff face ended abruptly turning westwards. Below the rocky face to the south now were oaks and occasional buttressed beech trees, old trees, more like the wood near Puddlefork. To their left, the silver of the birches was soon swallowed up by elm and ash, slender for the most part, competing greedily for sunlight. Hazel and brambles matted the forest floor there, an untidy, difficult path. The natural path they'd followed turned west below the cliff and though this wasn't the path they sought, Seth encouraged them along it, for he had rumour that this path was a good one.

Sure enough, the rush of water he'd heard was the source of a stream.

"The Puddle Stream, I'll wager," called Seth, who'd gone on ahead as the welcome sound grew louder in their ears. Here, the waters rushed out of the rock face through a deep cleft in the wall and tumbled on over stony shoulders. Then, trickling more lazily into a shallow bed below their feet, it ran onward in a gentle valley, flowing south. The path had disappeared, but the oak wood afforded many paths over the leaf mould of countless autumns. They picked their way within sight of the trickling waters and as light faded they came across a fork where other waters flowed to join their stream. Here they made ready for the night, weary yet feeling safe.

"No need to watch tonight, eh, Seth?" said Kaleb.

"No indeed," confirmed Seth, but he was the last to settle under his blanket. Restless, he tried to sleep but his thoughts wouldn't permit it, tired though he was.

Glancing across the water to the further bank, the patchy moonlight showed him a huge old tree, toppled by some storm ages since. Seth startled suddenly, for he spied an old man in ragged robes, sitting on the fallen giant. The white-bearded fellow beckoned him with bony fingers to join him there. The face was aged and thin and Seth almost felt he knew those thoughtful eyes. He warily forded the stream and sat some distance from the stranger, careful not to lose sight of the camp.

"And why do you travel this road?" asked the old man.

The voice struck a familiar chord in Seth's mind and he perceived a genuine concern for the wellbeing of he and his fellow the travellers.

"We're returning to Puddlefork, my home," Seth found himself replying, "from journeying in the north."

"And you are concerned that your return is to ill times?"

"That's true," replied Seth, "for we bring a treasure to our village. A treasure that will cure those ills."

"Will it?" asked the old man. "Yet they do not seem to want your help."

Seth was shocked that this fellow knew so much, but he submitted to his words all the same.

"Perhaps you should never have contemplated your first journey to the north?"

"Oh, the cattle," said Seth, ruefully. "They could have been a boon if it were not for the Scar."

"Were you in need of a boon then? I fear not. You had boon enough before that time. Like your friend the mage in the hills of the north. He too had boon enough but went too far and like you paid dearly for restlessness. You are wise, yet you've more to learn. You've not yet cured all your ills... but you will in time, all being well. Go and rest now, for you'll need strength in the days ahead," the old man concluded.

And with a glance across the water he pointed an arm in a gesture of return for Seth.

Seth, reassured and yet not so, opened his mouth to say more, but found no more words. Warily, he rose and turned. Once more he lay beside the fire, and the old man was gone.

When he woke in the morning, Seth scratched his head, puzzling over his odd encounter. He'd become used to strange events in the north, but here so close to home? Surely not? Yet *there* was the tree, some way off, sure enough. He rubbed his waking eyes and, thinking on but saying nothing, joined the others in preparing a light breakfast. They were anxious to be moving on again.

The next day, after several detours caused by thickening undergrowth clustered around small streams that collected into the main flow, Seth was overjoyed. He knew the river here.

"That bend," he said. "The bank over there with the great willow. I know these parts. We're but hours from the farm."

And heartened, they made fresh haste. Above them, the trees fell silent as the breeze dropped, but then of a sudden, a great wind gusted overhead. The leaves sighed in one voice and heaved in like direction then whispered back again, others taking on the sigh. The gust was followed by a rising, howling wind above their heads. Yet down here they were sheltered from its blasts. Night fell, but on they travelled.

Windblown now and weary they emerged from the forest and crept quietly onto the greensward of the farmyard at Puddlefork. Seth motioned for the others to stand while he went cautiously forward, leaving his mount with Barny. All seemed calm, but care was best observed. Stealthily, he made to cross the cobbled yard, but as he did so, Tag let go a cry from his nearby stable and Meg echoed the call of recognition. The dog was woken and yapped and growled.

'So much for a quiet return,' thought Seth. *'But all seems well.'*
He tried the latch and realising it was bolted, called out.
"Sarah! Sarah!"

"Sarah! Sarah!" came the cry, and Sarah breathed a sigh of relief.

"Seth!" she called, dropping the axe and fumbling with the bolts. Ham at once knew who it was and retreated, relaxing the vice-like grip on his staff. Ruffles barked eagerly. The door opened and Sarah flung her arms around Seth, weeping now in relief. Nothing mattered now, and she found no words for their meeting. Seth returned her embrace and held her safely in his arms, he safe too in hers.

Will inched his way by Seth and Sarah. He called Ruffles to heel before kindling the kitchen lamp.

"Come now, Seth. Who's this young fellow? You've not mentioned him on our travels," said Henry who'd followed Will and had spied young Ham in the shadows.

Seth turned to look, not understanding Henry's words, and there, with a smile of recognition he met with that same bewildered look he'd seen in Fenny. Sarah answered Seth's puzzled glance.

"This is Ham," she smiled, "He's told me of your meeting in the north."

"Well met, lad," said Seth.

With this, Sarah told Seth enough of the boy and his journey south for him to understand. But she didn't yet mention the Scar.

"Food," she said. "It's late, but you must be in need of food."

"Yes, we all are tired and travel-torn, but a supper would be welcome," said Seth. "*We'll* see to the horses while *you* prepare a meal, and we'll talk as we must... but I'm forgetting," he added, hugging Sarah once more. "We've found it... the Ice Wolf."

"I know," said Sarah, smiling. "Barny sent word with Tom. He said that you hoped to be back some days ago. We were overjoyed, Ham and I, but we began to worry as the days passed without your return for we knew already that the Hamlet had turned sour. And if they could treat us here, and Barny, with such hatred, then what fate lay in store for you on your return?"

"Yes. We too were troubled, for Ely's return on the road brought desperate news," Seth hesitated. "But I don't think it's hate that drives the Hamlet to these actions. More likely it's panic. Despondency we all have felt, and frustration too, even though we had the privilege of searching for an answer. Back here, you must know more of the anguish they must be feeling in the Hamlet... held here in the Vale, many with the Scar and with all their hopes in others."

Sarah was surprised to hear that Ely had returned with Barny, for Tom had said nothing of it. Barny in fact hadn't wished to worry Sarah when sending the heartening news of Seth's imminent return.

"But Seth," Sarah replied. "If you've a cure then why aren't they elated at your return as am I?"

"Perhaps they *are*. Or at least perhaps they *will* be when their thought turn sober. Truly though, these last months have soured them. The news of what we bring perhaps didn't sink in at first and they do panic thinking there won't be enough for all. This is why we're later in returning. With Ely's unexpected news, we felt it best to find our way here through the woods. We didn't dare risk our precious load, without at first we talk some sense into the village. We even half expected to find some of them here."

"No, Seth. Quite the opposite. Even the milk has not been collected these last weeks."

Seth shook his head and thought on the new task ahead. He was reminded of the old man's words and said, "They'll know that all our ills *will* be cured... and soon."

Seth spoke these words with fresh purpose, but looking into Sarah's eyes, his new mood melted, for he perceive what she'd not told him. He held her tightly and, after a hollow silence, whispered in her ear with a quieter and yet reassuring resolve.

"All our ills *will* soon be cured. But first, the horses," he smiled, "and then that meal."

With this he went to aid the others who'd already, under Kaleb's direction, seen to most of what was to be done. Seeing Ruffles, Tag, Meg and the other horses brought back to Seth the reality of his return. He knew things must be steered back to the path the Hamlet trod before the Scar, or nothing would be worthwhile anymore. They brought the packs containing the bundles of leaves and the plants into the house for safety. Soon, a heartening meal was underway and the warmth of the fire, tended afresh by Ham, spread into their limbs.

Sarah tasted her first draught of the potion. The others were accustomed to it.

There was much that Sarah wanted to talk of, and though Seth wished to unload the trials of the journey, he was preoccupied with the problems they now faced... how to persuade the people of Myre Hamlet back to sanity, and then how to nurse them back to health.

No one who'd not been on that first expedition had yet died, but so many others were afflicted that this was little comfort. The travellers were grieved to hear of the deaths of Jack Marsh and Martin Wileman. Sarah hadn't known of Kelman's fate or of that of Amos until now. Thoughts of the lost men laid heavily on the gathering, but they talked on.

"First thing in the morning," said Seth, "we'll call to see Barny. He'll be glad to see Little 'Un back and *he* may know best how people are these last few days. Maybe they've come to their senses already."

"And maybe not," said Kaleb. "I must be away home first to see how things are."

"Yes, Kaleb," agreed Seth, "and Ely will want to see Helen as soon as he may."

Ely nodded in agreement, "If what Sarah says is right, even Helen is taken with sour thoughts. I must reassure her that all's well."

"Then, Henry... you and Will must stay here with Sarah and the boy. And Abe and I shall go to the village with Ely. Abe can speak with his brother, John and with Barny's help we must confront those who'll not follow sensible dealings for the benefit of everyone. The Wolf will be safe here, until we return. Perhaps if we meet with them before Felix opens his doors, they'll be cooler-headed. Meanwhile, we must all rest, though I fear you'll find the floor no more comfortable than the beds we've sampled on the road."

In fact, Seth had the worst restless night of all. Having become accustomed to the feel of rocks in his back and cold, damp, uncomfortable beds under the trees or the stars, sleeping next to Sarah in a warm bed was little comfort after all. He lay for much of the night thinking of all the wide world they'd travelled and how he wished Myre Hamlet had never sought to go beyond its own fair fields.

CHAPTER SIXTEEN

Passing Moon

As Seth, Abe and Ely mounted and left Puddlefork, still weary, darkness had yielded to a moonlit, calm and cloudless sky. Little 'Un followed almost as weary as the men.

It was mid-morning now and, as the three of them followed the familiar path, the birds were in full song. The party clattered onto the road, echoing their way to the forge. A column of smoke was rising there, glowing red in the morning sun and the ringing of hammer on anvil greeted them. Barny was at work.

As they approached, the hammering stopped and presently Barny peered out from the doorway. Rubbing his hands, he called to them heartily.

"You made it then. But where are the others?" Barny asked, his attention divided between his question and taking cheerful charge of Little 'Un who whinnied in recognition.

"It's alright," said Ely. "We came home through the Westwood. After our encounter we thought it best."

"The others are at Puddlefork. We come now from there," added Seth.

"Safest way," agreed Barny. "Folk are still as crazy, though they seem fair enough when they come asking for shoes. I've had more than one set-to though. Young Hal Wileman seems to be the one who's at the centre of it all. What with his father dying, it's understandable I suppose, but all this lunacy will get us nowhere. I keep telling them."

"We must convince them," said Seth, gritting his teeth. "Who can we rely on to help us?"

"Hardly anyone," said Barny, "if you really mean 'rely on'. Most are alright unless they're incited, but even so they won't *want* to help. They'll just expect you to sort out their problems for them. It's not like Hamlet folk at all."

"What about John?" said Abe. "Surely, *he's* kept his head through all this?"

"I don't know so much," said Barny. "*He's* been sharp enough at times too. I reckon he's had enough of the Scar from all sides. People stopped relying on his help long since. He's done his best I think, but it's hard Abe, it's hard."

"Then *we* must be hard as well," said Seth. "Abe, you must go to John and explain all he needs to know of the Ice Wolf and I'm sure he'll help us... now that there's something to work with. At least he'll see that it can help us all, the same as it's helped Barny. Now we must confront the village, young Hal in particular, and where better than at the Pig, before the ale starts flowing."

They didn't need to go and look for a crowd, for soon after they'd spoken with Felix, a crowd came looking for *them*, headed by Hal. He'd stayed that night with Samuel Dale's son in the village as he'd done for the last three nights. The loss of his father had taken him badly and he was intent on causing trouble now... *'why should others be cured when my father couldn't be?'* he'd thought. Hal had led his followers to thinking that Seth would keep what cure they had for himself and his close friends.

Felix looked upon the angry gathering with fear, for he'd suffered enough *inside* the Pig already.

"You'll meet them out here, Seth? Not *in* the Pig?" he beseeched, as they stood on the threshold, watching the crowd approach... some twenty or more, shouting and jeering.

"Where's this amazing cure then, Seth Linden? This cure that will cure all ills."

It was Hal sure enough who spoke these words.

"We *have* the cure," replied Seth with a confident air, "but it'll stay safe with us for the present... until you see sense enough to allow its proper use for everyone."

The crowd resorted to murmuring.

"You see," retorted Hal. "He hides it from us as we feared."

The crowd jeered again in support. Seth looked anxiously at the ugly gathering which had stopped several paces short of the threshold.

"And if I showed you the cure now," he replied, "would you take it all and fight over it, as you did with the precious little we sent ahead for you?"

"There are many people here that need this so-called 'Ice Wolf', and you send such a small token of it," said Hal, barely controlling himself. "People have died whilst you've been away roaming the countryside."

With this, he moved to take Seth by the throat in an insane rage.

Barny pushed him back, "Do you forget Amos so easily?" he shouted angrily, rising to a rage himself. "*He* died whilst bringing you back this cure."

"It's true, Hal," said Seth. "You're not the only one who's lost something through our sad encounter with Kelman. And I wager you yourself haven't even the need for a cure. I'll tell you *this* much... In all my travels I've been lucky, for I've not yet been taken with the Pox of Icelar. I've stood aware of the very womb of evil and still I'm lucky. But I've lost Amos. And Sarah is now taken with the foul thing. I've faced many lonely nights wondering if she was yet ill and now I know it. And so, I tell you," and with this he pointed at the crowd also, "I'll not see *your* hopes disappear with foolish squabbling any more than I'd see *my* hopes disappear. As one who approved of that first journey, as also did your father, Hal, I'll not let this second journey be in vain. You'll learn soon, if you'll listen, of men who took the path towards evil many years ago, unwittingly, through their desire to know more of things... and they found that greed even for immaterial things, however innocently intended, can lead to disaster all too easily. *We* too have seen that for ourselves, in our own way. So let's do our best to put things aright. That way, we may have a future… one in which we can trust in what we have and not go looking for things beyond our needs. So, Hal, *with* you or *without* you, I'll see that our treasure is meted out fairly. There *is* enough to go round, I assure you."

With this, the crowd fell to whispering again. Hal pointed a finger back at Seth, as if to threaten him further but, perhaps in recognition of both Seth's anger and his wisdom, or more likely because the throng's fiery support for him had cooled to a flicker, he turned and walked away through the crowd, followed by his friend the carpenter's son.

'That at least is a start,' thought Seth.

The crowd dispersed and with it went the murmuring and whispering. Seth wasn't sure whether they'd been turned from Hal's folly altogether, but he felt encouraged again.

Ely had now made his way home to Helen and the children. Barny and Seth together made their way to meet John Arden, hoping that all was well now that Abe had had a chance to speak with him, but as they arrived, they could hear the two men exchanging heated words.

"…and I tell you, John, it *will* work. Yes, you've tried everything you know but, without the Wolf. Your efforts were bound to be as nothing."

"Then, if *you* have the Wolf, retorted John to his brother, "and if *you've* cured Barny, then *you* can cure the rest. *I've* had enough of it all."

Seth and Barny entered the dismal shop.

"Well met," Seth offered, but the look he gave the apothecary hinted that this might not be so if the present attitude continued. "It seems you're reluctant to help us now."

John shrugged his shoulders and with this gesture his mood softened somewhat. He wouldn't speak so readily to Seth of his indifference as he had to his brother, but even so it seemed he

Passing Moon

was still reluctant.

"Look, Seth," he said at last. "My energy is all spent. I've achieved all I can and that's precious little. Surely, Abe has learned much of herb lore. He'll stand in my stead well enough.

"But John," replied Seth, facing him squarely, knowing enough of spent energy himself. "Your energy may be all taken, but your efforts are *not* in vain. You've surely learned much of the Scar. And with that knowledge and your years of learning *you'll* know best how to use the Wolf sparingly. There's enough for all if Barny's speedy recovery is to be counted on, but we must go with caution nonetheless."

With this, Seth placed a hand on John's shoulder.

"But I've been concerned increasingly this last week or so," Seth went on, "for Abe, Kaleb and Will have shown little if any improvement. Though there seems also to be no worsening, the Wolf does not seem as potent as it was. Frankly, John, though I dare not show my thoughts to the crowds, I sometimes begin to think it altogether impotent. If my fears are founded well, then others will soon find out and if my fears are ill founded, then we'll need you all the less, John."

He hesitated and turning he brought down a clenched fist in desperation on the counter.

"What can it be, John, that slows the cure? Has the potion been weakened by the aging of the leaves? Maybe Abe has forgotten some of his newfound lore? Maybe he hasn't the skills of Tavar. I fear we're going to need you dearly, John."

"Very well," said John with a sigh of resignation. "If Abe will work alongside me, and if we keep the Ice Wolf well-guarded, should it prove that the Hamlet folk persist in their foolishness."

"We'll keep much of it at Puddlefork," Seth agreed, "and supply you as you need more. Those who can travel to you here must do so and those who *can't* come, Abe can travel to."

Myre Hamlet & the Ice Wolf

Sarah was relieved to hear that the people of the Hamlet had seen some sense. Seth didn't let on to her his fears. On Seth's return, Will made his way home. Henry was to stay here with Seth, Sarah and the boy.

The rooted plants had been unwrapped and Sarah and Ham had planted most of them in a hidden, sheltered corner of the greensward, beyond the chicken coops. The leaves were limp and the plants looked the worse for their long journey. Several, Sarah had planted in indoor pots, hoping *they* at least would recover from the necessary abuse they'd suffered. Sprigs they separated into several bundles. One was for John Arden and the others were hung safely out of sight, for when John should need them.

Seth visited John frequently in the next few weeks but his heart was laid heavy, for it became obvious that his fears were being realised. No one was improving, for all the redoubled efforts of the brothers. In truth, Abe himself had worsened. Will and Kaleb too. Sarah had shown no sign of recovery but despite all this, Seth had looked for some small sign of hope in others. Now, it seemed only a matter of time before someone died, despite the 'cure' of Icelar.

There'd been little sign of the earlier hostility in Myre Hamlet, but now impatience was threatening to overwhelm restraint afresh, and Seth knew it. Hal had started to hold forth again in the Pig, by all accounts, and the precarious peace became ever more fragile.

The life of the community had change so much since Kelman's arrival and, with the continuing persistence of the disease, little thought was given to all but the more essential chores. And this apathy served only to swell the cloud of depression engulfing people who had been so naturally gregarious.

Seth now came closer to despair despite having a real friend in Henry who seemed to him less reassuring away from the sea and the Northern Lady. Even despite Ham's continuing high spirits... since Ham had regained his tongue, the boy's appetite for learning had found no bounds, but Seth couldn't show him the enthusiasm he might normally have done.

Visits to the village and the Pig became infrequent. Henry had sampled Felix Cavey's brew in Barny's company, but in less jovial circumstances than they'd each hoped. And Seth wouldn't leave home without Henry staying to protect Sarah and Ham. Sarah was slowly but surely getting worse and, despite her resolute will, she became as drained as any by the hopelessness of it all. Despair spread with the Scar.

The harvest was brought in with little enthusiasm, except from Ham. It was just one of those essential chores. Some left the fields to waste, for they saw even this chore to be unnecessary now. No thought was given by anyone to the Dance. The coach continued to pass through, for tidings in the Hamlet when it *did* stop were full of woe and ill fortune.

September had come and gone. John Arden continued his efforts, but poor Abe was becoming very ill now and those unable to travel to John were neglected, though most of them saw no virtue in such a journey anyway.

Will had managed to shrug off the advance of the disease, but still he was no better, while Kaleb, like Abe, was badly scarred now. Seth was driven deeper into sorrow for Ely, along with his eldest child had been to seek help from the apothecary. And so too had Josiah Cavey's wife. There were several now close to death and ugly talk was heard again in the Pig.

One morning early in October, a morning filled with grey drizzle, and dreary skies, found Seth leaning on the gate, mindless of the rain, staring at the drab stone walls of the house.

"You've more to learn, Seth Linden," he said aloud to

himself.

His thoughts had wandered to his encounter with the old man, and in that moment he knew he must journey into the forest again, to find the old fellow. He wandered back into the house and spilled his thoughts to Sarah.

"Perhaps the old man will tell me what I've to learn, if it's more than to be content in a bleak future," he said.

"But, Seth," protested Sarah, as she tended the plants on the window sill of the kitchen. "This is foolish. We need you *here*. Not wandering off again."

Until now, he'd told no one of his mysterious meeting with the hermit fellow... not even Sarah. And now, Sarah maybe thought that their troubles were leading him to delusions. But Seth had become so desperate. He collected together what he might need and was ready to leave.

"I'll come with you, Seth," Ham declared, but Seth would have none of it.

"I go alone," he insisted.

And so he did, leaving even Ruffles behind him. Henry, who was tending the horses, shook his head in disbelief as he watched his pathetic friend scurry across the yard and disappear under the canopy of the trees. Thankfully the rain had ceased but Seth would have ignored it anyway in the frame of mind he was in.

Sarah was overcome, for it seemed her husband had gone quite insane. She sat, head in hands, lost to her surroundings. Neither she nor Henry saw another, diminutive figure accompanied by Ruffles follow Seth.

It wasn't long before Ham had lost sight of the farmer, but the path he took was obvious... it followed the stream. But, as the morning wore on, the path became less clear and the boy wasn't so sure. Even Ruffles found it difficult to keep to his master's scent. Ham was worried now. He stood and called out, but his tiny voice was snuffed out by the canopy of leaves. The dog, sensing Ham's fear, turned and barked. He turned once again, barking and yammering loudly. They were lucky, for Seth was barely within earshot, but he perceived the cry and turned in search of the dog.

"I *told* you I was coming alone," shouted Seth when he found the boy with the dog.

"But... I wanted to see the old man," Ham stammered.

"Very well. I can't seem to leave you anywhere, Ham, without you turning up. Perhaps you'd better come with me now," the farmer smiled, as if reluctant but in truth in need of some company. "But the food I brought won't see us all provisioned."

The boy smiled and pointed to the bag he'd brought with him. That evening, they huddled together in the chill October air. Rain threatened once more but came to little, and they were sheltered from it by the thickness of the trees.

By nightfall on the next day, they'd reached the fork in the stream. Seth soon spied an enormous fallen tree... a tree Seth remembered from his recent return. After lighting a fire, he sat atop the trunk of the felled tree and waited, hoping the old man wouldn't let him down. Ham and Ruffles settled together against the trunk and left Seth to his waiting.

When Seth woke, he couldn't remember climbing down from the branch, but sure enough he'd slept deep. The night had passed and he'd had no visitor, but something told him he'd heard a voice whilst he'd slept. *'The voice of the old man?'* he asked himself. Vague and distant was his recollection of the voice and he thought he remembered the words it had spoken.

'Seth! So you despair. So you despair. Well, my friend, if you're to win through in all this, you must follow your instinct. Little else will help you, Seth. Follow your senses.'

He scratched his head as these words came to him, and as he did so, he looked about him for the boy, who'd left his resting place.

"Hi there, Ham," he shouted at length. "Let's have some breakfast," he called, as he spied the lad sitting by the stream's edge.

Ham ran back to Seth, still clutching a handful of weeds that he'd dragged out from the water's edge and draping them over the tree trunk, he sat down to join Seth in a frugal meal.

"We had more than enough meals like this on the road. What a fool I am, forcing more upon myself. But then I imagine you too knew such meals, and worse, in Fenny... when you were Tim, eh, lad?"

The boy listened happily as he shared a biscuit with Ruffles.

"Things are grim, but I shouldn't be running away like this, looking for answers far from home. The answer is surely back in the Hamlet."

Seth was talking to himself now.

"Use your senses, Seth. Follow your nose. Follow your..."

And at that very moment, a chill sensation took hold of him, for his nose indeed had scented something on the air... the reek of foul smelling vegetation. The weed that Ham had dragged from the stream. The chill was one of sudden realisation. The stench, though different, reminded him of that smell he'd not come across since they'd left Icelar. The *smell* of the Ice Wolf... of the free-growing plant! And, in an overwhelming flood of thoughts, he realised. Barny must have been cured by the smell... the evil smell of the living, growing plant. It had been absent all this time. The potion had never had a smell to it... not even that administered to Barny by Tavar. He laughed aloud and the woods echoes his calls.

"We've found it, Ham! You and I! I'm sure of it."

Ruffles ran about excitedly, barking and wagging his tail madly. The boy looked at Seth, only half understanding, and disappointed that he'd not seen the old man.

Seth was cut short in his rejoicing. Lowering the boy to the ground, he knelt on one knee despondently.

'But, have we found it?' he asked himself dejectedly. 'We still don't have the smell, for the present at any rate. We left it back in Icelar. If the plants we have survive and grow, we may yet retrieve it, but that could take until next spring, or longer still. All the same, we must return with all speed for, if we've hope at all, it lies in the living plants. We must look to them with double care.'

So they hurried back, by elm and ash and over brambles, flying almost all the way. They passed the old willow and by noon on the next day, they were home.

As they ran out into the open, they were greeted by a great commotion. There were a dozen or more men of the Hamlet in the yard, jeering and shouting. And before them on the path that Seth now stood upon was Hal Wileman. Facing Hal, between he and Seth stood Henry, wielding the wood-axe from the kitchen, firm against the wrath of the crowd.

"What is it?" cried Seth.

"They've come to find you, Seth. But they had to make do with me," said Henry, glancing over his shoulder.

"Where's Sarah, then?"

"Fear not, Seth. She's safe indoors. But young Wileman here is after your blood this time."

"Yes, Seth Linden, I *am*... you and your hollow promises. Nothing have you brought back from your little adventure. Nothing but a short future. The Ice Wolf is no good to us. It's no good to anyone."

"They know about the plants, Seth," interrupted Henry. "Sarah mentioned them innocently... to give them hope of fresh potions, but they made to destroy them rather than to pour fresh hope into the Ice Wolf."

"If the Wolf is no good to anyone, then why must you destroy it, Hal?" shouted Seth, moving forward and challenging Hal face to face.

"Because it's *your* false hope, Seth Linden. In it we see *your* false hope, but now you're here and you'll stand in its stead, for you too are a false hope."

Hal raised his arm to strike Seth but, with a single blow, Seth sent him sprawling on the turf. In a second, Henry moved forward and lifting the hostile youth held him firmly with an arm around his throat.

Seth shouted to the ever-restless gathering, "There will be no destroying... of *me* or the Ice Wolf, for I know now what we must do."

"We've heard *that* before," called a voice above the commotion.

"We must still be patient," Seth went on, ignoring the voice, "for I know now how Barny was cured."

The noise fell to a muttering and they listened restlessly.

"I give you my word! If you'll only be patient and let these plants grow, then we'll be free at last of the evil fingers of the north. Their *smell* is all we wait for."

"But we can't afford to wait," called a voice from the crowd.

"You can't afford *not* to wait," called a softer voice behind Seth and Henry.

It was the voice of Sarah. She'd been watching and listening at the window. She ran the short way to Seth and embracing him, she looked into his eyes.

"We needn't wait for long," she said, leading him aside to the bed where the Ice Wolf was planted. She stooped and picked up a pot. "Here, Seth. A plant from the house. I brought them out here yesterday, for they've started to smell awfully. I despaired, for I thought the evil of the Icemere was here returning, though the smell is as if the roots are rotting.

Seth leaned forward and took a whiff of the sweetest foul smell he'd ever smelled.

All went well from that day on. Hal apologised openly to Seth and the others for calling their journey wasteful and pointless. Seth sympathised, for Hal's emotions were understandable, despite their overflowing as they had.

Within a few days, the plants were smelling magnificently. It seemed they'd established and were growing *before* winter set in. Or perhaps it was in spite of the coming winter, for winter here was no doubt as warm as the summer they'd been used to. They'd recovered well from the long journey and were thriving in this normal autumn weather.

As with Barny, Sarah improved now daily and was back to health within weeks. That his dear Sarah had seen off the evil bane was in truth Seth's true salvation.

Potted plants had been taken to John Arden, and many folk made regular journeys to Puddlefork where the planting was, for they daren't disturb the plants again.

After all, the journey north *was* worth it, for the virtue of the 'cure' had been proven at last. The plants grew well, though their progress slowed as winter came. Seth had gazed out to where they stood and he'd recalled poor Kelman who, in a way, had brought them here. He dwelt too in thoughts of Amos who'd found the Wolf and Seth brought two heavy, rounded stones and laid them in among the Ice Wolf's leaves. The plants would stay there always should they again be needed, and the stones too would stay there always, under the soft shadow of the trees.

The coaches were calling again now and had brought no ill news of the Scar from Fenny or from Ambleton, but Seth wondered if Tavar and his people had yet realised that the plant's virtues were hidden in its growing stench. He knew in his heart that the men of Ironmound were in safe hands, and soon it was confirmed for Tavar came to Seth in a dream.

Their room in the Blue Pig was as kind and comforting as it had been the year before. Felix busied himself again with food and ale.

'We've been on the very edge of disaster and we've cleared the

chasm. Or have we merely retreated from it?' thought Seth, drawing on his pipe. He looked around at his companions, who talked and laughed in good heart as they looked forward to the summer. The winter solstice had passed and the new year was upon them. The spring was still far off, but the Hamlet could at last expect a return to something nearing a normal existence. There were those who'd suffered great loss and they were slow to feel enthusiasm again. There were those who'd forgotten the anguish of the ordeal readily and looked to the future most eagerly. This coming year, the harvest Dance would be an occasion to make amends for last year's being put aside in the face of their dilemma.

Ironically, the cattle of the plains, as useful and successful as they were proving to be, were a constant reminder of the tribulations they'd brought with them and if few others did, then Seth thought on the great pity that they'd ever considered the first quest. He recalled quite often, the words of the old man, 'You paid dearly for restlessness.' He was nonetheless reassured to think that they'd now cured the worst of their ills and hopefully learned something along with it.

Seth found great strength in Barny, for the smith had soon become his old self again... 'party clothes' and all. There he stood by the mantle, now cheerily recounting some of their ordeals... even the grim encounter with Kaan. And when Kaleb brought him back to earth with sober corrections of the events, Barny would dismiss such amendments with contempt as irrelevant, or at best uninteresting, brandishing a new hoof-pick, brought to the Pig to support his tales.

Will Sparrow looked full of heart as he talked with young Tom. More heartening than anything to Seth was the sight of Ely fully hale once more. After the trials of travelling twice over, he'd suffered deeply, but now he, and his family, were safe again.

Seth's greatest sadness was for Amos, for he alone was

missing from their gatherings now, though in many ways Henry Harding brought memories of the resolve that Amos always had.

Henry had been a good friend to Seth. He'd accepted the initial deception on the boat, then had given Seth all the support he could on their travels and back here in the Hamlet. But he was anxious now to be back to the Northern Lady.

"I smell the salt-spray and I see the silver waters in my dreams," he'd said many times to Seth and Sarah, "and I feel the morning breeze in my hair. I must be away before too long, though perhaps I'll wait until the spring is with us."

Seth smiled when Henry said, "You and Sarah will find enough help in young Ham. He's a good soul and will serve the Hamlet well."

In fact Ham was already part of the family and all who now knew him were amazed at how eager he was in all that he did. Unlike Henry, he'd few good memories of Fenny and so had no thoughts of returning there.

Seth was nudged from his thoughts by Henry. The fire was dying and it was late. The others were making ready to leave for home amid continuing laughter at Barny's tales which refused to end despite those gathered all now making for the door.

They said their goodnights and, after tapping out his pipe, Seth followed Henry into the street.

"I'll bring the horses round from the yard," Henry called back as he disappeared through a gateway.

Seth hesitated. It was a night not unlike that when he'd looked to the north and had longed to journey from the Hamlet. He smiled to himself and shook his head, his thoughts straying.

'The stars and the moon here always were as beautiful as those we saw in the north. The old man was right of course... 'our boon is here for us to see and always has been.'

Myre Hamlet & the Ice Wolf

He tugged at his feather-beard with his slender fingers and thought on.

'Perhaps I'll meet the old man again one day... when I'm older myself...'

But he knew well enough now that the familiar old man was already close at hand.

Henry appeared with Tag and his own gelding.

Seth caught a glint of metal at his feet... Barny had let fall his new hoof-pick unnoticed in his carefree departure. He smiled and bent down to pick it up for safekeeping.

The two friends mounted and with a clatter of hooves they were in the lane and all the light they had was from the moon, now two days into waning.

'Madman's moon is passing in more ways than one,' thought Seth.

~The End~

Printed in Poland
by Amazon Fulfillment
Poland Sp. z o.o., Wrocław

Corrected Index (Chapters 5, 6, 7, 8, 9, 10)

MYRE HAMLET & THE ICE WOLF

Chapter:	Title:	Page:
One:	The Blue Pig	1
Two:	The Homecoming	16
Three:	Harvest Home	39
Four:	The Home Leaving	52
Five:	The Sea and the Breeze	67
Six:	Scar Bringer	91
Seven:	Pulse	110
Eight:	Sentinel	127
Nine:	Respite	145
Ten:	Dunbeck	154
Eleven:	Blizzard	166
Twelve:	Icemere	187
Thirteen:	Sharfell	203
Fourteen:	Boy	220
Fifteen:	Bright Messengers	236
Sixteen:	Passing Moon	249